INEVITABLY

RiffRaff Records – Book Eight

L.P. Maxa

2

ALSO BY L.P. MAXA

RiffRaff Records
Royalty
Legacy
Infamy
Loyalty
Sanctuary
Piracy
Certainty

The Devil's Share
Play Nice
Play Dirty
Play Fair
Play Softly
Play Hard
Play For Keeps

St. Leasing
Mouth Watering
Breath Taking
Jaw Dropping
Heart Stopping

Other Novels
Happy Place
Stumbled into Love
Rescued

www.BOROUGHSPUBLISHINGGROUP.com

INEVITABLY

ISBN: 978-1-951055-32-5

Devil's Share

Dash and Lexi
Conner
|_____|
|
Halen Grace
Avory Leigh
Marley Van

Smith and Dylan
James
|_____|
|
Evangeline Marie
Emeline Claire

Jacks and Bryan
Cole
|_____|
|
Landry Hope
Beau Weston

Luke and Harlow
Matthews
|_____|
|
Cash Marshall
Crue Bradley
Jett Wilson

Spawn

For everyone who believes in meant to be

ACKNOWLEDGMENTS

As always and forever, thank you to my husband and my daughter. You two are incredibly understanding and supportive, and I'd be lost without you. Thank you to all my wonderful readers who have followed along this amazing Devil's Share and RiffRaff Records journey with me so far. I can't believe we're almost at the end. To my mom, thank you for helping me get this story out. My spectacular Smitten Kittens, you guys are the BEST. I truly appreciate you.

INEVITABLY

8

"You can't be wise and in love at the same time."
—Bob Dylan

Chapter One

Kasen

My parents had been married for a thousand years. At least, it felt that way. It seemed they'd been in love since the beginning of time, and I understood how rare that was. The type of love they had was admirable...to people like my sister. Katie had always aspired to find a love like our folks, Mason and Payton Cadence. Katie wanted a partner in life, someone to hold her hand through the ups and downs. And she'd found it. She'd found her soul mate. Her better half, the one for whom her heart beats.

She was marrying the poor asshole this weekend.

Marriage wasn't for me. Happily ever after wasn't really my cup of tea. I fucking adored my parents, and I felt lucky to have been raised in a happy, cohesive home. But that shit was for the birds. I was taking a page out of my Uncle Pax's book. I was going to see the world and live every moment. I was going to take chances and stay up to see the sunrise. I wanted to have fun, nonstop, up until the day I died.

What was that famous quote? *I hope to arrive to my death late, in love, and a little drunk.* Well, mine would go like this: I hope to arrive at my death late, a little drunk, and on top of some banging hot chick in the middle of a Balinese jungle.

And speaking of the Balinese jungle, that was where I was headed on assignment as soon as this three-day wedding extravaganza was over. Yeah, you heard correctly, three days. I was expected to attend the welcome lunch, the rehearsal dinner, the wedding day brunch, the groom's pre-game, the wedding, the reception, and the morning-after breakfast. I put my Tom Ford boot down at the morning-after breakfast.

I was not about to sit across from my sister and the dude who'd had sex with her all night. I had to draw the line somewhere, and awkward jokes about consummating a marriage was where I did it. Plus I had a flight to Bali to catch. It was work. There was nothing I could do to get out of it. Insert conspiratorial wink.

"Sir, we're here."

I picked my head up off the back of the seat at my driver's announcement. I'd been dozing on and off since I was picked up from the Austin airport. I'd flown in from South America and jet lag was going to be a bit of a bitch.

"Thank you." I opened my own door. I wasn't *that* spoiled. I also got my own bags out of the trunk because my driver was pushing eighty and it seemed rude to have him take them up to my sister-in-law's front door. I shook his hand, slipping a fifty in there for karma.

He drove away and I climbed the low-profile concrete steps, sighing. Katie insisted that I stay at Luke and Harlow's house, her soon to be mother- and father-in-law. I was a groomsman and all of us were staying here tonight. My parents and uncles got to stay in what was reported to be a *lavish* pool house.

I hadn't seen my family in months and I'd much rather be spending the extra time with them. But this was important to Katie, and Katie was important to me. So, here I was, staying with her soon-to-be husband's 'rents. I was a damn good brother.

Katie had met Cash Matthews a few summers ago when she'd been banished to the Devil's Share compound for safekeeping after our dad lost his shit because he caught a guy almost kissing her. Our dad had just started a new tour—yeah, rock star parent—and he couldn't handle the thought of what might happen to his eighteen-year-old baby if she stayed on the road with him.

Ultimately, that'd been a parental fail on my dad's part. While she was here, she lost her virginity to another rock star's kid. But they were *in love*—insert eye roll and singsong voice—and they were going to ride off into the sunset tomorrow night.

"Kasen. Hey, man, glad you made it." Cash opened the front door before I could knock, a big smile on his face. Cash and his twin looked like Thor from those old Avenger movies. No surprise the guy ended up getting into my sister's pants. "Come on in."

He grabbed one of my bags, holding the door open. "Thanks." I stepped past him, peering through the house into the backyard through the large floor-to-ceiling windows. "The gang's all here?"

Crue, Beau, Jett, Brody, and Talon were all in the backyard, standing around a smoking barbeque pit.

"Yeah, we're cooking all the meat for lunch." He set my bag down in the entryway. "Come on, let's get you a beer and I'll show you to your room later."

I dropped my second bag before following him out onto the patio. I'd met all these guys before. Katie and Cash had been dating for a while now. We'd had some family holidays together, and Jett came to Cali to visit his older brothers while they'd been living with my sister.

But still, the last thing I wanted was to spend the whole day with a group of men so disgustingly in love I'd get a fucking toothache.

Love wasn't for me. No thanks.

I had better things to do with my time, and my dick.

Chapter Two

Kasen

I was standing off to the side with my Uncle Pax, sipping a beer and wishing this welcome lunch would end so I could get the guys' night over with. I stood around the backyard in the Texas sun while Cash and his friend Benson had smoked enough meat to feed an army. You'd think that would count as enough time with "the guys," but alas.

If I was being completely honest, all this togetherness was starting to grate on my nerves. I lived on my own, traveling the world, and answering to no one in particular. So to be constantly surrounded by people and on a tight schedule was sort of killing me.

"You look miserable." That was Uncle Pax. He could read me like a book 'cause the man was me, only older.

I cracked my neck, then shook out my shoulders. "I'm feeling twitchy, man. I've got to get out of here." And this was only day freaking one, how was I going to feel by the time the actual wedding rolled around?

"Where you headed after all this lovey-dovey crap is over?" He lifted his glass to his mouth, sipping on his scotch as he watched the party around us. Uncle Pax was like me, not too keen with the happily-ever-after tract.

"Bali." I loved Indonesia, the culture, the vibes, it was one of my favorite places to work. And I'd purposefully scheduled this trip for the week after my sister's wedding. I knew I'd need a little peace and quiet after being with the Devil's Spawn for three days straight.

"Nice."

I turned to him, jumping on the chance to have some fun with my favorite uncle. "You want to come with?"

Uncle Pax liked to travel as much as I did, and more often than not he'd meet me if I was somewhere cool. We both had the same outlook on life, and he never bothered to stop my good time. To sum it up, he was the coolest uncle a boy could ever have.

"Maybe. It's been a while since I've done a travel piece." Pax was a writer. He had a blog that had turned into a three-book deal. They'd all hit the NYT Best Seller list, because it turned out people enjoyed reading about an aging playboy's sexcapades.

I took another sip of my beer, deciding to give this lunch five more minutes before bailing. I didn't see anyone here but Devil's Share peeps and my own family. Not sure who the hell they were *welcoming*. Most of these people either lived on this damn compound or across the street. I'd sneak over to the pool house, maybe go for a swim. If I was lucky, I'd have a few hours to myself before I needed to head back to Cash's for guys' night.

Looking around the large field, I took inventory of all the famous rock stars and the kids they'd produced. There was a stocked tank to one side and several long farm tables elegantly set with vintage glassware. Fancy barbeque.

Cash had his arm around my sister, his mouth near her ear, she was smiling at whatever he was saying, no doubt something incredibly sweet. He was a good guy, and I approved. She could have done worse, that was for sure. Like Crue, Cash's twin. That dude was a broody asshole from what I'd seen. He reminded me of a depressed caveman, barely talking, walking around with all his muscles. More brawn than brains.

Their youngest brother Jett was pretty cool: cocky, but cool nonetheless. He was with a cute chick in glasses, making her laugh out loud every few seconds. Talon and Marley were seated across from them, she was balancing a glass of water on her pregnant belly. Those two seemed like an odd match, but so did Landry and Brody for that matter. And that couple? They had a gaggle of little boys constantly running circles around them like mini tornados. Wyatt, Weston, and Walker? I could never remember the youngest one's name. This family was growing by the damn second. I swear, I wouldn't be surprised if there was another baby born before the wedding.

Kids weren't really my thing.

It's not like I hated them or anything. They simply weren't for me. I liked my life the way it was, and I didn't plan to give it up any time soon. Or, like, ever.

Nicky, Evie's husband, was talking to my dad across the tank. He'd worked his magic, inking spectacular tats on almost every member of this massive family. The massive family I was now part of, I guessed.

I polished off my beer, choking on the last sip when a beautiful girl stepped out of the tall grass and onto the bank of the pond. I didn't remember ever seeing her before, and no lie, holy shit, I would have remembered her. She lifted her long flowing dress, holding it in place as it blew in the summer breeze. Lexi and Dash greeted her, giving her a hug and smiling like they were happy to see her. One of Landry's little boys ran to her, and she scooped him up, making him giggle like a madman.

"Who's that chick?" I couldn't tear my eyes away from her, drinking in everything about her, cataloging it in my head: her long blonde hair, her even longer, slender, shapely legs. Her elegant jaw line and her pouty pink lips.

"That *chick* is Smith James's youngest daughter Emmie, so stop looking at her like that." Uncle Pax stepped into my line of sight, shaking his head in warning.

I leaned to the side, looking past him. "She's fucking gorgeous."

He moved to block my view of her again. "I don't think she's even eighteen yet."

"Her legs, that blonde hair. Is she a dancer?" I put my hand on his head, pushing it out of my way. I couldn't get enough. The way she floated across the field, the way she smiled at everyone.

"Ballet." Uncle Pax sighed. "But if you don't put your eyeballs back into your head, Smith is going to come over here and remove them with a rusty spoon."

"She looks like a sexy angel." Maybe I could use my contacts to get her some white wings. She could wear them, and nothing else. Fuck, what I wouldn't do to that sweet little ass.

"Goddammit, Kase."

Uncle Pax could protest all he wanted, but my mind was made up. And my weekend got a hell of a lot more interesting. "I'm going to go introduce myself."

"I really wish you wouldn't."

I patted him on the shoulder as I stepped away. "I know, man. I know."

Chapter Three

Emmie

Katie and Cash were getting married. Another member of the Devil's Spawn paired up and headed for marital bliss. And babies. All my cousins seemed to be keen on having a lot of babies. Landry and Brody had three. Beau and Halen already had one, and Marley, of all people, was pregnant. I knew that my older sister Evie and her husband, Nick, had plans to try for a baby at some point soon.

Jett was coupled up with Devin, and that looked solid as in forever and ever. Avory was dating some tech genius she'd met at UT. She didn't bring him around to large family events. And that's what told me she was actually into this one, which was a surprise. If she didn't care for the guy she was dating, she let Crue or the rest of our family scare him off so she didn't have to end it.

Yeah. Everyone was in love, except for me. Emmie James, the youngest, purest, shyest, most obedient of the Devil's Share offspring. My life wasn't empty though, not at all. I had ballet, and for as long as I could remember dance had taken up every single moment of spare time I had. It'd paid off. I'd been accepted into the Austin Ballet after graduation.

"Em, can we go on an adventure walk? Pretty please?" Wyatt, Landry and Brody's oldest son, was clinging to my leg, pleading up at me with his gorgeous blue eyes.

I tickled his ribs, making him giggle and let go. "After we eat, okay? We don't want to miss lunch."

"Come here, you little hooligan." My uncle Jacks scooped his grandson off the ground and tossed him up into the air. "Em just got done with rehearsal, crazy kid. Let's let her sit down for a minute."

"I don't mind taking him, I'll eat real quick." I loved kids, which was good since I was surrounded by them constantly. "Give me a few minutes, Wyatt." He nodded, grinning wildly as Uncle Jacks carried him to a nearby table to sit with his brothers.

I picked a spot at one of the other farm tables, taking my plate over to the large buffet-style serving area. I piled it high with ribs and cream cheese corn. Normally, I didn't eat like this. Ballerinas were *not* curvy girls. I allowed myself this indulgence knowing I'd burn off almost every calorie I was about to eat after I took my nephew on his adventure walk. Wyatt was a tiny hurricane of blond curls, a small force of nature who never slowed down until he basically fell asleep standing up.

I turned away from the buffet to head back to the table I'd selected, then stopped short when a guy I'd never seen before stepped into my path. He had dark hair and nearly black eyes. His features were sharp. Especially his jaw and nose. He filled out his dress shirt and slacks like they were handmade and sewn onto his body. His muscled arms were visible despite the long sleeves he'd rolled up. He was taller than me by a few inches and his smile was more of a smirk.

"Hey." He looked me up and down, his tongue darting out to wet his bottom lip.

"Uh, hello." I smiled politely and then moved to the side to go around him. He was hot and he was smirking at me. I didn't really know what to do with his attention.

"I'm Kase." He held his hand out, then pulled it back when he realized mine were full of food. "Katie's younger brother. I don't think we've met."

Katie's brother? I was an idiot. He wasn't hitting on me, he was introducing himself to his massive new in-law family. "Oh, right, I'm so sorry." I transferred my plate to the top of my vintage goblet full of sweet tea. "I'm Emmie, Smith and Dylan's youngest daughter." I shook his hand when he held it out a second time. "It's nice to meet you." I kept my smile firmly in place, making sure I was pleasing and polite as I'd been raised to be.

"Here, let me help." Kase took my plate, carrying it for me over to a completely empty table farther away from the rest of my family.

I sat, and he sat opposite me.

I wanted to be with my family, away from Katie's gorgeous brother, who was still smirking. He reminded me a bit of Jett in the way he carried himself. Beau said Jett was a cocky little shit and I wondered if Kase was too. Maybe all incredibly hot guys smirked like they knew the effect that it had on the female population. Since I'd had no experience, all I could do was go by what my cousins told me.

"How have I never met you before?"

I folded my hands in my lap, not sure how I could eat ribs in front of him. "Uh, I'm not sure. I miss some family functions when I have rehearsals and shows. And I never got a chance to visit California when Katie and Cash were living there." Mainly because I was the baby and my parents refused to let me go party with my older cousins. But I wasn't going to share that piece of information.

He nodded, licking that bottom lip of his again. "Rehearsals? You're a dancer, right?"

"Ballet, yes." I glanced behind my shoulder, not sure if I was looking for an escape or checking to make sure my dad wasn't shooting daggers into Kase's head for talking to his baby girl.

"Do I make you nervous, Emmie?"

I turned back to him, my eyebrows rising at the new slightly deeper tone in his voice. "What?"

He leaned forward, his forearms resting on the worn wooden table. "Do I make you nervous, Emmie?"

Yes. But could I say that? I didn't know how to talk to guys who weren't part of my family or my ballet company. "No." I cleared the lie from my throat. "I was looking for Wyatt. He has the patience of the four-year-old he is and we're supposed to go on a nature walk."

"Can I come?"

No? Yes? Did I want him to come? Kase made my heart beat a little faster. He made me want to run away and move closer at the same time. "Sure."

He grinned, getting to his feet and holding out his hand. "Then let's go on an adventure, Emmie James."

My body responded immediately, forgetting my food as I put my palm in his. The breeze brought his enticing scent to me and blew my dress all around my legs. I could have sworn time stood still for a moment.

"Em! Em! Are you done? Can we go now?" Wyatt came flying toward me, his arms outstretched, sure that I would catch him.

And I did. "Yep. Let's go, little man." I placed him back on his feet, smiling when he slid his small hand into mine as we set off on our walk.

Wyatt looked at me, then past me to Kase. "Who's that?"

"That's Kasen." I jiggled his hand. "He's Katie's brother."

"Kase. Kasen is what my mom and my sister call me when they're mad at me."

"I have two brothers." Wyatt nodded, like he was commiserating with Kase. "They're both younger than me and they can't do anything cool like come on our adventure walks. Right, Em?"

"Right, kiddo." The truth was Weston was old enough to come with us, but Wyatt wouldn't allow it. I understood though. I didn't think Wyatt was into sharing his special aunt. Plus, it felt nice to steal a few moments of peace when people constantly surrounded you.

Most likely, that was why I'd chosen ballet when I was young. I needed a break, a reprieve from the chaos of growing up on the Devil's Share compound. My cousins were a noisy, out-of-control bunch, and I tended to be quieter, more reserved. When I was at the studio, it was my "me" time. And then one day, it was *all* my time.

"Thanks for letting me come on your adventure, Wyatt." Kase had his hands in his pockets, his eyes on the woods we were walking toward.

"You're welcome." Wyatt let go of my hand and skipped ahead, reaching the edge of the trees and stopping to wait for me like I'd taught him to do.

Kase and I walked in silence, watching as Wyatt bent down, collecting rocks and sticks, which was one of his favorite parts of our walks. I'd found a big vintage glass water jug at an antiques store and I'd placed it on his front porch. He put all his treasures in there.

Music started playing back at the welcome lunch, the sound carrying on the wind through the field to the three of us. Kase reached for my hand and before I had to a chance to process the frisson that traveled up my arm, he twirled me around.

Butterflies. Whether it was from the sweet gesture or the touch of his hand, my stomach was instantly filled with them. Kase made me nervous, but in an excited way. A little dangerous, but not scary: more like forbidden. I couldn't remember the last time a guy paid attention to me, sought me out and requested my company. I didn't know how to act or what to say.

Part of me wanted to skip ahead and let Wyatt be a buffer between us, but the other part wanted to keep dancing with Katie's handsome brother.

"Show me some moves, tiny dancer." Kase spun me out again, then brought me back closer to his chest.

A little dizzy from the contact, my laughter sounded strained to my own ears as I rested my palm on his back and swayed to the soft beat. "Ballet is different than slow dancing with a boy." No doubt technically true, but slow dancing with a boy was something I'd never done in my entire life.

He dipped me dramatically, then pulled me back up. "You feel good in my hands, Emmie James."

Those butterflies turned into dragonflies. Or, like, small birds.

We stayed pressed together, looking at each other, locked in a staring contest that I was almost afraid to win.

"Em, can we go to the woods now? *Pleeeese?*"

I blinked. And took a step back, smiling at Wyatt, who was once again clinging to my legs. "Yeah, buddy, let's go."

"Is he coming with us?" The tiny blond boy glared up at Kase, daring him to ruin our adventure walk. I couldn't help but giggle.

Kase squatted down, eye level with my nephew. "You two go ahead. I think I have to head to guys' night anyway." He glanced at me, then back to Wyatt. "Take good care of her. I think I'm going to need to dance with her again before this weekend is over."

Wyatt narrowed his eyes and crossed his arms. "I always take care of Em."

Kase bit his lips together like he was having a hard time keeping a straight face as he stood. "Can I have your number?"

I clenched my jaw to keep it from dropping open. "Uh, yeah, sure." Why did he need my number? Was he into me? Weren't we family now? Although family was a loose term when it came to the Devil's Spawn. Ask Halen and Avory.

He pulled his cell out of his pocket, handing it to me so I could add my number. My hands were shaking a bit and I hoped like hell he didn't notice.

When I gave the phone back to him, he looked down and said, "See you around, kid." He winked at Wyatt before walking away.

I let Wyatt pull me deeper into the woods, my mind still on the way it'd felt to have Kasen's hands on my body.

Chapter Four

Emmie

Girls' night: a house full of girls drinking champagne and getting facials.

Tomorrow was the rehearsal dinner, and our moms had decided that there wouldn't be time to have full spa services tomorrow night. It took time to pamper thirteen women. Time and money. Which we had plenty of. Exhibit A: the ten-person team of estheticians loaded down with everything a spa could offer.

I was sitting on the couch in Aunt Lexi's living room. Marley was lying with her head in my lap and her feet resting in Avory's. She was about six months pregnant, and not in the mood to be surrounded by wedding vibes and over-the-top declarations of love. That wasn't Marley. She was quietly head over heels for her husband, Talon, and not a girly girl in the slightest. But she was putting up with it for Katie, like I was.

My cell buzzed next to her head and she picked it up, passing it to me. She didn't bother reading my text, which was something I wasn't sure any of my other cousins would have done. Maybe it was because we were the closest in age, but she'd never treated me like a baby like everyone else did.

Unknown: Hey tiny dancer, it's Kase.

My stomach dipped when I read the message. My first text message from a boy. Well, my cousins texted me all the time, and the guys in my dance troupe texted, too, but that was about our schedules and stuff. *This.* This was my first text message from a guy who seemed to be interested in me. *Butterflies.* It'd been hard to keep my brain from wandering to all things Kase. I hadn't seen him when Wyatt and I got back to the field after our walk. And I hated that I'd been disappointed.

Emmie: Hey.

I quickly added his contact to my phone, glancing around to see if anyone noticed I was blushing.

Kasen: How was your adventure walk? See anything cool?

Emmie: A couple lizards and one hawk. Wyatt was pretty pumped.

Kasen: Wyatt is a protective little guy, huh?

Emmie: He gets lost in the mix of kids, cousins, aunts, uncles, etc. His time with me is like his little escape.

Kasen: And I invaded his territory. I get it. I'd be pissed if some dude interrupted my private time with you too.

Oh wow. Was he flirting with me? Was I supposed to flirt back? I was sure I didn't even know how to do that. I'd spent more time dancing than I did dating. And by more time, I meant that I've never been on a date. Ever. Hell, I'd never been kissed.

Emmie: How's guys night?

Kasen: Incredibly tame.

Emmie: So no blow or strippers.

Kasen: You didn't strike me as the kind of girl whose mind would go straight to coke and topless chicks.

I covered my mouth, stifling my giggle. Yes. Kase Cadence was making me giggle, and I was embarrassed for myself.

Emmie: I was raised by a group of former rock stars, surrounded by promiscuous teenagers.

Kasen: Fair enough. You at girl's night?

Emmie: Yes.

Kasen: You guys have any good drugs?

Emmie: We have nail polish and face masks.

Kasen: For a bunch of rocker offspring, these two make a lame bride and groom.

Emmie: Cash is probably the most chill of all of us, neck and neck with Beau. Now if this was two nights before Jett or Crue's wedding? You guys would probably end up in a Mexican jail cell.

Kasen: Now THAT would be a good time. I'll see you at the rehearsal dinner right?

Emmie: I'll be there.

Kasen: Have a good night Ems.

I didn't want to stop texting him. I wanted him to flirt with me some more. I wanted him to make my stomach dip and butterflies take flight. This was all new to me, having a handsome boy pay attention, compliment me, and seek me out. But I could get used to it, that was for sure.

"Why are you smiling like that?" I glanced down to find Marley studying me, eyes narrowed.

I shook my head, brushing her question off. "No reason."

"Who were you texting?"

"No one."

She snorted. "You're a shit liar."

I tapped her nose. "And you're a cranky pregnant chick."

She opened her mouth, either to be snarky or ask me again who I was talking to, but luckily she was interrupted by Aunt B. "Okay, Em, you're up."

I grinned at Marley, getting up and putting a pillow under her head.

Saved by the facial.

Chapter Five

Kase

The rehearsal dinner was in full swing, food had been eaten, and parents had made heartfelt toasts. Cash and Katie had stood and thanked their wedding parties and passed out thoughtful gifts for each of us. Katie had gotten me a new watch, which made me smile. She'd bought me my first watch when we were younger, and she'd given me a new one every couple of years since then. It was our thing.

I talked a lot of smack about all this wedding bullshit, but I really was happy for my sister. I loved her. She was my first friend, my first partner in crime. And Cash was good for her. He made her live, made her try new things and have more fun. Tomorrow he'd promise to spend the rest of his life doing those things for her, the things I'd been the one to do when we were kids.

Katie had always been cautious, always followed the rules. I, on the other hand, had encouraged her to bend them every chance she got.

I smiled when Emmie caught my eye. She was sitting next to her mom and laughing at something Jett was saying. He was talking with his hands and Devin was next to him blushing.

Emmie must have sensed me watching her because she looked my way, biting the corner of her mouth. I gestured her over to me with a slight jerk of my head, and then I sat watching the war she was waging in her mind. She wanted to come to me. Her body had immediately lifted from her chair at my suggestion. But then she'd stopped herself, her gaze darting between her family and me.

I held my breath, waiting for her to make her decision. I *wanted* that girl. There was no other way to put it. I wanted to know what she looked like when she came. I wanted to hear the sounds those sweet lips would let escape as I fucked her. Emmie was reserved, prim. I wanted to witness the moment she came completely undone.

Finally, she excused herself, smiling politely and then making her way over to my table. I pushed the chair next to me out, casually resting my arm over the back of it as she sat. "You're beautiful, you know that, right?"

Her blue eyes got wider. "Oh, um, that's really sweet, thank you." She tucked a blonde lock behind her ear, like I was making her nervous.

"Do you want to hang out after this?" I didn't want her to be nervous around me. I wanted her to let go and feel free. And if that meant I needed to play an extended version of my usual MO, then that was fine by me. "My family and I are staying at the pool house on the compound. Maybe we could go for a swim?"

She swallowed, the movement of her sexy throat drawing my attention. "I don't think my parents would be okay with that."

"I was under the impression that the Devil's Spawn didn't really do rules."

She sighed, her shoulders relaxing slightly. "Well, my cousins certainly don't."

I moved my hand so my thumb could graze her bare back. "They seem to get away with it."

"Yeah, I guess our parents don't really pay very close attention to what we do." She laughed quietly, not like she had when she'd been listening to Jett's story, which told me she didn't want anyone to notice the two of us sitting close. "Pitfalls of raising a herd of kids together on a secure compound."

I dipped down, making her meet my eyes. "Then what does it matter if your parents approve or not?" I smiled, my thumb sliding from the base of her neck to the space between her shoulder blades. "Meet me at the pool house."

She was at war with herself again. Would she say yes? Would she turn me down? The suspense might be the death of me. My dick was already hard, straining to get to her. I wanted to touch her. I wanted to taste her. I wanted to fill her.

"Um, yeah, okay."

Emmie James was going to be the highlight of my weekend, of that I was sure.

I dipped my head and whispered, "I'm going to get out of here." She nodded and I put my hand on her thigh under the table. "Text me when you get home?"

I squeezed her leg and then got to my feet, winking at her before I headed for the exit. I was hoping she'd leave soon as well. I knew we couldn't share a car back to the compound, but I wished we could. I wasn't going to sneak around. I didn't do that shit. But I had no problem avoiding roadblocks. I wanted to fuck Emmie, and I could guarantee that every member of our families would try to stop me if they had the chance.

"Where you headed, kid?" Uncle Pax came down the hallway that led to the bathrooms right as I reached the doors to freedom.

"Pool house." I put my palms on the double doors, prepared to push them open and escape.

"Not so fast." He grabbed the back of my shirt. "Why are you leaving so early?"

"It's a fucking rehearsal dinner, Uncle Pax, not an all-night kegger." I turned, shrugging him off and crossing my arms over my chest. "I've done the damn barbeque, welcome lunch, guys' night, and rehearsal." I grinned humorlessly. "I'm all family'd out for the moment."

"Oh yeah?" He raised one eyebrow. "So you're not headed back to the compound to spend time with another new *family* member?" He pointed back into the dinner area. "Because it looks like Emmie is telling everyone good-bye."

"Maybe she's fed up with the festivities too." I wrinkled my nose. "And she is *not* a member of my family. Don't say that shit."

"Why?" He rolled his eyes. "Because it'll make it harder for you to justify hooking up with her?"

I sighed, pushing past him and opening the doors into the warm night, knowing that he would follow me. I headed down the walkway flagging one of the town cars they had on standby.

"Kase."

I turned to face my favorite uncle, the one who had never in the history of our life together tried to stop me from doing something I so clearly wanted to do. "I know you're against this, I get it. But I don't care."

"She's young and we both know she's more innocent than what you're used to." He stepped closer, dropping his volume. "You can't hurt her. You *can't.*"

I nodded, moving out of the way so the driver could open my door. "I'll be honest, like I always am, like *you* taught me to be." I shrugged. "But if she's still game, I'm playing." I climbed into the sleek black car, the windows so heavily tinted that I could no longer see the hesitation on my uncle's face.

Chapter Six

Kase

She'd texted me when she got home, and I felt like a tiger in a cage waiting for her to get here. But it didn't take long for Emmie to join me at the pool house. I watched as she walked up through the fields, opening the side gate. My eyes were on her, but hers were on her feet. I didn't say a word as she kicked off her shoes and gathered her long black dress before sitting next to me, and then put her feet in the water. Her shoulder was resting against mine and that touch alone was doing things to me mere contact never had before.

There was something different about Emmie James. My life was one grand adventure after the other, and I pretty much did what I wanted whenever I wanted to. But the *want* that crawled inside my chest for the timid girl sitting next to me was altogether different: stronger, more persistent.

"Talk to me, Ems." I needed her to relax and I wanted to hear her voice.

She licked her lips, her eyes on the dark water in front of us. I'd left all the pool lights off, not wanting anyone to see us if they decided to come home early. I was like Wyatt, refusing to let my time with her get stolen.

"Um, Katie says that you travel a lot for work. What is it that you do?"

I smirked, curious to see the reaction my answer would cause in her. "I'm a model."

"I could see that." Her hands went to her mouth like she was shocked she'd said those words out loud.

"You think I'm hot, little spawn?" I couldn't help but give her a hard time. Gently, I pulled her hands away. Before she could answer, which seemed like it would take a while since she was blushing, I told her, "I'm kidding. I'm not only a model. Agencies book me for jobs, and then fly me all over the world where I capture and create content. I take pictures of the beautiful locations, do drone videos, you name it. And then I turn around and sell that content to different companies to use however they want."

"That sounds really interesting."

"It's a good setup." I put my palm next to hers on the rough concrete, letting my pinkie touch hers. "I get to see the world, my travel expenses are covered, and I make double the money on each modeling booking. My fee, plus what content I sell."

She finally looked at me, a smile on her lips. "You're smarter than you look, Kasen Cadence."

"I guarantee you there's much more to me than meets the eye." I winked, and those smiling lips of hers parted in a gasp, drawing my gaze to her tempting mouth.

I put my hand on her neck, gently pulling her closer. I gave her time to tell me no. To pull back. I gave her time to stop what was about to happen between us. But instead, she watched with avid interest as I leaned in to kiss her. She let my lips move against hers, she let me part them, slipping my tongue inside her sweet mouth. She tasted like cake and champagne, and I fucking loved it.

She whimpered, and I lost my mind for a second. I grabbed her hips, pulling her into my lap. She weighed nothing. A hummingbird perched on my knees. My hands traveled to her tiny ass, enjoying the way her core felt against my dick as she straddled me. She groaned, her fingers tightening on my shoulders.

I kept kissing her, my palms squeezing her ass, helping her grind on my cock. I was impossibly hard, and images of laying her out beside the pool danced inside my head.

I moved my lips to her throat, licking her rapid pulse. I pulled back to study her. Her eyes were closed, and her lips were parted. She was trembling in my arms. I smirked, loving the way her body was responding to mine. She was going to come, it was written all over her beautiful face.

I whispered against the shell of her ear, "You feel so good, Emmie."

She let her forehead drop to my shoulder, panting.

I kept my hand on her ass, not letting her stop her increasingly intense grinds. I wanted her to come. I wanted to make her feel good. And more than that, I wanted her to want more when she woke up tomorrow.

I started moving against her pussy, feeling its heat through her panties and my pants. Fuck, this girl was on fire. I groaned, fighting the urge to pull her panties to the side and slide inside her core.

I wanted more. I wanted it all.

But she was right. I was smarter than I looked. The wedding wasn't until tomorrow, and if I hooked up with Emmie James right now, I would end up all alone tomorrow night. I couldn't fuck her two nights in a row, chicks tended to take a double to mean more than it was. One-night stands were where it was at. The sweet spot.

I grabbed her hair, bringing her head up so I could kiss her, swallowing her moans. Her body moved against mine and she pushed against me as she came.

I held her, waiting for her to come down and catch her breath. "You okay, Ems?"

She nodded, avoiding my gaze.

Emmie could try to hide her reaction to me all she wanted, but I knew my way around a chick's body. She wouldn't be shuddering in my arms right now if I was wrong. So, reluctantly, I pulled back, satisfied that I'd given her a good preview.

"Stay with me tomorrow night."

Her eyebrows drew in. "Is that a question?"

"I was hoping it'd be more of a given."

She nodded, biting her lips, lips swollen from my kisses. "Can I think about it?"

"Of course." I stood, reaching a hand down to help her up. "You need me to walk you home?" I looked past her to the field that stood between the pool and her house in the distance.

"One thing we all learn at an early age is to navigate this compound so well that darkness doesn't make much of a difference."

I let her fingers slip across mine as she turned and made her way to the gate she'd entered only thirty minutes ago. Her long hair blew in the breeze, her dress dancing along with it.

Fuck, she was stunning.

I chuckled, shoving my hands in my pockets as I headed back inside the pool house. I couldn't wait to have long ballerina legs wrapped around me tomorrow night.

Chapter Seven

Emmie

I felt foolish leaving like that, but I'd been embarrassed. I mean I dry humped him, came, and couldn't say a word after. Three times I considered turning back, but then I thought if I wasn't cool enough to carry on a conversation after a little fooling around, I'd only embarrass myself more by reappearing after rabbiting. So, I went to bed thinking about Kase's lips on mine, and I woke up thinking about the same thing. I'd never felt the way he made me feel. It was consuming, in a good way. I was excited and I was nervous. I'd never been kissed until Kase. I'd never been touched until he'd put his hands on me. But I wanted more. I wanted his attention and his words. I wanted to come again.

And why shouldn't I get what I wanted? I was an eighteen-year-old virgin and I was entitled to a little fun, right? I mean hell, my cousins had been having a damn ball while I sat quietly on the sidelines and watched. It was my turn to be reckless and selfish, to do something that made no sense and my parents would hate. It was my turn to live like a Devil's Spawn.

Emmie: *Your offer still open?*

Kasen: *Hell yes.*

Emmie: *Good.*

Kasen: *There's a few things that you need to know first though, Ems.*

Ems. No one else called me Ems, and I sort of liked that Kase did. It made me feel like he and I were at least friends. I wasn't thinking about giving my virginity to a complete stranger. No. I was thinking about having sex with my friend Kase. We had nicknames and he kissed like he was made of magic.

Kasen: I want you, real fucking bad. But I need you to understand that one night is all there will ever be between us. I travel all the time, and I don't plan on settling down until I'm old and gray. I'm not the guy that's going to call you. I'm not the guy that's going to do long distance. But I AM the guy who makes an excellent one night stand.

I took a deep breath, pausing for a moment while I tried to sort through everything Kase's text was making me feel. I was excited, turned on, and a little taken back. I didn't think he'd be declaring love for me or anything, but to straight say it'd be one night and one night only? It was like a preemptive rejection, and it stung a bit. Maybe Kase was exactly what I needed though. A guy I wanted, who wanted me. There would be no complications and he'd never break my heart because he wasn't going to let me give it to him.

And I was tired of being the inexperienced sweet baby of the family. I was eighteen. I was one of the most talented dancers in my company. I was an adult, and I could make my own damn decisions.

Emmie: Sounds perfect.

Kasen: Yeah? You're not just saying that because you desperately want my dick?

Emmie: Desperately? Not really how I operate.

Not that I had any clue how to operate. I'd never even gone to first base with a guy, let alone entertained the idea of having sex. Luckily everyone in my family talked about it nonstop, so I'd picked up on a few things.

Kasen: Then I'll see you tonight gorgeous.

I left him on read, smiling at my reflection in the mirror over my dresser.

Chapter Eight

Emmie

Katie and Cash's wedding was beautiful, romantic, and heartfelt. She'd walked down the aisle to a recording of her dad singing an old David Essex song, *Rock On*. Cash had cried, Crue had put his hand on his brother's shoulder, and Jett had chuckled, but then secretly wiped his eyes through the whole damn ceremony.

There were flowers everywhere in the gothic church in downtown Austin. The interior was transformed into a living, breathing garden. Katie and Cash loved this space, and they wanted to have their reception here as well. The diocese told them that wasn't possible, so their dads had pulled out their wallets and made an insane donation. After the ceremony, we'd all moved out to the back courtyard where a large white tent held a million fairy lights.

"Would you like to dance?"

I looked up to see Kase, his palm out with a smile on his hot model face. I nodded, putting my hand in his and letting him lead me to the dance floor. "Is dancing allowed though? I thought I got one night and nothing more."

"We danced at the welcome lunch." He twirled me around, bringing me back tight against his hard body. "And you technically got two nights, Ems." He put his cheek next to mine. "We both know you came last night."

I was blushing. I had to be. I'd never been talked to the way Kase spoke to me, and it made my heart pump faster than any opening night performance. And he was right. Last night as I straddled his lap, his hard length hitting my clit on repeat had made me come. He'd given me my first orgasm, or at least the first one that wasn't self-initiated.

As we danced pressed close together, I wondered if anyone noticed us, moving in sync around the dance floor. Kase was gorgeous, and a good dancer. I felt like I was floating. I took deep breaths, willing my pulse to slow. He'd be gone in the morning, and we weren't falling in love.

"Ems?"

"Yeah?"

"You sure you're okay with this?"

Was he reading my mind? Could he feel the tension in my muscles? I was sure, I was so sure that it was supposed to be Kase and that it was supposed to be tonight. But I was nervous too.

"Of course I am." I let out the breath I'd accidentally been holding. "One more night, and then you're gone." I was saying it out loud for myself, to make sure the butterflies in my stomach heard me. "Don't worry, Kase, I won't be crying into my pillow once the sun comes up."

At least, I hoped I wouldn't be.

Chapter Nine

Kasen

Emmie was probably the hottest bridesmaid I'd ever seen. And I'd been to a fuck ton of weddings. She outshined her cousins, that was for sure. I couldn't say she looked more beautiful than the bride, because the bride was my sister and she'd punch me in the junk. But she was definitely sexier than the bride.

The wedding was full of sweet moments, flowers, and old-school Texas country music. Katie and I both grew up listening to the stuff with our Uncle Pax, who was currently twirling Avory around the crowded dance floor. Crue was in the corner, drinking from a silver flask and scowling. Cash's twin needed to find someone else to wet his dick before his face got stuck like that.

After the song ended, Uncle Pax came over and sat next to me, and my uncle Parker, and Pax was winking at Crue to fuck with him. "That kid needs to get his shit together."

"I was thinking the same thing." I took a sip of my whiskey. "You dancing with his girl was a prick move. I like it."

Uncle Parker scoffed, "Those two are a damn mess."

I swirled my cocktail around in the crystal tumbler. "How is it that you old scoundrels know about their drama but their parents still haven't figured it out?"

"Well, I had to listen to Crue bitch and moan every time I visited Cash and Katie out in Cali."

Uncle Parker pointed across the room to the table where Smith, Dash, Jacks, and Luke were passing around a bottle of scotch. "And in case you haven't noticed, the Devil's Share keeps their heads firmly in the clouds."

Let's hope so, because I was about to take their youngest upstairs and do unthinkable, delicious things to her perfect ballerina body. I tracked Emmie, watching as Nick, her brother-in-law, pulled her out onto the dance floor. I couldn't help but enjoy the way he made her laugh.

"Speaking of, did you hook up with the youngest James last night?"

Uncle Parker choked on his champagne. "What?"

I shook my head. "Not really."

"Good."

Parker, the more reserved of the two uncles, glanced between his brother and me. Parker had been married twice and was currently between wives at the moment. I didn't see him as much I saw Uncle Pax, but I loved him all the same. "Is there something I should know?"

Pax and I both shook our heads, choosing to keep last night's disagreement to ourselves.

My parents danced into my line of sight, blocking my view and waving to me. Mason and Payton Cadence were the complete fucking opposite of the Devil's Share crew. They watched every move my sister and I made, which was probably the reason I chose to have all my fun out of the damn country.

"Hey, man, can you cover for me with my dad?" I finished the whiskey in my crystal tumbler, knowing the only person who would question where I was about to go was my father. "I have, uh, plans."

Uncle Pax raised one eyebrow. "Plans?"

I grinned. "Naked plans. In a hotel bed."

"With who?" Uncle Parker searched the room, as if the chick I was about to fuck would be waving a red flag in the air.

"Kase." Uncle Pax said my name like he had last night, like it was a warning in and of itself. "I thought you said you didn't hook up with her. I thought you'd changed your mind."

I scoffed. "Why the hell would I change my mind? *Look* at her. I said I didn't bang her last night, not that I didn't plan to."

"Look at who?" Parker was on his damn feet now, so I put my hand on his shoulder, pressing him back into his seat.

Uncle Pax turned to me. "No. I won't let you do that, or, well, her. I won't let you do *her*." Uncle Pax gestured around the room.

"There are tons of chicks looking to fuck away their single lady blues. Pick one of them."

"I don't want one of them." And I didn't. I wanted Ems, and I planned on having her as many times as possible before it was time for me to catch my flight. "Emmie is not as innocent as everyone thinks, she knows what's up. I was nothing but honest with her, and she's still game." I leaned in closer. "It's one night, and I'm gone tomorrow."

Uncle Parker's eyes got wider as they darted between Pax and me. "Holy shit. That's a terrible idea."

Uncle Pax sighed, dropping his chin to his chest. "As I'm sitting here listening to my nephew spit my own words back at me, I'm starting to wonder if I did these kids a disservice by being so open and honest about my life choices."

"Yeah, you've really fucked them up, bro." Parker shook his head sadly, like he was disappointed in his brother.

Pax rolled his eyes. "Like you have room to talk, two divorces guy." He turned to look at me. "Kase, Parker is right, this is a terrible idea. It's your sister's wedding night and that's the youngest girl in her new family. I'm still not even convinced that chick is eighteen."

"She is." I stood, done with this cock-block. From Uncle Paxton of all people. "I googled her birthdate." I wasn't an idiot.

"There's nothing we can do to change your mind?" I shook my head, a smirk on my face. "I want the record to show that we tried." I nodded, letting Uncle Pax know it was noted. "Make sure you wrap it up. You put a baby inside their baby, they'll fucking kill you."

"I always do." I clapped a hand on his back, tossing the black bow tie that had been hanging loose around my neck onto the table in front of Uncle Parker, and went in search of that sexy little ballerina.

I found her at the bar where she was laughing with the bartender. He was into her. I could tell by the way he leaned forward when he spoke to her. He kept finding reasons to touch her arm, her hand, where they were resting on the bar top. There were people in line behind her, but he was ignoring them completely. I watched for a few more moments, enjoying the hell out of the fact that I was about to take her away from him.

I cleared my throat as I stepped up beside her, speaking loudly so the bartender would hear me. "You ready, beautiful?" She glanced behind her shoulder, eyeing all the people in line. I leaned in, putting my lips against the shell of her ear. "I'm sorry, would you rather me whisper?"

"You better take a step back before my dad sees you." She turned her back to the bar, and the bartender. "And they haven't even cut the cake yet."

"I'd rather lay you out on the bed and eat you for dessert."

The old lady standing in line behind us gasped.

Emmie covered her mouth, trying to hide her laughter. "You're going to give that sweet lady a heart attack." Discreetly, I brushed my hand up the side of her thigh, making her breath catch. "I'll, um, go first." She cleared her throat, speaking quietly. "I told my mom I was tired from rehearsals this week."

I nodded, slipping my hands in my pockets so I would keep them off her until the coast was clear. "I'll be right behind you."

And then on top of you, and under you, and behind you again.

"Leaving so soon, pretty girl?" The bartender with the stupid ponytail stuck out his bottom lip, pouting when Emmie took a step to leave.

"Yeah." She shrugged, smiling at the poor guy. "It's been a long week."

"My shift is over in about ten minutes, do you want to go for a cup of coffee? There's a place a few blocks over that should still be open."

"Oh, um, that's a really nice offer and normally, I'd love to but it's late and I've got brunch plans with my family tomorrow." She took another step away, trying to let him down gently.

"One cup? My treat?"

My treat? How much was a fucking cup of coffee? This guy needed to take the damn hint.

"Dude." I knocked my knuckles on the bar, getting his attention. "She said no thanks, let her go."

Let her go all the way up to her hotel room so she can get naked and wait for me like a good little girl.

The bartender turned to me, looking a little pissed. But luckily he kept his mouth shut and Emmie used the distraction to hightail it out of the room. My eyes tracked her until she was no longer in sight, and then I surveyed the crowd. Did anyone notice that she'd gone?

My gaze collided with Uncle Pax's. He shook his head and let out a deep sigh.

I winked at him, throwing a twenty in the tip jar.

Chapter Ten

Kasen

Emmie opened the door, wearing a thin white nightgown that stopped mid-thigh, leaving her sexy legs on full display. She'd taken out the pins from her golden hair and it was falling down her back in soft waves, all the silly flowers tossed on the dresser behind her.

"You're so fucking sexy, Ems." I kicked the door shut behind me, wasting no time as I palmed her tight little ass and lifted her slender body into my arms. I turned, putting her back against the wall, attacking her lips with mine. I wanted to fuck her hard and fast, and then I wanted to slow down and take my time. I didn't want to leave her body until it was time for me to fly away.

I moved my attention to her neck, placing kisses on her throat, her collarbone. "You sure you're good with this?" She whimpered, her nails digging into my shoulders in response. "I need to hear you say it, Ems, I need to hear that you want to be fucked."

"Yes." Her voice was breathy, like a plea.

And that was all I needed.

I kissed her, my tongue stroking hers as my hands slid up her silky thighs. I moved her panties to the side, slipping one finger inside her soaking wet pussy.

"Holy shit, you're so damn tight." Her walls were clenched around my finger, making my dick weep in anticipation.

I'd wanted to taste her the moment I'd seen her, and I was done waiting. I spun again, dropping her onto the soft white blankets covering the bed. I yanked her panties down her legs, ripping them as I tugged them over her feet. I pumped my finger in and out, placing kisses on her delicious thighs before flicking my tongue against her clit. I dropped to my knees, fully prepared to worship her perfect, unbelievably sweet pussy.

She was so wet for me, so ready. But she was so damn tight. Carefully, I added a second finger, trying to prepare her for where I needed her to be. I looked up, wanting to make sure that I wasn't being too rough. "Tell me if I'm hur—"

I stopped short, freezing. Emmie's hands were covering her face, her chest heaving like she was having trouble catching her breath. I was good, but I'd barely started. "Ems? What's wrong?"

"Nothing." She answered too quickly, slapping her hands to the mattress and shaking her head, her eyes still closed. "I'm fine. Keep going."

She didn't sound fine. And as much as I did want to *keep going*, I wasn't a total prick. "We have all night here, beautiful, tell me what's up."

She opened her eyes but kept them trained on the ceiling, like she couldn't stand to look at me. "I, um, I've never had anyone…" She waved her hand toward my head that was still between her legs. "Down there."

"Oh." What the hell kind of guys had she been with? Who wouldn't want to bury their face in her pussy? I flicked her clit with the tip of my tongue again, causing her hips to jerk. "If you want me to stop, I will, but I promise you're going to like the end result." I was my own hype man, and I was assured in my abilities to rock this girl's world. I attached my mouth to her core, sliding my fingers in and out again, reminding her how good I could make her feel.

"Don't stop." She was louder this time, some of the shyness gone from her tone.

I sucked her swollen clit. "You sure?"

"Yes, Kase, don't stop."

There we go. That was more like what I was used to hearing.

I loved that I got to do this for her, that I got to give her this first. Before I left we needed to have a serious discussion about the type of guys she was dating. All those assholes were missing out because Ems tasted like a fucking dream.

I worked her over, my fingers, my lips, my tongue. Goddamn. She had the most delectable pussy I'd ever tasted. I pulled out all the stops, *needing* to blow her mind. Her hands were in my hair, her hips moving, seeking out her release. She rode my face and I fucking couldn't get enough. Her whimpers were growing louder with every second. She was close. I started going faster, finger-fucking her harder. She was still tight, but at least I felt like I could move without hurting her.

"Kase." I'd heard my name shouted as I made girls come more times than I could count. But hearing it from Emmie's mouth was different. She sounded confused, and bewildered. Her pussy clenched around my fingers, pulsing as her orgasm hit. "Kase," she said it again, louder, fucking music to my ears.

I waited patiently for her to come down, for her to catch her breath. My dick was straining against my slacks. I pulled the small box of condoms from my pocket and then kicked my pants off, letting them join the pile of clothes where my shirt had already been tossed.

I'd shredded her panties and let the scrapes of lace rest on the mattress. She could keep the sweet white nightie on; it made me feel like I was corrupting a princess.

I moved up her body, placing kisses on her hipbones, her toned stomach, her small but perfect breasts. In that moment I thanked whoever the hell was in charge of this universe for allowing me to spend the night with this gorgeous girl.

I tore open the condom wrapper with my teeth, watching her face as I rolled it on. Her eyes were on the ceiling again; she was biting her cheek. She looked nervous, but she'd looked nervous the whole time I'd been in her room. I thought after she'd ridden my damn face, she'd loosen up a bit. But maybe that was her personality. Maybe she hadn't been with a lot of guys. She was the baby of the family, she had so many people protecting her and watching her every move. To be honest, I was pretty shocked that no one had come up here to check on her.

"You still good with this?" I needed her to know that if it was too much, too far, we could stop. I didn't want to stop. I wanted to stay inside her all damn night, but I'd walk away in a heartbeat if that was what she asked of me.

She nodded. "Yeah. I'm good."

"Ems. Look at me." I hovered over her, pushing her hair back to the pillows. Her blue eyes met mine and I could see her pulse threading in her neck. "Tell me you want this." I nudged her opening with the tip of my dick, holding my breath so I didn't let out the moan that wanted to tear from my throat. The anticipation was killing me. Me and my dick.

"I want this." She nodded, swallowing thickly. "I swear I do."

Welp, that was all I needed to hear.

I pushed inside her still-slick pussy, slowly because she was so damn tight. I couldn't break her already. We were only getting started. I studied her face as I added every inch; she winced, her eyes closing as a soft whimper escaped her lips. Fuck, I was hurting her. I couldn't possibly be any gentler, I was—

Wait.

Why can't I go any...

"Emmie."

"Hm?"

I was stopped halfway inside her, being as still as I possibly could. I was almost afraid to breathe for fear of what would happen. I cleared my throat, beads of sweat forming on my forehead. "Were you going to mention that you were a virgin? Or were you hoping I wouldn't give a shit?"

I should have noticed it earlier. How had I not put two and two together? She was so shy, nervous, and quiet. When she said she'd never had anyone between her legs, I thought she'd meant she'd never had anyone go down on her. But she meant that no one had ever touched her. Anywhere. At all.

"Emmie." I pulled my hips back, only the tip of my dick left. "You need to start talking." I didn't want tonight to be over. But I also wasn't sure I wanted to keep going either. I'd been with plenty of chicks, and virgins tended to get a little clingy. I couldn't do commitment. I couldn't even do friends with benefits. And the last thing I wanted was to end up breaking her heart.

"I was kind of hoping you wouldn't give a shit, if I'm being completely honest." She finally opened her big blue eyes. "I'm not drunk. I'm not high, and I'm saying yes. Does my virginity really matter?"

"Yes."

"And yet." Her gaze moved down my body. "You're still inside me."

"I said it matters, not that I wouldn't take it." Fuck me. Was I really considering this? The smart thing to do would be to put my overeager dick back in my pants and walk out of her room.

But. On the other hand.

Someone was going to take her virginity, so why not me? I was a nice guy. I'd make sure she felt good. I'd take my time. I knew how her body worked. I'd been paying attention. I could make her come again. I knew I could.

"Tell me you understand that this doesn't change things." I reached up, taking her chin in one hand, making her look at me. "One night, and I'm gone."

She nodded, biting at that plump lower lip of hers. "I understand."

"And this is what you want? You want me to fuck that barrier away." My dick twitched, excited at the idea.

She nodded again.

"Say it, Ems."

She took a deep breath, letting it out slowly as she hiked her smooth thighs farther up my hips, opening herself and making more room for me. "I want you to fuck it away, Kase."

I let my weight settle between her legs, entering her slowly. She didn't close her eyes like I thought she would. She didn't look away. Instead her gaze stayed glued to mine, searching. There was so much trust in her beautiful face, and it made my heart ache in a way that it never had before. It softened me. It made this *feeling* sink into my soul. This feeling that made the smirk fall from my face. I couldn't be that guy, not tonight. She deserved more. Emmie James was giving me her virginity and even though I knew I probably shouldn't take it, I *wanted* it. I wanted this forever connection to her. I wanted to be part of her life, her stories, always. But I'd be more than myself. I'd be more for her tonight.

I stopped, taking a moment so she could adjust to the fullness. I brushed her wild blonde hair back from her face and traced her perfect lips with my fingertips. "You ready, baby?" I knew this was going to hurt, and for some reason her pain was tied to mine at the moment.

She nodded.

I pulled out, hissing at how good she felt every time I moved inside her tight pussy. I took a deep breath, and she did the same. Then I surged forward, doing exactly what I told her I would. She winced, her whole body stiffening with tension. I waited, patiently still, until she started to breathe again. "Good girl." I placed a sweet kiss on her lips. "Try to relax for me." My mouth trailed across her jaw, down the column of her graceful neck.

Ever so gradually, the tautness disappeared from her muscles, allowing me to move, to make her feel better, to make her feel pleasure. I was careful, leisurely, taking my time because we had all night.

She arched her back, her hands digging into my hips. "More, Kase. I'm okay."

I nipped at her collarbone, hiding my smile against her skin. I picked up the pace, pushing up on my arms so I could watch her body react to me inside it. Her breasts were bouncing, her bottom lip caught between her teeth. Her hands were gripping my forearms, holding on for purchase. I studied her face, checking for signs that I was hurting her. But there were none. So I did want she asked. I gave her more.

I pulled most of the way out, her pussy tightening like a fist, not wanting me to go. Then I surged back in, burying myself as far as I could possibly go. She whimpered, clawing at my arms, dragging her nails down my skin. "Oh my god, Kase."

My smirk was back. I couldn't help it.

I fucked her harder, tingles of pleasure licking their way up my spine. She was so fucking tight, so fucking perfect. I'd never felt anything like Emmie James. I wanted to set up camp inside her pussy and never fucking leave. The more she whimpered and whispered my name, the harder I drove into her.

I kept watching to see her features twist in pain, in discomfort. But it never came. She loved everything I was giving her. She loved to be fucked, and I was quickly falling in love with being the one to do it.

Lust. Falling in lust. Love had no place between the two of us on this bed.

Her pussy fisted my dick, squeezing me so hard I saw goddamn stars. She was panting, her lips parted, her pulse threading wildly in her neck. She was close, chasing her release toward the edge, not at all scared to fall. "That's it, Ems, just like that, baby." I wanted her to own her orgasm, to take it from me, not wait for it to be given. I wanted her to recognize what she liked, catalogue it.

"Kase." Her blue eyes were closed now. Her eyebrows drew in like she wasn't sure of what to do next.

"Tell me what you need, what you want." I was close too, her pussy holding on to my dick so tightly I could barely move. Every push and pull like fucking ecstasy.

"More, don't stop, please don't stop." Her words were whispered, and they made me smile. Why chicks thought we'd stop right before they came was beyond me. Our pleasure, if we were doing it right, was tied to theirs. Why the hell would I want to come *without* her pussy milking my dick?

I curved my spine, resting my forehead on her collarbone. "You feel so good, Ems, so fucking perfect." And she did. She was like pure nirvana.

She moaned, her nails scratching down my back. "Kase." It was my name on her lips as she came, her core clenching in intense waves, dragging me toward that inevitable edge with her. "Oh my god...Kase."

My orgasm hit me hard, like a fucking ton of bricks. I buried myself inside her, not wanting to leave the warmth of her body as I came.

Yeah, her virginity might not have been for me to take, but I was so fucking glad I had.

Nothing felt as good as Emmie James.

Nothing.

Chapter Eleven

Kase

I slipped out of Emmie's room, closing the door as quietly as I could. I wasn't sneaking out. I didn't want to wake her. She hadn't been asleep long and the sun would be up soon. I had a plane to catch and I didn't have time for any more good-byes. If she woke up, I'd want to fuck her again and I'd miss my flight.

I hadn't been able to get enough of her, of being inside her. I fucked her over and over. She was sore, but I couldn't stay away, so I went slow. I took my time and made sure that she was okay every step of the way. I tried to leave an hour ago, but she'd been asleep on my chest, her blonde hair covering my arm and her toned thigh hiked up over my dick. Instead of sliding out of bed, I'd rolled us over and slid back inside her.

"Kase?"

I jumped about a foot in the air, spinning around. "Shit. Fuck. Damn." I sighed when I came face-to-face with my sister. "Hey, I need to head to the airport, but I'm glad I got to see you before I left." I pulled her in, hugging her tight and trying hard not to think of all the things Cash did to her in the room next door. Had they heard Ems and me? I sure as hell hadn't heard them. "You were a beautiful bride, was your big day everything you wanted it to be?" Distraction. I needed her distracted so she wouldn't ask me too many questions.

"Kase, that's Emmie's room. What were you doing in Emmie's room?"

Well. There went that. "What? That's not Emmie's room." I wasn't above lying if it got me out of this stupid hallway and on my way to Bali before consequences could catch up with me.

"*Kasen.*" Oooo, she said my full name, that wasn't good. "I did the hotel blocks with the wedding planner myself. I know for a fact that is Emmie's room, so don't even flipping try to lie to me. Now, why the heck were you sneaking out of her room?"

Well, Katie, because I took her virginity and then continued to bang her six ways from Sunday.

Yeah, the truth definitely wouldn't work here. I narrowed my eyes. "Why are you sneaking out of *your* room? The sun isn't even up, and it's your wedding night. Is something wrong? Do I need to give Cash some pointers? Is the magic gone already?"

She crossed her arms over her chest, her lips going thin and pissed off. "What the heck were you doing in Emmie's room? Stop lying, and stop trying to distract me. It's not working."

"Um, nothing happened?"

Her eyes went wide. "Did you just end that sentence with a question mark?"

"No?"

"You did it again." She poked me in the chest. "Kasen, I know that game. I invented it. Tell me what's going on right now." She stomped her foot and raised her voice. If she didn't fucking chill, she was going to wake up the rest of the family sleeping on this floor.

I motioned for her to be quiet. "What does it matter, Katie?" I spoke softly, hoping she'd take the hint. "Come on, don't you have more important things on your mind? Emmie's fine. I'm fine. Everything is fine."

She glanced at the door to the room I'd done everything but slept in. "Why wouldn't she be fine? What did you do to her?"

What didn't *I do to her?*

"Look, Katie, it's not a big deal. Emmie and I started talking at the welcome lunch. And she's a fucking gorgeous ballerina. I didn't bang her on night one. I took the time to get to know her first, like a gentleman." Which wasn't how I normally operated, but she was part of Katie's new family, and I respected that. To a certain extent.

She rolled her eyes so hard I was surprised they made it back to straight. "Yes, Kasen, thirty-six hours, you're such a gentleman. How did you ever manage to restrain yourself?"

I snorted at her sarcasm. "Well, I can't unfuck her, so why don't you drop it and go back inside your room." Definitely couldn't undo what I'd done in there. Granted, I did feel a little guilty that I'd taken her virginity when she'd offered it to me on a silver fucking platter.

"You're right." I jerked back, surprised to hear those words come out of my sister's mouth. "You're an asshole, but you're right."

Yeah. I was right. And I was also running late. "She's fine. Your family is fine. But I've got to go. I'm on a plane to Bali in like three hours." I'd stayed with Emmie longer than I'd intended, and if I didn't hurry, I'd never make it through security in time.

She nodded, taking deep breaths like she was trying to stave off a panic attack. "There is nothing I can do about it and it's my wedding night. It's fine. We're all going to be okay. You're leaving, and she's okay."

"Right, there you go." I rubbed my hands up and down her arms, trying to reassure her that this wasn't going to matter tomorrow. "I love you. Congratulations. See you around Thanksgiving?

She pursed her lips. "Did you end that sentence in a question mark?"

I winked and headed for the elevators.

Chapter Twelve

Four weeks later
Emmie

I was two weeks late. Which was fine. I put my body through so much that I rarely had normal periods. One time I went six months without having one when I was working like hell to get a spot in the company I danced with now. I trained nonstop days and days in a row. That kind of strain took its toll in all sorts of ways.

But this was the first time there was a possibility that it was something else. Kase and I had been careful, but we'd had sex. A few times. I refused to spend too much time thinking about it though. The chances were so incredibly slim.

I was tired because I was rehearsing for six to eight hours every day and then coming home to work on the two college courses I'd picked to take online. I'd be concerned if I *wasn't* longing for a good nap.

"Em, dinner is ready." My mom poked her head into my room, frowning when she saw me with my head resting on my desk beside my laptop. "You okay, baby girl?"

I nodded, sitting up so she wouldn't go find the thermometer. "Yeah. I'm burning the candle at both ends, that's all."

"You know that Dad and I are fine with you putting off your degree." She stepped into my room, taking my hand in hers and pulling me down the hallway toward the dining room. "No one expects you to try to do both right now."

"I can do it." And I could. I knew I could. "I need a good night's sleep, that's all." She kissed my forehead as I joined my family at the dining room table.

"What can she do?" Evie picked up the large bowl of quinoa, scooping some on her plate and then some on Nicky's. They came over for dinner once a week now that they were living in Austin.

"Take those online classes and keep up with her rehearsals." My mom rubbed a soothing palm on my back. "She's been so sleepy lately though."

She passed me the platter of grilled salmon and my stomach turned in protest. I clenched my jaw, working past the sudden aversion to my favorite meal. Ignoring every single warning bell that was starting to chime inside my head.

"You're a rock star, baby girl." My dad plucked a tomato off the end of his fork, chewing and swallowing before continuing. "I don't know how you do it all, but we are very proud of you."

I smiled tightly, trying like hell to not vomit up the bowl of Fruity Pebbles I'd snuck out of the pantry when I'd gotten home from practice. My dad liked sugar. My mom insisted we make healthy food choices as often as possible. Surreptitiously, he kept contraband on the top shelf of the pantry where my mom couldn't reach. And today, sugary cereal had been the only thing that sounded even remotely appetizing.

"You not hungry, Em?" Nicky glanced to my untouched food. "You sure you're feeling okay?"

I nodded, scooping up a small bite of the super food filled with kale and feta cheese. "I'm fine, guys, I promise." I choked down the quinoa, choosing it over the fish until it was all gone and I had no other choice. I took a deep breath, silently praying for my stomach to cooperate. "I um, wow, I think what I need is a full night of sleep. I've been studying until at least midnight, trying not to fall behind, you know?"

"Oh Em, baby girl. Why don't you go ahead and get in bed?" My mom put her hand on mine, squeezing it gently. "I'll come tuck you in, okay?"

I wiped my mouth, putting my napkin on the table beside my uneaten salmon and thanking all things holy that I hadn't even attempted it. I kissed her cheek, and then my dad's. "Sorry, guys. Rain check on dinner?" I smiled at my sister and Nicky, trying to sell the fact that I was simply tired. If anyone would question me, it'd be one of them. My parents believed every word I said, because unlike every other kid in this family, I'd never given them a reason not to.

"Sure, Em." My sister returned my hug and Nicky gave me a solid high five. "Get some rest."

A few minutes later I was snuggled under my covers in the dark, silent uncertain tears spilling down my cheeks. I was tired. That was all. My brain was tired. My body was tired.

That's what was happening.

That was all that was happening.

Chapter Thirteen

Emmie

Salmon wasn't the only thing I couldn't seem to stomach. In the last two weeks I'd also added beef and tuna fish to that list. Most meats made me queasy, but luckily I could choke down chicken and pork. And all things sugar. Cereal, cookies, ice cream, fruit. If it contained sugar, it was fine.

I still hadn't started my period. But again, it was totally normal, it happened to athletes all the time. No big deal.

"Em? You napping?" Beau.

I opened my eyes, shielding them from the bright sunlight. I'd told my parents I wanted to swim some laps in the family pool. But really, I'd wanted a place to sleep where no one would question me. Because I was tired. All. The. Time.

"Uh, no." I stretched my arms over my head, sitting up. "I was taking a break. I swam laps for about thirty minutes." *Lie.* I'd taken a quick dip to cool off and then promptly fell asleep.

"You feeling okay? You look a little pale."

I grinned, holding my arms out wide. "Thus the sun I'm soaking up. I spend most of my time in the studio these days. I need some vitamin D." Or the *D* was what was making me feel like constant crap. I snorted at my own joke, even thought it was a terrifying thought. Maybe I was losing my mind.

"Did you just snort?"

I shook my head. "Nope." Was he buying this bull I was slinging? "I have to get back to the house, I have homework." Now *that* wasn't a lie. I did have homework to do.

"Are you sure you're okay, Em?" He pushed my sunglasses up to the top of my head and put his hands on my shoulders. "You can tell me if something is bothering you, you know that, right?"

No, I couldn't. I couldn't tell anyone anything, because that would mean that I'd have to admit it to myself first.

"I know, thanks, Beau." I shoved my glasses down to hide my eyes and gave him a quick peck on the cheek before hightailing it back to my house. Maybe I could get a nap there before my parents got back from their meeting in Austin.

I needed sleep. That was all.

Sleep and a big bowl of cereal.

With whipped cream on top.

Chapter Fourteen

Emmie

Four weeks, one solid month of no period. But that wasn't what was worrying me. It wasn't even the exhaustion I was still feeling. No. It was the fact that I couldn't eat. I hadn't thrown up, not once. The constant aversion to most foods was too strange to brush aside though. My family had all commented on my lack of appetite. And a few of my cousins had caught me sleeping in the middle of the day. I knew my parents would happily remain in the dark, but the rest of my family was starting to ask questions.

I was hiding in the bathroom at my studio. It was our lunch break. I had fifteen more minutes until I had to go back to rehearsal. I had three more hours here before I could go home. But I couldn't wait three more hours to know.

Waiting the two minutes the instructions had suggested was hard enough. My knees were bouncing while tears were silently falling down my face. My heart knew even if my brain was still clinging to hope. The timer on my cell went off and I picked up the test off the top of the toilet paper holder.

I was pregnant.

No. No, no, no. That couldn't possibly be right, could it? I closed my eyes, then opened them again, but there were still two lines. I shook the test frantically, like it was an Etch A Sketch I could erase. No such luck. No matter what I did, that stupid stubborn second line refused to go anywhere.

I'd done something wild and fun for myself, and it'd come back to bite me in the ass. Hard.

My hands were shaking, and my heart was pounding. Tears were pouring off my face and landing in my lap. I was losing my shit as quietly as possible.

But I needed to get it together. The damage was done, and there wasn't anything I could do about it until after rehearsals were over for the day. I sniffled, wrapping the test in toilet paper and shoving it down deep in the trashcan. I wished I could shove all my feelings in there too. All my stupid inconvenient feelings.

One night and then I'll be gone.

Well, Kase, you left something behind, you big handsome jerk.

I hadn't talked to him since the night of the wedding. He hadn't texted. He hadn't called. He'd kept his word. For the first few weeks after the wedding, before I'd started to feel sick, it was almost like he'd never existed at all. Like a dream.

And now, he was like a damn nightmare.

I wiped my eyes, took three deep breaths, and walked out of the stall with my head held high.

I didn't have time to lose it right now. No one could know. I couldn't cause a scene here or at home. This was mine and mine alone. I'd finish rehearsal, and then I'd call a clinic. I needed confirmation, and then I needed to move on.

Eighteen-year-old dance prodigies didn't get knocked up by one-night stands. I had my whole life ahead of me, my whole career. I had a plan, and this? This did not fit into it.

Chapter Fifteen

Emmie

I closed the front door, locking it behind me. Everyone on the compound refused to knock, and I really rather my family think no one was home. My parents were out of town again, and I planned on sleeping from now until tomorrow.

At least now I could eat more than just cereal.

Ten weeks. I was now ten weeks pregnant. I knew that because I'd gone in last week for an appointment at the clinic near my dance academy. They showed me a tiny peanut on an ultrasound. I heard its heartbeat, and I cried. It was so small, so innocent.

That baby didn't fit into my life, but I was its whole world.

And I couldn't go through with it. I'd gotten off the table and walked out. I'd still been wearing the gown.

I dropped my duffle in the entryway, taking my hair down from its tight bun on my way to my room. My bed. Oh how I loved my bed these days. I stopped short. "What are you all doing here?" I frowned, taking in all the spawn sitting around my bedroom. "I don't think half of you have ever been in my room before."

I was the youngest child, the baby. By the time I was old enough, and cool enough, to hang out with my cousins, they were all grown. And the ones closest to my age, Jett and Marley, they had each other and there was no space for me. Which was fine. I had my own life. I had dance, and I was busy. But that made all of them scattered around my room all the more jarring.

"We're here because we love you, Emmie."

"Great. I love you guys too." I moved to my best friend, my bed, and shoved Jett to the side. "But I've danced for a total of seven hours today and I need to lie down for a little bit." I climbed onto my mattress, hoping they'd get the hint and save whatever odd talk this was for later.

Like. Way later. The twelfth of never, maybe.

"She's not taking in enough calories." Jett patted my head. "Her body is out of fuel."

I swatted his hand away. "What?"

Beau stood from his seat at my desk. "Emmie, we've noticed that you've lost some weight recently."

"Lost some? Really?" I wasn't convinced that was true. I felt bloated as all get out.

"You push away dinner." Evie was sitting next to Nicky on the floor beside my bed. "Salmon is your favorite and you refuse to eat it."

I clenched my jaw shut, my mouth watering with the threat of throwing up. Fish was my one remaining aversion.

"You're either at practice or sleeping, none of us see you at mealtimes anymore." Landry was on my windowsill, Brody sitting between her knees on the ground.

This was all getting a bit dramatic. And this baby made me a hell of a lot less pleasing than I normally was. "Uh, do you normally see me at meals? Other than family dinner? Because I don't remember any of you inviting me over for a big bowl of spaghetti recently." Spaghetti, now *that* sounded amazing. With some garlic bread? Yum. I gave myself a mental headshake, bringing my attention back to my room.

Why were they all here? Did they suspect I was pregnant? Did they think I was hiding an illness?

"She sort of has a point." Talon winced. "You guys never invite her to dinner." He was glaring across the room at Jett, like this was all his fault. "You should make more of an effort."

Jett flipped him off, then put his hands on my cheeks. "Emmie, are you throwing up everything you eat? Or are you the other kind of eating disorder where you don't eat at all?"

Talon threw his hands in the air, like he was exasperated. "Jesus, Jett, what the hell is your problem?"

They thought I had an eating disorder? Good Lord. I closed my eyes, wishing them all away. *You hear that, tiny baby? Your fish aversion is making everyone think we're bulimic.*

"Tiptoeing around the issue isn't getting us anywhere and she's about to fall asleep during her own intervention."

My eyes popped back open at Jett's words. "Intervention? You guys staged an intervention because you think I have an eating disorder?" That's why they were all here? Not to confront me, but to send me to some kind of rehab facility? Maybe I should take them up on it. I bet there was a lot of time for naps in whatever cushy rehab place they had in mind.

"Yes, Emmie. You don't eat and you're losing weight." Beau steepled his fingers under his chin like a therapist in a bad movie. "You're tired all the time, you—"

"I'm pregnant, you morons." I rolled onto my side, adjusting my pillow. "Now please go away so I can sleep." I wasn't planning to blurt the truth out like that. But they were all crowding me and I was too exhausted to keep up the lies. They'd all find out eventually, right? What was I expecting to happen? Let the baby introduce itself once it got here?

"Holy fuck." Beau sat back down at the desk.

Jett rubbed my stomach over the covers. "Well, that's better than an eating disorder, isn't it?"

"Do Mom and Dad know?" Evie came to sit next to me.

"No. And I'm not ready to tell them, so keep your big mouths shut please."

Evie shook her head, frowning. "I think you should tell them, Emmie. Keeping this a secret isn't a good idea."

I looked around the room. Landry, Beau, Talon, even fucking Nicky were all nodding in agreement. And that straight pissed me the hell off. How dare they come in here and demand that of me. I rarely lost my temper. I was always controlled. But right now? I was feeling a little bit crazy.

"So let me get this straight." I sat up, throwing my covers off and over Jett's head. "Every other member of this family can fuck up? Sex tapes. Drug addiction. Covert op tunnels. Sneaking around and lies that went on for years. Lying for *each other* constantly. But the second I toe one damn foot out of line, everyone loses their shit and wants to run and tell my daddy?"

Beau glanced at my sister, then back to me. "Em, you didn't toe a foot out of line, you got knocked up."

I pointed across my room. "So did Landry."

"She was an adult, living on her own, in a surgical residency program." Talon stepped forward, going up a few notches on my new shit list.

"And I was well on my way to becoming a prima ballerina in the ABA." I threw my hands in the air. "But things change."

"They don't have to change, Emmie." Nicky got off the floor, coming to join the party on my bed. "You don't have to keep this baby, there's adoption, there's—"

"Don't you dare say it." I shook my head, my eyes narrowed. "I might be the youngest in this family, but I'm not a child. While all of you were busy helping fix each other's mistakes, I grew up." I pointed at myself, my emotions running high. "I have money, like the rest of you. I can have this baby. I can raise this baby. I can do this. I *will* do this. And I don't need anything from any of you."

I pushed off the bed, needing to get away. This was too much, too intense. Everyone was worried about me, and no one agreed with what I wanted. It was like they all still saw me as a five-year-old girl with pigtails and a fluffy pink tutu. But that wasn't me, not anymore. And for the first time in my life, I was fully prepared to walk out on my family.

"Emmie, wait, we're sorry." Cash gently grabbed my wrist, stopping me as I tried to walk past him. "You shocked us, that's all."

"Is this what your parents feel like all the time?" Talon rubbed his chest, like he was about to have a heart attack. "I gotta say, it's not fun."

Nicky had his arm around my sister, like he was comforting her. But I was the one with the life-altering news. "What about the baby's father? Does he know? Is he going to stick around?"

The baby's father. Yeah. I was not about to get into that with my family. Especially since Katie had been the only one not chiming in and pissing me off. She was standing with Cash in the corner next to my desk, looking a little pale. Did she know?

All eyes went to Jett when he raised his hand in the air. "What he really means is, who is he?"

I swallowed past the bile that was rising in my throat once again. Talking about Kase with my family, now that might actually make me throw up.

"He's, um, a friend, sort of. It was one night and he doesn't know." I shrugged like it was no big deal. "I have no plans to tell him. He wouldn't want this. He has his life and I have mine. I don't need anything from him either." But it was a big deal. It was something I'd lain awake night after night thinking about, both before and after my appointment at the clinic.

"The chicks in this family, I swear." Brody got to his feet and then crossed the room to stand right in front of me. "Em, he deserves to know." His blue eyes were more serious than I'd ever seen them. "Landry didn't plan to tell me about Wyatt, and it broke my fucking heart. I was as wild as they come, but if I'd never had the chance to know my son… I can't even wrap my mind around it, Emmie. You get to make the choice whether you keep that baby or not, but *he* gets to make a choice too."

I had made a choice, and I'd made it for me and me alone. Keeping the baby was what was in my heart. It was what my soul chose to do. I hadn't even thought about Kase in that moment. But Brody was making me think maybe I should have. I didn't like the guilt that was starting to gather in my gut.

"Who *is* he?" Jett was pleading with me.

Nicky popped him on the back of the head. "You're a nosy fucker, you know that?"

He nodded. "Yes."

"She doesn't have to tell us until she's ready." Evie sent me a soft smile, the sibling form of an apology. Good. She owed me one after trying to demand I tell our parents about the baby. She kept secrets for years. Big fucking secrets. Why couldn't I keep this one for a little longer?

"Bullshit." Jett crossed his arms over his chest. "She wants us to lie for her, to cover for her, she has to be honest with us. That's the way it works. Us against the world, but she has to let us in."

I rolled my eyes. "I'm not part of your little club. I never have been."

Beau wrapped me in his arms, kissing the top of my head. "Emmie, that's not true. You're one of us, from the second you were born, you were one of us. And that baby? That baby is one of us too."

I hid my face in my big cousin's chest, taking deep breaths. I wasn't prepared for everyone to see me cry. But Beau's words were sweet, and exactly what I needed to hear. I needed to know that I wasn't alone, that I never had been. I didn't need them forcing decisions on me. I didn't need them ratting me out. I needed them to love me, to be there for me, to reassure me. And I hadn't realized how badly until Beau had offered it to me.

He rubbed my back. "This is the first time you've really needed us. You don't mess up on the daily like the rest of these yahoos. You were always more a Devil's Angel than Devil's Spawn. But let me be the first one to officially welcome you over to the dark side." He put his hands on my shoulders, pushing me back and grinning. "Knocked up at eighteen by a one-night stand with a guy none of us know? Pretty spectacular first offense."

Landry raised her hand. "Mine was breaking curfew *and* wrecking my car in the same night."

Beau snorted. "I started having sex with the underaged girl next door."

Jett sighed. "Marley made me her accomplice in burning down a shed."

I'd told them about the baby, and although their initial reaction hadn't been the best, they'd moved past it. They were giving me exactly what I needed in this moment: acceptance and love. I wanted their offer. I wanted *us against the world*. It was making me emotional, making me want to let them in. I took a deep breath. "You do know him. You know the father."

"Are you going to tell us who he is?" Jett rubbed his palms together. "Holy fuck I'm so excited."

I winced, my gaze darting to Katie.

She gasped, shaking her head. "No, please tell me it's not him."

Brody's eyes went wide. "Holy fuck, is it Cash? I think I'm going to be sick." He bent at the waist, resting his hands on his knees, gagging.

"What? It's not me, you dipshit." Cash pushed his shoulder, sending him toppling to the ground.

Katie groaned, her head falling back as she gawked at the ceiling. "I'm going to freaking kill him."

She *did* know, or at least she'd suspected. That was why she'd remained quiet this whole time. Had Kase told her? Why? It was a one night and he acted like he didn't want anyone to know, which had been fine by me. So why had he told his sister?

"Wait. *Kase?*" Cash's attention jerked back to me. "Is it Kase?"

I nodded.

"Katie, get in line," Beau ground out, "because I'm going to fucking kill him first."

"How did this even happen? How did the two of you end up…banging?" Brody was back on the ground, leaning against the wall between Landry's knees again.

Talon looked to his best friend, a bewildered expression on his face. "You paused to find the right word and came up with *banging*?"

"Fucking felt dirty." Brody wrinkled his nose, reminding me of Wyatt when someone tried to get him to eat broccoli. "Sleeping together? Is that better?"

Jett scoffed. "From what I've heard of Kase's reputation, I'd say fucking would be more accurate. Doubt he slept."

"Dude." Talon shook his head.

"What?" Jett turned to me, his eyebrow raised in question. "Emmie, did he stay the night? Did you wake up with him and go for a nice brunch?"

"No, he was gone when I woke up."

Jett gestured toward me. "See?"

"I'm going to kill him." Talon pointed at Beau. "You first, then me."

Brody held his hand up. "Let's cut off his dick, and *then* kill him."

"I saw him come out of your room, the morning after our wedding." Katie looked sad, like she was disappointed. I wanted to tell her that it wasn't her fault, that it was no one's fault. No one's but mine. I'd made the choice, and I was going to be living with it every single day from here on out.

But there were so many people talking, no one seemed to require input from me.

Cash frowned at his wife. "You knew? And you didn't say anything?"

"What was I supposed to say? *Hey, Cash, I know it's our wedding night but Kase was next door banging your little cousin?*"

"You get that in your head, it would have killed your boner." Jett nodded sagely. "She did the right thing."

"Shut up," Cash snapped at his youngest brother.

Great, now my family was arguing with each other. Cash wasn't happy with Katie. Katie was disappointed in her baby brother. And

Jett, as he was prone to do, was close to pissing everyone off at this point.

"So, a one-night stand at a wedding with a fuck-boy groomsman?" Brody sighed. "Cliché, baby girl."

He wasn't wrong. I was like a bad romantic comedy, except that night wasn't Kase and my meet-cute. Nope. Far from it. We wouldn't be living happily ever after, laughing over all this one day as we watched our child dance in her first recital. This wasn't the beginning of my fairy tale, and I'd accepted that.

Now I needed everyone else to.

"I thought Emmie'd save that virginity of hers for her husband." Jett pointed at Talon. "Marley and I had a bet. I owe your baby momma fifty bucks."

"I did too...wait." Beau turned to me. "Emmie, was that your first time?"

Really? Did we need to get into all this too? Why was this day the absolute worst?

Cash took my silence as a resounding yes. "And you chose Kase? For fuck's sake, why?"

"Because he would take it." My sister hung her head for a minute, then picked it up and met my eyes. "Emmie. Are you okay? Was he..."

"Oh my god." I cut my hands through the air, silencing their questions. "Yes, I was a virgin. Yes, I chose Kase because I didn't think he'd care. But yes, he was good to me, and kind and sweet, and all the things I needed him to be. So can we please stop talking about it?"

"Have you spoken to him since he, you know, knocked you up?" Talon glanced at my stomach.

"I haven't talked to him since that night. I wasn't going to tell him about the baby."

Katie reached out and took my hand in hers, squeezing it. "Emmie, I don't know what to say."

"You're not responsible for your brother any more than Cash is responsible for me. And he didn't do anything wrong, neither one of us did. We were careful."

We were careful. Kase had worn condoms, he'd even pulled out, I think. We weren't reckless. We didn't throw caution to the wind. We were responsible. As responsible as we could be.

"You chicks are hella fertile." Brody shook his head. "Landry and I use a stupid amount of condoms, and I keep knocking her up too." He pointed at Talon. "That what happened to you guys too?"

Talon closed his eyes for a moment and took a deep breath. "For the last time, our pregnancy was *planned*."

Brody snorted. "Whatever you say, man."

Chapter Sixteen

Emmie

It'd been a few days since my family had gathered in my room and tried to stage an intervention. But Brody's words had been on my mind long after they'd all gone home. He made me question my decision to not tell Kase about the baby.

I'd started to think that he was right, that Kase deserved to make his own mind up about becoming a father. So I'd called him, three times. I left voice mails, and he never called me back. I'd since resorted to text messages.

Emmie: Can you call me back when you get a chance?
Emmie: It's kind of important.

He hadn't responded to those either. I'd tried convincing myself that his lack of a response was the answer I needed. I thought I could use that as him saying he didn't want to be part of our baby's life. But it didn't work.

Kase needed to hear the truth.

I knocked on Cash and Katie's door, hating that I was having to drag her into this. I knew she felt partly responsible, but it was unnecessary.

"Hey, Em, come in." She opened the door wide, inviting me inside.

I glanced around the room, glad that I didn't see Cash. Him knowing that Kase was ignoring me would only make him hate his brother-in-law more than he already did. "Can I talk to you for a minute?"

"Yeah, kiddo, what's up? You feeling okay?" She gestured for me to sit, doing the same herself.

"It's Kase."

She winced. "Oh no, you told him? What did he say? Was he an asshole? I'm so sorry."

"I can't get ahold of him." I cut her off, not wanting her to think the worst. "He, um, won't call me back."

"Oh."

"I was wondering if you could reach out to him." I smiled, trying to go for casual, like I wasn't a ball of nerves at the moment. "What Brody said the other day keeps running through my mind. How Kase should get to make a choice too. I want him to know, before I start to show and the rest of the world finds out."

"I'll see what I can do." She leaned forward, squeezing my hand like she'd done the other day in my bedroom. "He shoots in these crazy remote jungles and stuff. He might not have his cell turned on."

"Thanks."

"You want to stay for dinner? Cash is doing press this week. It's me here with the dogs." She looked hopeful, like she wanted me to say yes.

I hadn't spent much time with Katie one on one. She and Cash had spent so much of their life together living in California. But now she was here, on the compound, married to my cousin. And I was carrying her niece or nephew. We were connected, for better or worse, and it was probably high time we became friends.

I nodded. "I'd like that."

Chapter Seventeen

Kase

I ran out of the bathroom, towel drying my hair as I dove for my cell. "Yelllllllllo?"

"You're so lame."

I snorted at Katie's response. "Nice to hear your voice too, sister mine."

I wouldn't normally have hurried to answer the phone, but I'd flown in from the middle of nowhere today and this was the first time I had service or Wi-Fi. I was starved for connection with my family.

"Emmie said she tried to call you."

I put the call on speaker, carrying it with me back into the bathroom so I could put clothes on. "She called a couple times, but I've been traveling a lot."

"You need to call her back, Kase."

I rolled my eyes at my sister's dramatic tone. "I will. I'll be back in the states in a couple weeks." I was in between gigs at the moment, but I was staying in Europe until it was time to hop a train to Spain. No use doing that trans-Atlantic flight twice in that same number of weeks.

"Kase."

What was my sister's deal? I'd seen Ems's calls. I'd read her texts. But I'd been honest with that gorgeous girl, and she'd sworn that she understood. Changing the game plan wasn't going to happen. It was one night, and it didn't matter how incredible it'd been. I wasn't going to indulge some misplaced infatuation. It would only prolong the inevitable.

"Look, Katie, I know she's your family now, but Emmie knew what she was getting into with me. I was completely honest with her."

"See, that's the thing, Kase. I don't think she knew *everything* she was getting when it came to you."

"What's that supposed to mean?" Was she insinuating I gave that chick an STD? Because hell to the fuck no. I always wrapped it up. And I got tested monthly. If there was something going on with Ems, it was someone else's problem.

"Call her, Kase."

"I will, promise. I've gotta go, talk soon, love you."

I hung up the call, tossing my phone back into my room and letting it bounce on the bed. Who knew Ems would turn out to be a crazy clinger? I thought she seemed cool enough. But then again, I had been her first. Keeping my distance was probably for the best. If she thought she was in love, hearing from me would only make it worse. I hoped that she got over this shit before Thanksgiving. If not, I'd be skipping out on that big blended family activity.

I was not about to sit next to Uncle Pax and have him shoot me *I told you so* looks over the turkey.

Chapter Eighteen

Kase

I was finally home, and back in the United States, back in Texas and back at the ranch. My mom had done my laundry and my dad had grilled me a steak. I was lying in my own bed, watching good old-fashioned trashy American TV.

I took a deep cleansing breath and counted my blessings.

Life was fucking fantastic.

My cell rang on my nightstand, Emmie's name flashing across the screen bringing me down from my high a bit. I wanted to send it to voice mail, but Katie wanted me to talk to her. I'd indulge my sister and use it to restate my stance. One night, *no mas*, no matter how fucking hot Ems was.

"Hello?" I really hoped this phone call wouldn't come back to haunt me.

"Hey."

She sounded a little pissed, her tone clipped. "How's it going, Ems?"

"I've been calling you for weeks." Great, she was going to go the whole a woman scorned route.

"Yeah, I've been traveling, bouncing from country to country. I landed back in Texas a few hours ago." *And your clinger call ruined my bliss, thanks for that.* "What's up?"

"I'm pregnant."

"Oh." That was not the direction I thought this call was going to go. "Congrats, I guess?" Why was she telling *me* this? Was she hoping I'd confess my love? Beg her to get rid of her baby daddy because I wanted to be with her? Not gonna happen. "Who's the lucky guy?"

"What? You are."

That couldn't be right. It wasn't possible.

Well, it wasn't *probable*. "No. We were really careful, I'm pretty sure I even pulled out. So it can't be mine, you made a mistake."

"I've never been with anyone else, Kase, you know that."

"You hadn't been with anyone *before* me, but I have no clue what you've done *since*." My throat was dry. I reached for the beer on my nightstand and drained every drop.

"You think I'm lying about this? Are you kidding me right now?"

If she hadn't been pissed before, she sure as shit was now.

"Look, Ems, you're a great girl. But that baby isn't mine, it can't be. It would be a statistical anomaly." I didn't have the brainpower to do the math in my head at the moment, but condoms and pulling out? I mean one was 98% effective and the other was like 78% effective. So, you know, put those two together and that was *not* my baby.

"I don't even know what to say to you right now."

Good. Great. Loss of words, that was my out. "Congrats on the baby, but I've got to go."

"I never planned on telling you that I was pregnant, because I don't need anything from you. I never even *wanted* to tell you. But Brody made me feel awful. He made me feel like a terrible person. He said you deserved to choose whether you wanted to know your kid or not." She laughed in this manically scary way. "I *knew* you wouldn't want this, and I was okay with that. But to call me a *liar*? To *deny* that the baby is even yours? Fuck you, Kase."

I pulled my phone away from my ear, staring at the screen. She hung up on me.

My heart was racing. I needed another beer or, like, a whole fucking keg. She hadn't wanted to tell me? Did that mean that she wasn't lying after all? Brody made her tell me? Brody knew about the baby. Did that mean everyone else did too? Did they all think it was mine?

Holy fucking shit. No. There was no way that was my baby.

I called Katie, standing and pacing my room, getting more and more agitated with every unanswered ring.

"Hello?"

Thank fuck she finally picked up.

"Emmie's pregnant." *She's pregnant, but it's not mine. It can't be mine.*

"You talked to her?"

Shit. That was why Katie had called me a few weeks ago. That meant Katie believed her. "So you knew?"

"We all know."

We all know. Okay, so that was like what, twenty people, give or take? And they all thought the baby was mine. Holy fuck. "Her parents know?" Why hadn't her dad tracked me down and tried to murder me?

"No. Only the spawn."

The damage wasn't all the way done then. There was still time to fix this. Still time to make them understand. "It's not mine."

"Are you in denial or are you that big of an asshole?"

"I wore a condom. And I pulled out." *Right?* I knew the condom part was accurate. I can remember seeing the small pile of them in the hotel room trashcan. It was like an ugly gold color. But had I pulled out? I usually did. I don't know why I wouldn't. "It can't be mine."

"She was a virgin, Kase."

I snorted. "Yeah, that I remember." But then that comment felt super inappropriate so I tried to cover it with a cough.

"Gross."

"Maybe she was with someone after me?" And when I said maybe, what I meant was please god let that be the case. Let it be someone else's baby.

"Or maybe you knocked up the youngest member of the Devil's Share family."

No. I refused to believe that. "Have you seen her with anyone else?"

"I'm going to stop you right there." There was a brief pause and then she continued, adopting a slightly harsher tone. "You're my brother and I love you. More than I love a lot of things in life. But you need to pull your head out of your ass. Emmie decided to tell you about the baby because it was the right thing to do, not because it was something she *wanted* to do."

"She said she wasn't planning on telling me." Katie knew she didn't want to tell me, so that meant everyone else knew that she never wanted to tell me. Fuck you, Brody. Fuck you very much for making her do the right thing.

"We all had to convince her that you deserved to know. She said she didn't need your help, that she didn't need anything from you."

She didn't need anything from me. Made sense. In her mind I'd already given her enough. *Fuck.* Emmie didn't want me to know. It took her whole family to make her tell me. She wasn't lying. I knocked her up and she hated me for it. So much so that she wanted nothing to do with my rude ass.

And I'd made it worse. "I basically called her a liar."

"You're an idiot."

I nodded, even though my sister couldn't see me. "She hung up on me."

"She should have driven south and punched you in your stupid handsome face."

"Holy fuck." I sat down on my bed, closing my eyes when I felt the room start to spin. "I don't want to be a dad, Katie."

"Emmie figured as much." She figured as much because I'd told her over and over how I didn't want anything that even vaguely resembled commitment. "Me on the other hand? I was really hoping you'd surprise them all."

Fuck my dick. Why couldn't he stay away? Why couldn't he leave her the way he'd found her? And now she was pregnant. You know what the biggest form of commitment was? Being a fucking parent. "I'll call you later." I needed to freak the hell out and have a meltdown of epic proportions.

"Love you, dummy."

"Love you too." *Sorry I accidentally knocked up your new husband's youngest cousin.*

I pulled out the bottle of vodka that had been hiding under my bed since my senior year of high school. It was old, covered in dust and plastic. I knew it was going to burn going down, but nothing could possibly steal my breath the way realizing I'd gotten Emmie pregnant had.

Chapter Nineteen

Kase

I'd tried calling Emmie back nonstop for the last two days. She either silenced my call or sent it straight to voice mail. My parents thought I had the flu, but really, I'd been holed up inside my room binge drinking and watching reruns of *Full House*.

I needed to apologize for calling her a liar. It was the worst way to react to the news she'd shared. I'd been in denial, and then shock and terrified. It hadn't been my finest moment and I felt pretty bad about it. The vodka helped numb my pain, but not enough for me to ignore it completely. I was a lot of things, but a bad human wasn't one of them. The need to tell Emmie I was sorry was clinging to me like a second skin.

I jumped when my phone chimed in my hand. I knocked over the beer chaser that had been balanced at my side. I checked the screen, surprised to see Emmie's name flashing across the screen.

Emmie: Stop fucking calling me.

She said fucking. Ems didn't cuss, not like the rest of the people who surrounded her at every turn. She was polite and kind.

Kasen: I want to apologize.

Emmie: Don't care.

Kasen: You shocked me.

Emmie: Shocked me too, you asshole.

Kasen: Your language has gotten increasingly profane.

Emmie: I guess you bring out the best in people.

Kasen: I'm so sorry, Ems.

Emmie: I don't need anything from you. I don't want anything from you. Please stop trying to call me. Just go on living your life, Kase. We will be fine on our own.

We. Holy shit, that word hit me right in my poor player heart. *We.* Emmie and the baby. Emmie and *my* baby.

Kasen: You told me not to call you. Would it be okay if I kept texting?

Kasen: You're back to ignoring me, huh?

Kasen: I deserve that. I was such a prick the other day.

Kasen: I know you're reading these. You still have the read feature turned on like it's 2019.

Kasen: If I could take it all back, I would. Can I get a do over? Can you call me again and tell me you're pregnant like it's the first time you've ever said those words?

Kasen: Guess that's a no.

Kasen: How 'bout I tell you what I should have said?

Kasen: Wow. Are you sure? You are? Um. Do you want this? You want to keep it? Okay, then it looks like we're having a baby. Do you need anything from me? I know you don't need my money, but I mean, like emotionally. I don't know how I feel yet either. I think I need a few days to process all this. Is that all right? I'll call you soon. But. If you need me, I'm here, okay?

Kasen: That's what I would have said if I wasn't such a dick.

Kasen: I'm so sorry, Ems.

Kasen: I'll be in Colorado the rest of this week, working. I leave tomorrow. But then I'm back in Texas for a while. It's Thanksgiving, and I'm supposed to come to the compound with my family. Will I see you?

Emmie: Of course you'll see me. I live here, asshole.

Kasen: Holy shit, you texted me back.

I'd been texting her every few minutes for the last half hour but I honestly never expected her to respond.

Kasen: Can we talk when I'm there? Please, Ems. I made a mistake, but you shocked the hell out of me.

Emmie: You think about yourself an awful lot. I was right to not want to tell you about the baby.

Kasen: I just want to talk.

Emmie: Fine. But none of the parents know, so keep your mouth shut.

Kasen: You think I want your dad to snap my neck? I won't say a word to them, I swear.

Emmie: Meet me at Jett's house before you come to the compound, it's across the street.

Kasen: I'll be there. How are you feeling?

Emmie: Fuck off.

Kasen: Fair enough.

Chapter Twenty

Kasen

I was nervous to see Emmie. I kept having this recurring nightmare that her stomach would be massive, like ready to pop huge. But I knew that couldn't be the case, right? It'd only been three months since Katie and Cash's wedding. She probably wouldn't even be showing yet.

That was surreal to think about.

I'd gotten Emmie pregnant. She was pregnant. She wanted to keep the baby, and whether I wanted to be in the kid's life or not, I'd have a child out there somewhere. Did I want to meet it? Fuck if I knew. I wasn't ready to be a father. I didn't know if I'd ever be ready. I hadn't planned this for my life. The parent track wasn't for me. There were still so many things I wanted to see, to experience. I wanted to live for myself.

I wished I could go back in time and not accuse Emmie of lying to me. I felt pretty fucking shitty about it. But I'd been so careful. Had she been careful? Maybe she poked holes in the condom? No. That didn't make any sense. Why would she want to trap me? She had her own money. And both she and Katie had said she'd never wanted to even tell me. I guess if I was wishing for a time machine, maybe I should go back and *not* fuck Emmie James.

I parked my truck in front of Jett's house, rolling my eyes at the giant wall of windows that gave people a clear view of his massive bedroom upstairs. Of course Jett would want people to watch him fuck. I left my bag in the car, knowing that I wouldn't be staying here after our talk.

I knocked on the door, taking a step back as the large steel and glass piece swung open.

"Hey, is Ems here?"

Jett narrowed his dark eyes. "She's in the kitchen, eating an entire pan of fresh-from-the-oven sugar cookies. Those are her favorite lately. Not that you would know."

Okay. Jett wasn't a fan these days. Noted.

"Can I see her?"

He leaned forward, dropping his voice. "If you make her cry, I will fuck your shit up, bro."

I sighed, already feeling weary. "I only want to talk to her, man."

"Fine." He moved so I could come into the house. "Don't eat any of those cookies though. Those cookies are for *nice* people, and you are an asshole."

"Sure thing." As if I would come and steal her fucking cookies like some weird dessert bandit? I took her virginity. I'd leave her damn cookies the hell alone. I stepped past Jett, heading to the left where he was pointing.

The first time I had seen Emmie, I had been instantly enamored. She was beautiful and she'd had this air about her: angelic almost. It seemed like she'd been floating across the field down by the tank, the sun backlighting her golden hair in this ethereal way.

And this time wasn't much different. I let out the breath I'd been holding when I saw her again, sitting on the island in Jett and Devin's kitchen with her gorgeous long legs swinging. Her hair was piled on her head in a neat bun, her face perfectly made up. She had a giant cookie in her hands and she looked so damn young, so innocent. Emmie James was one of the most beautiful girls I'd ever seen, like a fallen angel gracing us mere mortals with her presence.

How had I ever accused her of lying?

"Ems."

"Kasen."

She was still using my full name. She knew that made me feel like I was in trouble, which meant her anger toward me hadn't thawed over the last few days. "Can we talk?" Devin was at the stove, spooning dough onto a cookie sheet with an ice cream scoop. "Alone?"

Emmie rolled her blue eyes, like she was already annoyed with me being here. Maybe it was hormones, or maybe I deserved it. She shoved the rest of the cookie in her mouth then braced her hands on the counter like she was preparing to hop down.

I moved forward, my arms out to help her.

She slapped them away and did it on her own.

That's what she wanted though, right? She wanted to do this all on her own. She didn't need help down, and she didn't need help raising the baby.

My baby.

Our baby.

Holy shit.

"You two can go out back. Jett has the fire pit going." Devin hadn't said hello to me, hell, she hadn't even turned around when I'd walked in. But she'd offered us some privacy, and I was thankful.

I knew the drill. You pissed off one spawn, you pissed off all.

I followed Emmie through the living room and out the floor-to-ceiling glass French doors. The back deck overlooked a vast empty field, the Texas sunset turning the sky vibrant shades of pink. Maybe it was an omen. Maybe the baby was a girl. Emmie sat on a cushioned rocking chair, tucking a leg under her and using the other to make the chair move back and forth in a steady rhythm. I sat across from her. My chair didn't rock, but I was nervous and my knees were bouncing.

"How are you feeling?"

"You actually care? Or are you attempting small talk and that's all you could come up with?"

"I care." I *did* care. Seeing her, being near her. It was different than I thought it would be. She was a real person, a person I'd been with. I'd taken her virginity. I'd been inside her. And left behind a womb-mate. "I care, Ems."

"I'm fine, I guess. Sleepy and hungry, but I haven't been physically sick or anything."

"That's good." *Right?* I mean, not vomiting was always a win, pregnant or not.

"How's work been?"

I raised an eyebrow, my lips twitching into a small grin. "You actually care? Or are you attempting small talk?"

"I'm attempting small talk."

I nodded, not really all that fazed by how much she seemed to dislike me at the moment. I hadn't given her any reason to change her opinion, so I wasn't offended. "At least you're honest."

"I thought I was a liar." Her chin lifted, her arms crossing over her chest.

She threw my words back into my face, and they exploded on impact, making me feel like a piece of shit. "Ems. I should have never reacted that way. There's no excuse for my behavior and I'm sorry." I *did* care, and I *was* sorry. I wasn't sure how long it would take me to convince her of that though.

"Stop calling me Ems."

I snorted at her odd request. "Why?"

"Nicknames mean something in this fucked-up family, and you don't deserve to give me one."

I decided to leave the "fucked-up family" comment alone, not wanting to dive into any Devil's Share drama. "Everyone calls you Ems." She kept calling me Kasen, like I was a child in trouble. Seemed only fair that I got to call her Ems.

"No. They call me Em, not *Ems*." The smile she sent my way was not friendly in the least. "You can call me Emmie."

"Are you serious?"

"Try me, asshole."

"Look. You have every right to be mad at me." I leaned forward, resting my forearms on my thighs and really wishing I'd thought to have a drink before I tried talking to the stunning ballerina I'd knocked up. "But I'm here, and I'll be here for a few days so can—"

"Why *are* you here, Kasen? I know for a fact that you bail on family stuff all the time. Before Katie and Cash's wedding, I'd never even seen you at a family function. You could have easily skipped Thanksgiving."

She had me there. I did bail on family functions pretty regularly, especially ones that included the entirety of the Devil's Share gene pool. But this time, it hadn't even crossed my mind to beg off an excuse to my parents. I knew that I needed to be here. I needed to apologize to Ems and I needed to figure out what the hell to do with the rest of my life.

"I wanted to see you." I couldn't let her keep thinking the worst of me. She and I would be connected in more ways than one now.

"What for, Kasen?"

"I wanted to apologize, and I guess I thought we could talk, figure things out." I'd screwed up with Ems from the moment she'd tried to tell me she was pregnant. I'd ignored her attempts to contact me for weeks, and then I'd called her a liar. I needed to apologize, I knew when I fucked up, and I always tried to make it right.

"There's nothing to figure out, Kasen." She gripped the arms of the rocking chair, pushing herself up. "I don't need anything from you. I don't want anything from you. I'm going to have this baby, and I'm going to raise it. On my own."

"But it's my baby." Holy shit, that was the first time I'd said those words out loud.

"No. It's *my* baby." She stepped forward and poked a light pink painted nail into my chest. "You're like a sperm donor or something."

"Don't say that." Is that what she'd tell it when it was older? When it asked where I was? That I was some asshole who knocked her up and then left? It bothered me more than I thought it would, being reduced to nothing in her and my child's eyes. "Please, Ems, don't say that."

"Can you honestly tell me that you want this, Kase? That you want to be here for me? For the baby? You want to change diapers and have daddy playdates? Teething, stomach bugs, scraped knees? First dates? You want to teach this kid how to drive, Kase?"

"I don't know. Fuck." I rested my head in my hands for a moment, not wanting to say the wrong thing. I needed to press pause. I shouldn't have come here without knowing exactly what I wanted. It wasn't fair to Ems. But when I got to the compound, the only thing on my mind had been seeing her. Maybe I thought once I laid eyes on her again, I'd *know* what I wanted. But no matter how fucking striking Emmie James was, she wasn't a magic eight ball. Peering into her eyes wasn't going to give me all the answers I needed.

She sighed, causing me to glance up in time to see her bite on her lower lip. "Look, this was clearly a mistake. I should have never told you about the baby." She put her hand on my shoulder, like she was trying to comfort me. Which made me feel like I was two inches tall. "I expect nothing from you, Kase, and I don't mean that in a bad way. I need nothing, I want nothing, so please, walk away from us and never look back."

The words she hurled my way this time hit me right through the heart.

Walk away from us. Us.

"No." I put my palm on top of her hand. "No, Ems, that I won't do. I can't tell you one hundred percent that I'm ready to parent this baby with you. But I can tell you that I'd like a chance to figure it out. I'd like to get to know you. I'd like to know how you're doing. How the baby is doing."

She pulled her hand out from under mine, her eyes narrowing. "So you want to, what, string me along until I give birth? You want to see the kid before you make your decision?"

"Ems. Give me a bit of a break here, will you?" I rose, standing in front of her, my fingers itching to intertwine with hers. But I knew better than to make that move, she'd probably bite them off. "You've had months to deal with this. I found out you were pregnant a week ago. This is the first time I've seen you since the night of the wedding. I'm about to be surrounded by your family and mine, with this huge secret between us. I'm asking for a little time. That's all."

I had to be honest. I was positive that she was going to tell me to fuck right the hell off. So it surprised the ever-loving hell out of me when she let out a deep defeated sigh.

"Fine." She licked her lips, pulling her lower one between her teeth before she spoke again. "But I need you to hear this, Kasen. I will not let you break this kid's heart. Either you're in or you're out. There is no in between. You understand me?"

I didn't want to hurt my kid, that much I *did* know. I'd never be half in when it came to him or her. They'd either get all of me, or none of me. I'd never leave them wondering where I'd gone or if I was ever coming back.

"Yeah, I get you."

She nodded, then pushed past me and walked back into the house. I sat down in the rocking chair she'd vacated, staring at the sun sinking into the wheat field. There was a tiny sliver of orange that was still lighting the sky.

How had this become my life?

Fuck.

One night with a beautiful girl and nothing would ever be the same.

Chapter Twenty-One

Emmie

When I got home from seeing Kase for the first time since he took my virginity and left me with a fertilized egg, his parents were at my house. I tried to slip past everyone sitting in my living room, but my mom spotted me before I could make it around the corner.

"Emmie, sweetheart, come in here and say hello to Mr. and Mrs. Cadence."

Lovely. First I had to discuss my pregnancy with Kase and now I was about to have to make small talk with his parents.

"Emmie, how is your training going?" Kase's dad smiled broadly when he saw me. Both his parents were actually really nice people. Even if their son had turned out to be a bit of a douche. "Your mom told us that you're taking college through correspondence? How in the world are you doing both?" He chuckled. "And can you share your secret with Kase? Because that kid refuses to get a degree."

I smiled tightly, thinking I'd already shared more than my secret with their son. "It's going well. The company I dance with makes sure I have time to study, they're really accommodating." I left the Kase comment alone.

My mom reached out and took my hand in hers. "We were sure Emmie was going to get her degree slowly so she could focus mainly on dance. But a few weeks ago, she decided to take a full course load. We're very proud of her."

I'd had every intention of going to college *after* I was done dancing with my company. That was, until I'd watched two pink lines form on the pregnancy test. I knew I wouldn't be able to keep dancing the way I was through this whole process. They'd never let me take center stage nine months pregnant. So I'd added three more classes to the online program I was already enrolled in.

"Are you planning to dance long term?" I liked Kase and Katie's mom, she was soft spoken and sweet, but I needed this line of questions to stop. All these reminders that my life was about to change were making me want to cry.

"I love it, of course, but a dancer's body only lasts them so long. I'll dance while I can, and then maybe I'll open my own studio one day. Who knows?"

Who knows? I knew. My company would have no choice but to sideline me until the baby was born. There were a dozen girls waiting to take my spot, girls who wouldn't have a pregnant belly jutting out over their tutu.

"You're only eighteen. I'm sure you have years of ballet ahead of you." She smiled, her eyes crinkling at the sides.

"I'm sure you're right."

You're wrong. I might be able to bounce back after the baby, and it would take hours every day and hard work. But it wasn't going to be only me anymore. I needed a schedule that was conducive to taking care of an infant.

Luckily, their conversation turned away from me and I was able to finally head to my room. I didn't want to talk about ballet. I didn't want to talk about my pregnancy. I didn't want to talk to anyone about anything. I wanted to curl up in a ball pretend that nothing and no one existed outside of me, and this tiny baby growing inside me. I could handle life when it was the two of us. What sent me over the emotional edge was other people and their opinions.

I groaned when my cell vibrated in my hoodie pocket. Great. Which one of my cousins was checking up on me now? Maybe I should preemptively send updates to the group text.

Kasen: *Thank you for agreeing to talk to me today.*

Oh. Not a spawn, but the actual devil himself. I sighed, feeling a bit like a brat. Kase wasn't the devil, that wasn't fair. It took two bodies full of lust to create this baby. It was as much his fault as it was mine.

Emmie: *You're welcome. Now leave me alone.*

Kasen: *We're having Thanksgiving lunch together tomorrow.*

Thanksgiving as one big happy extended family: his parents and mine. Would they think it was weird if I avoided him completely?

Would they even notice? Doubtful. There would be too many of us kids running around. It was hard to focus on one out of the whole pile. Plus, it's not like Kase and I were besties or anything.

Kasen: Leaving me on read huh? I deserve it.

Emmie: You deserve a junk punch.

Kasen: You been talking to my sister?

Was Katie mad at her brother? I didn't want to come between siblings. I understood that bond, and I never wanted to be the reason it was strained. I'd agreed to give Kase some time to think. I shouldn't be so mean to him while he did it. He'd apologized for calling me a liar, he was here, and he was trying. And I wasn't being reasonable.

Emmie: Lunch will be fine. My cousins know how to keep a secret.

Kasen: If you had a time machine, what would you go back and erase?

I rested my hand on my stomach, reading and re-reading his text. I felt guilty for wanting to erase the baby inside me. But if it had never existed in the first place, then that was okay, right? I wiped at the tears sliding down my cheeks and soaking my pillow.

Emmie: I don't know. What would you erase?

Kasen: Taking your virginity.

Emmie: You mean fucking it away.

If I closed my eyes and blocked out the rest of the world, I could still hear him saying those words to me that night. Kase had set my body on fire. He'd given me everything I never knew I wanted in that moment. He didn't treat me like I was a breakable china doll and I reveled in it.

Kasen: It wasn't mine to have, and I'm so sorry Ems.

It was always yours, Kase. I didn't know it until I met you was what I should have said, if I wasn't so afraid of his reaction. Either way, I couldn't regret him. I couldn't regret that night. If I could do it all over again, I wouldn't give him up. I couldn't imagine anyone else ever making me feel the way Kase did.

Emmie: If we really had a time machine, I'd go back a few months before I met you and get on the pill.

Kasen: Oh I like that one. That's a better plan than me going down on you for six hours and keeping my dick in my pants.

The sigh I let out sounded shaky as hell, my reaction to Kase's words making me feel things I hadn't felt since the night we'd been together.

Emmie: *Good night Kase.*
Kasen: *Good night Ems.*

Chapter Twenty-Two

Kasen

I was sitting at the largest, longest dining room table I'd ever seen. And these fuckers had two of them. We were having Thanksgiving at the pool house, the only patio large enough to accommodate everyone. All the parents were at one table, with some grandkids scattered on laps. My mom was obsessed with one of Brody and Landry's little boys. She kept sneaking him bites of pie when no one was looking, making him giggle. Payton Cadence was a fantastic mom, and she'd make one hell of a grandma it seemed. But it should be Katie making her one, not me.

Emmie was across from me. I'd tried to sit next to her but Cash and Crue had boxed me out. And I was now uncomfortably sandwiched between Jett and Beau. These spawns were a pain in the ass. It was obvious I didn't have any fans here. Not that I really expected any different, I supposed. I'd knocked up Emmie. And then accused her of lying about it. I'd hate me too.

"Em, you remember my friend Benson?" Cash speared one of her sweet potatoes, stealing it from her plate and then popping it into his mouth.

"Yeah." She knocked his fork away when he went for another bite. "He used to call me Rosemary's baby."

Jett snorted into his glass, making red wine splash on his face.

"Why did he call you that?" All eyes went to me the second I spoke, like the sound of my voice was offensive to every single one of them.

"It's an old movie, asshole," Beau answered after a few seconds of loaded silence. "Rosemary's baby is the devil's baby. Emmie is the youngest Devil's Spawn, *she's* the baby."

"Clever." Emmie being the youngest was really making everything more difficult, for both of us it seemed. They protected her, they thought of her as a child. But she wasn't a child anymore; she was eighteen and stunning. And pregnant. Thanks to me.

"Anyway, he was asking about you the other day." Cash smiled, but Emmie didn't turn to see it. Her eyes were focused on her plate, eating all her foods separately like a real weirdo. First the turkey, then green bean casserole, and then cornbread dressing. Looked like she wanted to save her sweet potatoes for last. Would the baby inherit that odd way of eating without me around to stop it? "You two hit it off when he was back home for our wedding."

At that she did look up, her eyes shooting daggers at her cousin.

"Was he the bartender that was hitting on you?" I knew that wasn't who they were talking about. I'd met Benson, how could I forget the man walking around in the cowboy hat? But Cash bringing up another guy to the chick I'd accidentally put a baby in sort of irritated me. My kid was growing inside her. I didn't want some other guy's cock in there too. "The one with the ponytail who couldn't seem to take no for an answer?"

Emmie's daggers shifted from Cash to me.

"Benson. He was *in* my wedding. You've met him like three times." Cash nudged Emmie with his shoulder. "What do you think, Em? Can I give him your number?"

I knew that Cash was doing this to get a reaction out of me. But it wasn't going to work. Ems and I weren't in love. And although I didn't like the idea of some dude dicking down the chick carrying my child, that certainly wasn't for me to say. Emmie barely tolerated me at this point. If I started trying to mandate what she did and didn't do with her body? She'd probably rip my nuts off, and my own sister would hold me down to help.

"No, you can't give him my number." She looked at Cash like he'd lost his damn mind. "I'm in no position to start dating at the moment." She jabbed her fork into a toasted marshmallow and shoved it into her mouth, speaking around it. "But thanks for bringing it up during an already uncomfortable family dinner."

"Sorry, Emmie." Cash did sound genuinely remorseful. I still wanted to hit him though. "I thought maybe hanging with Benson would cheer you up, that's all."

"No you didn't, you thought bringing him up in front of Kasen would make him jealous." Emmie was shocking me left and right today. Maybe the baby was a boy because that chick had sure developed some bigger balls since the last time I'd seen her. "But Kasen and I aren't together, and I don't need to be cheered up. I'm not depressed."

"Oh he's jealous, no doubt." Brody must have been listening in on the conversation from farther down the table, because he leaned forward, looking past Katie and Cash. "He might not admit it to himself or anyone else at this table. But that guy," he pointed at me with the beer bottle in his hand. "does *not* love the idea of another dude's dick inside the chick he knocked up."

Was he reading my mind? Were my thoughts on a ticker on my forehead?

"Oh my god." Emmie let her fork clatter to her plate as her fingertips went to her temples, a bewildered look on her face. "Could you all please shut the hell up? Our parents are one table away. And I am so done talking about *any* of this."

"Since when have your parents ever paid attention? Like, in the entire history of this family?" Talon glanced past Devin and Jett, sending them a disgusted headshake. "Jett's been doing god knows what to Devin under the table. Crue is drinking straight vodka instead of water, and Landry fed all her vegetables to the dog. Did any of them notice? No."

"But you did." Jett sent Talon some serious side eye. "You're such a narc."

"Em, you're going to have to tell them eventually, you know that, right?" Beau lowered his voice but didn't change the subject like Emmie had told them to.

"I said I was done talking about it."

"We're all here to support you." Cash put his hand over hers. "And Kase's parents are here. It's kind of the perfect time to come clean before you're forced to." He looked down pointedly, I guess insinuating that her belly was only going to get larger.

"Please drop it."

"Emmie, you know we're right." Halen reached across the table, putting her hand on top of the pile Cash had started. "You need to tell them, and we'll help you, okay?"

I wasn't part of the Devil's Share family, and Ems seemed like she could hold her own with no help from me, so for the most part I'd kept my mouth shut during this entire Thanksgiving bullshit. But now they were railroading her, basically ignoring her pleas. And it was starting to piss me the fuck off.

"I'm not ready and—"

"Emmie, secrets fester, believe me." Talon rubbed his hand on Marley's back. "The sooner you come clean, the sooner—"

"Hey." I didn't speak loudly, but there was enough edge behind my tone that all mouths closed and all eyes turned to me. "She's asked you nicely several fucking times to drop it. None of what's happening between Ems and me has anything to do with the rest of you. Stop treating her like she can't make up her own damn mind. Stop trying to push her into sharing something she's not ready to share. And stop eating all the food on her fucking plate." I grabbed Cash's fork out of his hand and tossed it behind me when he went to steal her last marshmallow.

"Kase? Everything okay?" My mom was turned in her chair, her hand resting on the back of it, a frown on her face.

"Of course." I smiled, but not too big. This was a family lunch at the Devil's Share compound. If I acted like I was loving the shit out of life, my mom would get real suspicious real fast. "Are there more sweet potatoes over there?"

She returned my smile in that sweet, warm way that only moms seemed to be able to accomplish. "Sure, love, here you go." She passed a clear casserole dish to Cash, who sat it in the center of the already crowded table. "Save room for dessert, okay?"

"You know it." I waited for her to turn back to the "adult" table and their conversation before dropping my voice. "My parents *aren't* fucking clueless, so stop throwing around phrases like *knocked up* and *other guy's dick*."

"Told you he was jealous." Brody nodded once, his beer bottle to his lips.

Emmie reached out and scraped the entire layer of toasted marshmallow off the top of the sweet potatoes with her spoon. She ate it, then licked her spoon clean. Ems was a sexy girl using her tongue. And I knew what that tongue felt like. So. My cock took notice and I had to adjust it under the table.

Jett snorted, which let me know he saw. "You into your baby momma?" He was whispering, thankfully. "Kind of complicates things, doesn't it?"

I ignored him, mainly because I didn't know what to say. I was at a loss for a witty comeback for probably the second time in my life. I was attracted to Emmie. It was impossible not to be. But I didn't know how I *felt* about her, about the baby, about any of it. And Jett was right. The last thing either of us needed was my libido to get involved.

"Ems."

She sighed, dragging her gaze up to meet mine. "What?"

"You want dessert?" I stood, taking her empty plate in one hand and mine in the other. I didn't know what I wanted or how things between us would end up. What I *did* know was she was carrying my baby, her family was stressing her the hell out, and she had an insane sweet tooth. Maybe I wouldn't be around three months from now, but I was here now.

"Uh, yeah." She smiled at me. It was small, but it was still a win. "I'm not picky."

"Bring her one of everything." Jett was talking out the side of his mouth, like he was being real covert op or some shit. "She's been eating like Willy Wonka put that baby in there."

Crue choked on his vodka when I walked away whistling the tune to "Candy Man."

Chapter Twenty-Three

Emmie

After Kase told my family to shut the hell up, lunch had gone smoother. Cash stopped trying to set me up with his friend Benson, Brody stopped accusing Kase of being jealous, and no one tried to steal dessert off the plate Kase had put in front of me.

Unfortunately, I'd been hiding in my room for the last three hours. Kase and Katie's parents seemed to have hit it off with mine. They were all hanging out in the living room, several bottles of wine deep and old photo albums opened on the coffee table.

I reached for my cell when it dinged on my nightstand, welcoming the distraction from the textbook I'd been reading to avoid the other people in my house.

Kasen: Hey, would you want to come hang with me tonight?

I did want to hang out with Kase, and his text made me smile. But I needed to lock that crap down real fast. He was the asshole who knocked me up and then accused me of lying about it. So what if he'd been a knight in shining armor during lunch today? He didn't deserve my complete and total forgiveness.

Emmie: Not really.

Kasen: What if I asked you nicely?

Emmie: Idk. Give it a shot.

Kasen: Will you pretty please with a cherry on top come hang out with me tonight?

Emmie: No.

I laughed quietly at my reply, because I was pretty sure we both knew I was kidding. I didn't hate him. It was obvious to anyone who was paying attention. There was something about Kase, something that made staying angry with him almost impossible. Maybe it was his sense of humor, or the tanned and toned abs I knew he was hiding under his sweater.

Kasen: You're breaking my heart.

Emmie: No, I'm not.

Kasen: Please Ems?

Emmie: Fine. But only because your parents are here again and I don't like spending time with two sets of parents I'm hiding things from.

Kasen: I'll take it.

I snuck out of my window for the first time in my entire life. I'd always used the front door, because I'd never been headed anywhere I wasn't supposed to go. Not that I wasn't allowed to hang out at Cash and Katie's new house on the compound. Of course I was.

But the reason I was going there had nothing to do with bonding with my cousins and everything to do with Kasen Cadence. And that? My parents wouldn't love that.

I left my car keys on my nightstand, choosing to walk the mile or so to their house at the edge of the compound. It was cool outside and the night breeze felt good on my constantly overheated skin. This pregnancy was making my body temperature run on the hot side, and I was so grateful that winter was around the corner.

"Did you walk over here?" Kase was on the porch, his brow wrinkled as soon as he spotted me. "I could have come to get you." He came down the four steps that led to the front walkway.

"And I could have driven." I rolled my eyes, ignoring his unnecessary concern. "I dance for six hours at a time. A leisurely evening stroll isn't going to hurt the baby you aren't sure you want." That was mean, and I instantly regretted it. Where was that damn time machine?

Kase chose to ignore my bitchiness though. "Where do your parents think you are?"

"My bedroom." I bypassed him, making my way up the stairs, trying really hard not to notice how good he smelled. "I snuck out."

"Thank you for coming here to talk to me." He reached past me, opening the door so I could step inside.

"Thank you for what you said at lunch, for sticking up for me." I sat on the soft leather club chair, not trusting myself to sit next to Kase on the couch. He was a smoke show, and he'd been nice to me. My hormones were taking notice, and I needed distance to keep them in control. "My cousins can be difficult when they get their minds set on something."

"They love you. But they baby you."

I shrugged. "I'm the youngest, it comes with the territory."

"You're more capable than they give you credit for." His dark eyes met mine, and chills traveled down my spine. Stupid hormones.

"They worry."

"You're strong."

I had to laugh at that. "Am I? Because right now, strong is the last thing I feel." It was like I felt heavier and heavier every day, the weight of the secrets and uncertainty exhausting me.

"Talk to me, Ems."

Talk to me, Ems. He sounded so sincere, so concerned. But I couldn't let go, not in front of him. Could I? No. "You're not sure if you want my problems to be your problems, we both know that. There's no use pretending otherwise. Like you said, I'm strong, capable. I can handle it on my own."

He nodded, agreeing with me and hurting my feelings a little. "I won't lie to you or blow smoke up your ass, it's not my style. I don't know what I want." It was in that moment of fleeting disappointment that I realized I *wanted* him to blow smoke up my ass. I wanted him to give me hope, I wanted him to tell he'd be here and that I wouldn't go through all this alone.

And that was dangerous. That would get me hurt, and it would get this kid hurt. I stood. "You know, I'm sorry, I shouldn't have come."

He grabbed my hand, his tone pleading. "But I'm here. And right now I'm going through all the same emotions you are. So how 'bout we forget that I'm an asshole, and you let me try to help?"

I sat back down, because he wasn't wrong. If anyone could possibly understand how I was feeling right now, it was him. Two kids whose lives had been thrown into another orbit trying to figure out exactly how to breathe in a new atmosphere.

I settled back against the cushions, tucking my legs underneath me. I could *share* with him. Sharing wasn't the same as depending. "For as long as I can remember, ballet has been my life. I started dance classes when I was three, and by the time I was seven, my teachers were telling my parents that I was one of the best they'd ever seen. I was supposed to graduate high school, join the Austin

Ballet Company, and dance until I was a principal. Meet a guy, fall in love, start a family."

I'd gone off course somewhere in the middle of that life plan I'd made for myself.

"But instead you spent the night with a hot guy at a wedding and got knocked up." I rolled my eyes at him referring to himself as hot but decided not to point out the fact that he hadn't spent the night.

"I'm not like my cousins or my sister. I've never climbed in my window three hours past curfew or smoked pot down by the tank. I've never been much of a partier. I've never gotten drunk." I gestured to him. "You were the first and only reckless act in my life. It doesn't seem fair. Everyone else can fuck up left and right, but the second I make one mistake…"

"Ems, come here, please." He reached across the coffee table between us, taking my hand in his, pulling me until I was next to him on the couch. "Do you want this baby? *Truly* want this baby? Or is this you thinking you're doing the right thing by keeping it, by raising it?"

It was a valid question, and one that he had every right to ask.

This was his life too.

"I found out I was pregnant at the studio in the middle of an eight-hour practice block. I was like five weeks late, which isn't abnormal because I put my body through so much. But I'd been feeling tired and nauseous, so I bought a test on my way in that morning. When we took a break for lunch, I went into the bathroom and sat in a generic gray stall. I closed my eyes and prayed that it would be negative. When I opened them, there were two pink lines staring back at me."

"You don't have to do this, Ems. You don't have to derail your whole life for this baby, there are options."

"I was in shock. I'd had sex with one guy, one night. And we were careful." He was right. I didn't have to do this. I'd *chosen* to do this. And he needed to know that I hadn't made that decision lightly.

"I made an appointment at a clinic and I told them that if I was in fact pregnant, I wanted an abortion that day. My life, the life I planned, wouldn't work if I kept the baby. My body wouldn't *work* the way I needed it to. I wouldn't look the way I needed to." I wiped a tear away, sharing all this with Kase was harder than I thought it would be.

"When I took the pee test it came out positive, but their test came out negative, so I was lying on the table, watching the tiny screen while they verified that I was in fact pregnant. I was trying to not feel anything. I tried so damn hard to turn it all off."

I wiped both eyes this time, drying my hands on my soft yoga pants. "But I couldn't. And the second I saw the baby, I got up and walked out of that room." I reached into my side pocket, pulling out the sonogram picture I'd grabbed before climbing out of my window, and handed it to him. "I'm not a victim. No one hurt me. I made a choice to have sex with a guy I thought was gorgeous and sarcastically funny."

"You tried to do it." Kase was staring at the black-and-white picture in his hand, his voice soft, almost a whisper.

"And I couldn't." I took a deep breath, straightening my spine and regaining control of my emotions.

Maybe that's exactly what Brody had been talking about. I'd made my choice. I'd made the choice I could live with. And I needed to give Kase the same space to do that for himself. I'd been angry that he'd assumed I was lying to him, but I'd refused to acknowledge what had been happening to my own body for weeks. I'd been shocked, and so had he.

"It wasn't fair of me to expect something of you that I hadn't even been able to do myself." I took his hands in mine, meeting his dark gaze. "You deserve time to figure out how you feel about this baby, and I promise I'll stop punishing you for it."

His eyes dropped down to the space between us where our hands rested. "This isn't something I'm taking lightly, you know?" He licked his bottom lip, and I hated how sexy the small gesture was. "I don't want to hurt anyone. I don't want to disappoint anyone. I feel like if I make the wrong choice, I'll be destroying everything...everyone."

"Take the time you need, Kase." I leaned forward, resting my forehead against his chest, fighting the tears that wanted to fall. "And whatever you choose, we'll all be okay."

We'd have to be okay.

There was no other option.

Chapter Twenty-Four

Kasen

After the job in Colorado, I went to Brazil. Now I was back in Texas. Usually when I came back to the States, I stayed at my parents' ranch. That was home. I traveled so much that I hadn't bothered to get my own place. I had plenty of money. I simply lacked the desire to pay for a house I never got to spend any real time in. Which was why I was currently in a hotel ten minutes from my family's ranch.

Being gone had been harder this time than it usually was. I'd spent the whole time thinking about Ems, and about the baby. I'd gone back and forth in my mind, trying to figure out what I should do. And in the end, I still wasn't sure.

I pulled my phone from the backpack I used as a carry-on, typing out a quick text to my family group.

Kase: Back in the US. Mom stop worrying that I'll be kidnapped and ransomed for all your retirement money.

Dad: Glad your home, kid. And no worries. We don't negotiate with terrorists anyway.

Mom: When will we see you? Are you headed to the ranch?

Kase: No, I grabbed a hotel room. I fly out again soon and need to get some editing done.

That wasn't a total lie.

Dad: Love you kid.

Mom: Love you.

Katie: Glad you didn't get kidnapped.

Cash: I have lukewarm feelings about it.

Yeah. My sister had demanded we add her stupid husband to the family group.

Kase: Love y'all too. Except for Cash.

Cash: Same, bro.

Well, I let my family know I was back in this country, I should probably let the chick carrying my baby know too.

Kasen: I don't know if you've tried to call or not. We were in the jungle and oddly enough, cell service was shit.

Emmie: I didn't.

Kasen: You're cold. Aren't pregnant chicks supposed to be emotional?

Emmie: I cried when Devin told me she ran out of ingredients to make my sugar cookies.

I smiled thinking about Ems eating her weight in cookies, sitting on that counter in Jett's kitchen. I took a sip of the beer I'd opened a few minutes ago, trying to drown the sudden desire I had to see her.

Kasen: How are you feeling?

Emmie: Fine.

Kasen: Don't be that girl.

Emmie: I'm fifteen weeks now, second trimester, and I seem to have a little more energy than I've had in a while. I can make it all the way through practice without needing to hide in the bathroom and take a nap.

Kasen: Maybe it wasn't the baby making you tired? Maybe it was constant sugar crashes from all the cookies?

Emmie: Maybe you can suck it.

I enjoyed the feisty side of Ems, the one that didn't come out to play nearly enough. She could tell me to suck it all she wanted, as long as she started standing up to everyone else in her life too.

Kasen: I'm back in the states. Can I come see you?

Oh wow. Okay. I guess my fingers were working independently of the rest of my body.

Emmie: Why?

Kasen: I don't really know. When I realized I had a break in my schedule, it was the first thing I thought about doing. I can stay with Cash and Katie again.

What the actual flying fuck? Why was I typing all these things? I *did* want to see her, but like, I shouldn't really want to see her. You know? No? Yeah? I didn't either. Dammit.

Emmie: If you want to.

Kasen: Okay, cool. Have you told anyone else?

Okay cool? Jesus. Way to play off the weirdness, Kase.

Emmie: No. Have you told anyone at all?

Kasen: No, but you're going to start showing soon, right?

Emmie: Eventually.

Kasen: Do you want to tell your parents while I'm there?

Holy fucking shit. When had I become so selfless? Maybe a bug had crawled inside my brain in the jungle and was making me act out of character. An Amazonian bug that specialized in mind control.

Emmie: Why would I do that? If you decide you don't want to be part of this, I'd rather them never know about you.

Yes. Yes, Emmie, you are exactly right. Why the hell would I want to be part of that terrible conversation between you and your parents? I sighed, flopping on my bed. Because being there with her was the right thing to do, and apparently, I was doing that these days.

Kasen: It's the right thing to do. Plus, our families are connected Ems.

Holy shit.

Kasen: Holy shit. Our families are connected. I'll have to see you, I'll have to see the baby. Even if I decide I don't want to be his dad, I'll still see him.

Why had that never occurred to me before this moment? I'd been so focused on the should I or the shouldn't I, that I hadn't even thought about anything else. Katie was married to Cash. Cash was part of the Devil's Spawn family, part of Emmie's family. I'd see her, and I'd see the baby. No matter what I chose to do.

Emmie: I guess so.

Kasen: How would that even work?

Emmie: You would just NOT walk up to it and say, hey kid, I'm your dad.

Kasen: But I am its dad.

Emmie: Sperm doesn't make a father. It's sort of a family motto around here. Look, I've got to get back to practice. If you want to come stay with your sister, you don't need my permission.

I closed my eyes, willing the room to stop spinning.

Chapter Twenty-Five

Kasen

I tried to put Emmie and the baby out of my mind, but it was virtually impossible. I couldn't concentrate. I couldn't get any edits done. This whole situation was starting to become bad for business. But since I wasn't the one giving up my dream to carry the kid, I should probably keep that little tidbit to myself.

I'd packed up and checked out. The hotel wasn't where I needed to be right now. And content of the Amazon shoot wasn't what I needed to be focusing on. Emmie had given me time, and I was pretty sure I'd used it all up. I wanted to do right by her, and that meant I needed to make my decision about being in the baby's life.

I pushed open the front door of my favorite uncle's house. If anyone would be able to help me figure out this shit storm my life had become, it was him.

"Uncle Pax?" I walked through the living room, and then headed into the kitchen to grab us a couple beers. He'd need alcohol for what I was about to tell him. "Where you at?"

"On the patio."

I stepped back through the living room, then out the double doors that led to his backyard where I found him grilling a big ol' Texas-size steak. "Take this, old man. Can't have you getting dehydrated standing over that hot grill, you might pass out." I popped the top of the cold beer before handing it to him.

"Funny." He took a deep appreciative pull. "What are you doing here? Your momma said you had plans to go visit your sister at the compound."

I texted my mom two hours ago, telling her I was going to visit Katie. Word traveled hella fast in my family. "You say *the compound* like you're talking about cult headquarters."

"Maybe I am." He waggled his eyebrows.

I snorted, buying myself a minute by drinking half my beer in two swallows. "I wanted to talk to you about something before I hit the road."

He gasped dramatically. "You're driving yourself? The spoiled Kasen Cadence is driving himself *four hours*? I thought for sure you'd charter a plane."

"Yeah, yeah. I'm slumming it with the mere mortals on I-ten today." I wasn't *that* spoiled. I was simply accustomed to flying everywhere I went. When you get used to having someone else charter you around, the idea of fighting traffic sounds particularly awful.

"What's on your mind?" He flipped his steak, taking another sip of his beer.

I took a beat, a few seconds to live in a world where my family didn't know that I was going to be a father. Once I told Uncle Pax, all this would be real. It was one thing for Ems's family to know, but it felt different telling mine. Letting mine in on the secret meant that I couldn't hide from it, and I couldn't wish it away. I'd have to own it.

"I knocked up Emmie James."

He spit beer out over the hot coals, making everything start to sizzle and smoke. "You put a baby in their baby? Didn't I specifically tell you *not* to do that? Like those actual words?"

"Yeah. I'm defiant like that." I finished my beer and tossed the empty into the trash. "Obviously it was an accident." Not a mistake, because we were adults who made a choice. *Right?*

"She keeping it?"

"Yep." I popped the *p*. "She told me it was up to me whether I wanted to be in their lives. No pressure, and no hard feelings if I chose to bow out on the dad life."

"Wow. I figured a young thing like her would be trying to drag you in, scared to go at it alone."

"Quite the opposite. Apparently her family had to talk her into telling me at all."

"Her family knows?" He let out a low whistle. "And you're still alive?"

"Her cousins know. Her parents do not." I took the tongs from his hand, pulling his steak off the fire and onto the waiting platter. Apparently this discussion was distracting him from cooking his dinner. Uncle Pax hated a well-done slab of prime beef. "Smith James has no clue I banged his daughter. And really, all of this might end up being a moot point because he might kill me before she can give birth."

Oh wow. *Birth*. Yeah, I guess the baby would need to come out at some point, right? Why did every step of this ordeal shock the hell out of me? Poor Ems. I got a night of tight pussy; she was getting nine months of pregnancy and then she had to get it out.

"That, or Smith will hog-tie you and make you marry her." He drank more of his beer and then sat in one of the patio chairs. "Tell me what's on your heart, kid."

This was what I needed. I needed to tell my uncle how I was feeling. I needed someone to hear me, to understand what *I* was going through. Someone who wasn't already team Emmie and calling me an asshole to my face every chance they got.

"When she told me, I reacted terribly. And I've basically spent the last couple weeks trying to repair the damage I did." I put the lid down on the grill, then took the seat on the other side, wishing I wasn't about to drive and could have another five beers with my uncle. "I don't know that I want to be a dad, like an active there-for-little-league dad."

"Biologically, you don't have a choice. And if she wanted to, she could force your hand down the road. Or rake your ass over the coals for money."

I waved away his concern. "She has her own money. She doesn't need anything from me."

"Just playing the devil's advocate here."

I grinned, unable to pass the setup he'd given me. "Playing with something that belonged to the Devils' is what got me into this mess."

"Glad you got jokes. It's good to keep the humor while you're on your deathbed." He smiled humorlessly, finishing his beer.

I had jokes, but I also had decisions to make.

"I was texting with Emmie the other day, and I realized, I'm always going to be in this kid's life whether I want to be or not. Dad's still under the RiffRaff Record label and Katie and Cash getting hitched shoved us all together. Hell, we were there for Thanksgiving." Thank goodness I was out of the country for Christmas and New Year. "If I'm not in it with her, I'll be there watching her raise this baby without me for the next eighteen years."

Uncle Pax crossed his arms over his chest, kicking his legs straight in front of him. "And how does that make you feel?"

He was like my therapist, if my therapist was the Big Lebowski. But how *did* that make me feel? I'd lain awake thinking about the next ten years of my life, and what I wanted that to look like. But every time I tried to picture me watching Ems and our kid opening Christmas presents, celebrating birthdays, while I sat at a distance with a polite smile on my face, it didn't sit right with me. It didn't *feel* right.

"Like a deadbeat asshole."

He nodded. "Good."

"Good?"

"You're not a child, Kase. You've been traveling the world on your own since the day you graduated high school. You've seen everything there is to see: the good, the bad, and the ugly. You've made a name for yourself, independent of who your father is. Hiding from your responsibilities would be a big step down for that fuck-boy soul of yours."

I chuckled humorlessly. "Karma? Really?"

"What goes around comes around, kid. It's time to man up. You don't have to be in love with Emmie to be a good man, a good dad." He clapped me on the back, getting to his feet and picking up his dinner.

I wouldn't be okay watching Emmie raise our child without me. Thinking about it had made me feel like the worst sort of person. She may not need me, but my kid would. That tiny baby deserved the best of both of us. We'd created it together, and we'd raise it together. Uncle Pax was right. We didn't need to be in love with each other.

Only in love with our kid.

I blew out a deep breath. "I'm going to be a dad."

"You're going to be a dad." Uncle Pax opened the patio door.

"Holy fuck."

He walked into the house, calling over his shoulder, "Yeah, holy fuck."

Chapter Twenty-Six

Kasen

I left Uncle Pax's house and drove straight through to my sister's. Lucky for me, neither she nor Cash were home at the moment. I couldn't deal with her disappointed smiles or Cash's asshole comments. I'd made up my mind, and the only person I needed to talk to right now was Ems.

Kasen: I'm here, at Katie's.
Emmie: Okay.
Kasen: Can I see you? Please?
Emmie: All the 'rents are off the compound, some "parents only" nostalgic trip to Florida.
Kasen: So...I can come over?
Emmie: Door's unlocked.
Kasen: Leaving now.

I left my bags where I'd dropped them and headed back out. I knew driving wouldn't be the smartest move. All I needed was to alert the whole fucking compound that Ems and I were alone at her house. They'd all shit a brick getting the wrong idea.

I was excited to see her, excited and nervous. I wasn't sure how she would take what I had to tell her. I didn't know if she'd be happy. I hoped she would be though. I hoped that this was a good thing, for both of us. I never wanted to make her life harder. I never wanted to hurt her. She was kind and pure and I'd fucked everything up for her. She deserved so much more than being knocked up by a guy like me.

Emmie James deserved hearts and flowers and romantic dinners. She deserved to be someone's whole fucking world, to be worshipped for being exactly who she was. And I couldn't give her that. But I could sure as fuck hang out with our kid while she tried to find it.

I locked her front door behind me after I walked in. The compound was secure. I wasn't worried about monsters or burglars. I was worried about her overprotective cousins poking their noses where they didn't need to be. "Hey," I called. Ems was sitting on the couch, cuddled up under a blanket with a glass coffee mug in her hand. "How are you?"

She smiled when she saw me, which made me hopeful that at least she'd stop calling me an asshole all the time. "Exhausted."

I'd never *tell* her she looked exhausted, but she did. She had dark circles under her eyes and she seemed half asleep at eight o'clock.

"You still training six hours a day?"

"Yeah." She sat up, putting her drink on the table beside her. "If I stop rehearsals, my parents will find out, and they'll start asking questions."

The blanket she'd been covered with had pooled in her lap. "Not showing yet?" She was wearing tight black leggings and a t-shirt that was cut off at her rib cage, like she'd come home from rehearsals and immediately collapsed on the sofa.

"Nope." She put her palm on her flat stomach. "Not showing, not ready to tell them."

"But everything is okay? With the baby?" I would also never tell her to stop training, but it seemed to be taking its toll on her body.

"Healthy and growing." She handed me her cell, showing me a short video of her last ultrasound. "My stomach muscles are tight, the doctor said it'll take a few more weeks for it to pop out."

I watched the video twice, smiling at the tiny little nugget floating on the screen, before handing her phone back. "Can we talk?"

"Talk." She gestured to the empty room before putting her hands back under the knit blanket and pulling it up to her chin.

"I want to be a dad."

Emmie's jaw dropped open a few inches, her big blue eyes blinking rapidly. "Are you sure?"

"Yeah. I'm sure. I've thought about it a lot over the last few weeks. We're always going to be in each other's lives and—"

"That doesn't mean you *want* to be this kid's dad, Kasen." Her eyes stopped blinking all cartoony and instead narrowed like she wanted to shoot lasers out of them.

"Wait, let me finish, please." She nodded still with squinty eyes and I continued, "I realized that I wouldn't be able to stand it. I wouldn't be able to watch you be a mom to this kid while I stood by and got to play a fun uncle part or something."

She pursed her lips. "I was thinking, like, fun but *distant* family friend."

"No." I shook my head. "Out of sight, out of mind? Maybe I would have made a different choice. But these were the cards we were dealt, and I'm here for it. I *want* to be here for it, if you'll have me."

"If I'll have you?"

I put my hand on her knee over the blanket, a little surprised when she didn't swat it away. "I acted like a dick. But that's not who I am, you know that."

"You were gone when I woke up."

"And I told you I would be."

I'd told her from the beginning that it was one night and that I would most likely be on a plane by the time she woke up. I made sure that she understood that. I double-and triple-checked that she wasn't expecting any more than what I was offering. So I wouldn't apologize, not for that.

"You going to be gone one morning when this kid wakes up?"

"That's not fair." I shook my head, removing my hand from her leg. "I never lied to you, Ems."

She sighed. "You're right, you didn't. I'm sorry."

"I didn't make this decision lightly." I reached for her hands, needing her to see the sincerity in what I was saying. "And I'm not going anywhere. I mean, other than traveling for work and stuff. But otherwise, I'm not going anywhere."

"Okay, then, I guess we're doing this. Together. Sort of."

"We're doing this. We're having a baby." Saying it out loud was as weird as I thought it would be. Would I ever get used to this shit? Maybe I should practice in the mirror or something. *I'm having a baby. We're having a baby. I'm going to be a father.* If I said it enough times, maybe I would stop wanting to tag *holy fucking shit* along at the end.

Ems nodded, licking her lips then dragging her teeth over her bottom one. It was sexy. Everything she did was sexy. I pushed that shit down to the depths of my soul though. I wouldn't fuck this up. Well, I wouldn't let my cock fuck this up.

"How long are you in town this time?"

"Couple weeks." I took my cell out of my back pocket, checking my work calendar. "I'm in Italy next month." I pulled up her contact, sharing my schedule with her. "I sent you the link, that way you'll at least know which country I'm in."

"Maybe we could tell my parents before you leave? I'll be eighteen weeks soon, and honestly, I don't know how much longer I can train the way I am."

The thought of telling Smith James that I'd gotten his daughter pregnant was utterly terrifying. That was a conversation no guy ever wanted to have with a chick's father. But I'd man up. I'd be there for Ems and I'd be there for my kid.

Starting right this second.

"To be honest, I'd rather you stop training now." When she opened her mouth, to most likely hand me my ass for trying to tell her what she should and shouldn't do with her body, I held my palm up. "I'm not here to tell you what to do, obviously. But if you're going to stop soon anyway, why put yourself through any more than you already have?"

"If I stop training now, my parents will find out in a matter of days." She winced. "Which means you'll be here for the duration of their wrath."

So not only would I be telling Smith I banged his daughter, I'd be sleeping within shotgun range. This kid better know that I put my life on the line to make sure its mom stayed healthy.

"That's okay."

"Really?" Her blue eyes narrowed again, the way they seemed to do every time she didn't fully believe what I was saying. "You aren't going to tuck tail and run? You're going to stand next to me, look my dad in the eye, and tell him you got me pregnant? And then stay for another week so he can torture you?"

"Yes." I nodded gravely. "I'll consider it my first selfless parenting act."

She snorted, rolling her eyes.

"Look. I know that the guy you hooked up with at the wedding and the guy sitting next to you right now seem like two different people. But they're both me. I can be a player, and a selfish bastard. But I can also be a nice guy, a loving brother, and a caring son. All I'm asking for is a chance to prove to you that I can be a good dad too." A chance to prove it to her, and a chance to prove it to myself. I'd made my choice, and I planned on giving it my all.

"Okay."

"Okay?"

"Yes. I'll stop training, and we'll tell my parents together." She threw off her blanket like she was suddenly burning up. "You can be in the baby's life. And we can work toward being…co-parents."

"How 'bout friends and co-parents?" I shrugged. "Seems like us at least enjoying each other's company would go a long way in giving this kid a kickass life."

"Friends and co-parents." Emmie held her pinkie out, nodding once when I hooked mine around it. "It's a deal."

I'd never pinkie promised on a friendship before, but then again, I'd never gotten an eighteen-year-old ballerina pregnant.

"Can I, like, talk to the baby? Can it hear me yet?" I'd also never talked to someone's stomach before either. But this was my life now. I might as well start living it.

"I don't know. I haven't had time to read any of those pregnancy books. By the time I get home from rehearsal, I'm too tired. And on my days off, I have to do all my homework. I'm like a walking, talking, knocked-up zombie." She put her hand low on her stomach. "But you can talk to it all you want. I do."

"You do?" I wasn't entirely sure why, but that made me smile, thinking of Emmie sitting alone talking to our kid.

"Yeah." She leaned back against the pillow, cradling her head on her arm like she was seconds away from passing out. "I talk to it. I turn on classical music while I study, and then hard-core rock for balance. We want a well-rounded kid, right?"

I laughed, climbing off the couch and getting on my knees in front of Emmie. "Can you like close your eyes or something? It feels weird talking to my unborn child with its mother listening."

She smiled a sweet, sleepy smile, her exhaustion seeming to make her guard fall. "If I close my eyes, I'll fall asleep."

"It's okay. You sleep. I'll watch the baby."

Emmie and I stared at each other, both seemingly happy with this new truce that had settled between us. I was going to be a dad, and if I could keep making my kid's mom smile like that, then we were going to be okay.

She lifted her shirt, tucking it into her sports bra and closing her eyes. "Good night, Kase."

"'Night, Ems."

I reached out, slowly putting my hand flat on her stomach. It was the first time I'd really touched her since the night we'd created the baby I was now trying to gather the courage to talk to. Her skin was smooth, her muscles tight. I spoked quietly, embarrassed and not wanting to wake Emmie. "Hey, kid. I'm, uh, your dad." I let out a soft sigh, the weight in my words not lost on me. "I know it took me a couple months, but I'm here and I'm not going anywhere. So. Try not to be too hard on me when you come out, okay?"

I didn't know what else to say, so I sat there next to Ems with my hand on our growing baby long after she'd fallen asleep. She was so beautiful, so damn angelic. I'd been drawn to her the first moment I'd laid eyes on her. I'd been infatuated with her purity, her grace. She was everything I wasn't, and I'd wanted a piece of her for myself.

I'd gotten a little more than I'd bargained for.

Chapter Twenty-Seven

Emmie

I'd been avoiding my whole family for two days now. They knew Kase was in town and they all wanted to know why. They were constantly texting, dropping by to check on me. Luckily, our parents were all still in Florida, and they weren't around to witness the over-the-top hovering that was taking place.

I hadn't seen Kase since I fell asleep with his hand on my stomach. I told him I had homework to catch up on, but really, I'd been hiding. He wanted to be part of this kid's life, and that meant he was always going to be part of my life too. It was noble, and I was proud of him. But I was also terrified for myself.

Kasen Cadence was handsome and funny. He was sexy, and he turned me on without even trying. He was my first, and he was the father of the baby taking over my body. Every time I saw him, I was overcome with emotions. Anger at the situation we were in, desire for his hands on my body, and longing for his heart to belong to me. And that was probably part of the reason I never wanted to tell him I was pregnant. The more he was around, the more he had the power to destroy me.

I needed to get it together. I needed to stick to our agreement. We were friends and co-parents. There was no room between us for more. I'd only end up hurt when everything was said and done.

I rolled over, wiping my eyes from the tears that seemed to flow nonstop when I was alone, and grabbed my cell out of its charger. Speaking of my baby daddy, I needed to talk to him. Brody had cornered me today, refusing to leave my house until I agreed to his terms.

Emmie: I stopped training today, I told them I was sick and couldn't make it in.

Kasen: How long you think we got?

Emmie: I don't know, two days? Max.

Kasen: Okay. Well, tell our kid stories about my bravery.

I was almost positive that my dad wouldn't kill him. Although I couldn't even wrap my mind around how disappointed he was going to be. How heartbroken. I'd never let them down before, and this was a hell of a first offense.

Emmie: Brody and Landry invited us to dinner tonight.

Kasen: Us? Like you and the baby? Or us like you and me?

Emmie: You and me. I think Brody is playing peacemaker.

Kasen: Do they not know we already made peace?

Emmie: No. I've avoided all my cousins since you've been in town. They ask too many questions and I haven't had the energy to deal with them.

I left out that I'd been avoiding him too. Maybe he hadn't even noticed. He probably didn't think of me nonstop the way I seemed to think about him these days.

Kasen: Then let's go to dinner with Brody and Landry.

Emmie: You sure?

Kasen: When I leave here in a week, I want to make sure that no one is calling me an asshole behind my back.

Emmie: To be fair, they call you an asshole to your face too.

Kasen: When do those pregnancy hormones kick in? The ones that make you all sweet to the man who gave you the baby?

I couldn't be sweet to the man who gave me the baby. It was called self-preservation and I was clinging to it like a life raft after a plane crash in the middle of the Atlantic.

Emmie: Those aren't a thing when your one-night stand knocks you up.

There. Distantly sarcastic.

Kasen. Hm. Too bad.

Emmie: I do appreciate what you're doing though, helping me with my family. And you're right. We need to let them know that you're the baby's father and that you aren't going anywhere any time soon.

Kasen: Ever. I'm not going anywhere ever. I'll be its dad, always. Teething, scraped knees, broken hearts, all of it.

Emmie: When you're not in Italy or Bali.
Kasen: You gotta bust my balls every time I attempt to be heartfelt and nice?
Emmie: I keep my expectations low so I don't get let down.
I don't get my heart shattered.
Kasen: That seems awfully sad.
Emmie: But smart.
Kasen: I'll come pick you up in a bit.
Emmie: Sure.

I got out of bed, heading to my closet and flipping on the light. It was a chandelier and it was so elegant it was almost embarrassing. My mom and sister re-did my room a few years ago, and it was like a department store threw up a bunch of pink bubble gum. It bothered me that this was what they thought I liked, what they thought of me. It was childish and ostentatious. I was neither of those things. I would have preferred clean and vintage.

I moved my clothes along the racks, trying to find the perfect outfit. What did one wear for dinner with the guy who you gave your virginity to? I glanced down at my stomach. It wasn't board flat like it used to be. Instead it looked like I'd had a big lunch. I could still fit into all my clothes. I didn't need to choose something that would hide it yet.

I smiled, plucking a thin tan slip dress out of the back of my closet. I wouldn't be able to wear this in a matter of days, so I might as well dazzle Kase while I could, right? Pretty soon I'd be obviously pregnant. He wouldn't be able to look at me without seeing our child. It may have been silly that I wanted to remind him that I was still me. That I was still the girl he'd wanted.

Even if it was for only one night.

Chapter Twenty-Eight

Kasen

I swallowed past the lump in my throat, and that lump was pure fucking lust. I'd pulled up in front of Emmie's house to find her standing on her front porch. Her hair was down and wild, her lips were like glass, and that dress...holy shit that dress. It was almost sheer, accentuating her every soft curve and angle. Was she trying to kill me?

I got out of the car, opening the door for her as she made her way down her front steps. The wind blew her hair, carrying the delicious scent of her shampoo directly into my brain. I felt dizzy, like it'd been laced with some unheard-of narcotic.

"You look beautiful, Ems."

I had to tell her, she had to know that she was gorgeous. I'd leave out the fact that she made it difficult to breathe and my dick was so hard it was about to bust out of my jeans.

"Thank you." Her smile was small, sweet.

I helped her into the car, and then spent the short journey to the driver's side willing my cock to stand down. *She's not for us. We've already been there and fucked up her life.*

Ems and I were both quiet on the drive over to Brody and Landry's. I hated that I didn't have the right words and that I didn't know exactly how to talk to her. We'd made our choices, and we were now living in the middle of our new normal. But neither one of us seemed to know exactly how to navigate.

Luckily, once we got inside, Brody and Landry picked up the conversation. Asking Emmie about how she was feeling, about the classes she was taking. Brody wanted to see the drone videos I'd shot on my latest trip overseas. And before I knew it, it was time to eat.

I was sitting next to Ems, and across the table from Brody and Landry. I'd always thought they were an odd pair, but tonight was making me rethink that assessment. They complemented each other in a way that was hard to ignore. Brody was hilarious and over the top, with no filter. Landry was quietly brilliant, and he made her laugh.

"Where are the kids?" Emmie was eating her dinner, one food at a time. I noticed that she always seemed to save her favorite part for last. This time it was the strawberry vinaigrette salad that was still left, which made sense because that was the only part of dinner that contained sugar.

Landry smiled, letting out a content sigh. "They are with Devin and Jett. Isn't it great? It's so quiet." She put her hand to her ear. "You hear that?" When the rest of us stayed silent, she nodded, her smiling growing. "Exactly. It's only the four of us and this nice meal, and this delicious wine. No one is screaming. No one is fighting. No one is peeing on the potted tree in the living room."

Brody pouted out his lower lip. "I kind of miss them. Call Devin and tell her to bring them back."

"Not a chance." Landry picked up her glass of wine and took a healthy swallow.

Brody pointed across the table while addressing his wife. "You're going to scare them." He looked at us. "It isn't all bad, you know? They're great, and we wouldn't trade those little monsters for anything in this world."

Landry rolled her eyes. "Em knows how much we love our kids." She took another big drink of her red wine. "She also knows the chaos that ensues when all three of them are at a dinner table together."

"Well, then you're going to scare Kase." Brody and Landry were talking back and forth like I wasn't here, listening to every word spoken. "Em is going to need him, and he'll regret walking away. So keep the *our kids are terrors* stuff to a minimum."

"Uh, you're not going to scare me away." I'd seen those three little blond-haired surfer spawn, and when they were together, they were a force to be reckoned with. But Ems and I weren't having three kids. We were having one. And we could handle one. *Right?* I put my arm along the back of Emmie's chair, rubbing my thumb along her enticingly bare shoulder. "I'm not going anywhere."

Emmie wiped her mouth in that small, polite way she had about her, and put her napkin back in her lap. Which drew my eyes to the fact that her dress was short, and most of her perfect thighs were exposed. Fuck. Now I had a semi at the damn dinner table. "Kase and I are going to raise this baby together."

Brody and Landry didn't say a word, but their eyes grew a bit rounder.

"Yeah, I want to be in the baby's life." I kept rubbing her shoulder, unable to stop touching her smooth skin. "We'll co-parent as friends."

"No shit?" Brody finally found his voice.

I nodded. "No shit."

"Good for you, bro." He held his hand out over the table for a high five. I'd take it. That was at least one other person in my kid's life who was happy I was sticking around. "You tell your parents yet?"

Ems cleared her throat, and I went from rubbing her shoulder to squeezing it. We were two adults about to have a baby. But when it came to telling our parents, we were reduced to two teenagers unsure of our every step. "We're telling mine this week."

There was a constant pit in my stomach. The thought of admitting out loud to Smith James that I got his youngest daughter pregnant made me almost physically ill. But I did the, uh, crime? So I'd pay the time. Was that even the right analogy? Probably not.

"Do you want us to be there?" Landry had finished her first glass of wine and was pouring herself a second. "We can come over, all of us."

"I think we can handle it." I did not want an audience for that conversation. And why the hell would a room full of extra people be helpful? "Thanks for the offer though."

Landry's eyes narrowed and Brody's smile grew. "I wasn't offering it to you, I was offering it to Em. If she wants us there, then we'll be there. That's how this family works, not that you would know."

Us against the world. Who *didn't* know this family's decree by this point? But right now, I was Emmie's person. We were the ones having the baby, we were the ones who needed to man up and tell our parents. We couldn't keep hiding behind our siblings, and behind our fears.

"I think our kid needs its parents to have big enough balls to announce its existence without a backup crew."

Brody clapped his hands, once, loudly. "Yes." He pointed at me, grinning. "That's exactly right, bro. We've all announced our shit in this ridiculous way, across the table at family dinners. It's always dramatic and everyone's fucking opinions get thrown in the mix. It's unnecessary chaos."

I wholeheartedly agreed. But Ems was sitting silent and stiff beside me, and Landry looked like she wanted to stick a knife through her husband and into me.

"Ems? Do you want them there?" It was her life too. If she wanted to be surrounded by her cousins, then I'd deal with it. What I couldn't handle was her staying quiet, afraid to voice her opinions. That wasn't how things were going to work between us.

She shook her head. "No." Her hand found mine under the table. "We can do it, together."

My chest swelled with pride. She trusted me to be there for her, she gathered strength from us. And that mattered, a lot. I pulled her closer. We were a team. We were going to be a team for the next eighteen years. It wasn't us against the world. It was us there for our kid from day one. I kissed the side of her head, allowing myself one small moment to breathe in her scent. Suck it everyone who doubted me, who doubted Ems. The fuck-boy and the ballerina, figuring their shit out.

"You two boning?"

"Seriously, Brody?" Ems sat up straighter, tossing a broccoli stalk across the table. He caught it before it could hit him in the chest, and he popped it into his mouth, smiling.

He chewed, talking around his food. "He's been looking at you like he wants to eat you for dessert. You're wearing a sexy-ass slip of a dress. And you two have announced that you're raising this baby together and formed your own little team. What else am I supposed to think?" I opened my mouth to defend us both, but he cut me off before I had a chance. "I know what it's like to be completely turned on by the chick carrying your kid." He gestured with his thumb to Landry, like we wouldn't know who he was referring to otherwise. "I get it. It's hot."

He wasn't wrong. There was something about knowing Ems was carrying my baby that made her hot level go from smoking to fucking on fire. I tried to ignore it as much as possible because it made me feel like a caveman.

"I'm wearing this dress because I won't be able to in a matter of days." Ems leaned back in her chair, her palms going to her stomach. "This is only going to get bigger. And then I won't be dessert. I'll never be dessert ever again. It's *not* hot."

The table went silent. Brody looked terrified.

I had to bite my lips together to keep from smiling at her adorable outburst. "Ems, is that what you honestly think?"

She sighed, her eyes trained on her lap.

I lifted her chin with my finger, forcing her to meet my gaze. "You are gorgeous, and you will always look like dessert, Ems." I smiled, cupping her cheek. "And the pregnancy thing? It's hot. I swear I'm not just saying that to make you feel better. It's stupid hot."

I might not be able to act on any of it, but I didn't want her to think otherwise. I'd remind her how beautiful she was every day if that was what it took for her to believe it.

"You sure you two aren't boning?"

This time Landry popped him on the back of the head.

Chapter Twenty-Nine

Emmie

Dinner at Landry and Brody's house was last night. And I'd been thinking about Kase's hands on me ever since. The words he'd spoken, the compliments he'd given me. But more than that, I thought about how he made me feel. He made me feel like I could do anything, like I could own my life without anyone's help. He made me feel capable and beautiful, and I was so grateful.

So far, Kase had kept his word. He was there for me, and he was there for the baby. He wanted to be part of this, and he wasn't going anywhere.

"Emmie, can you come in here, baby girl?"

And now, he was really going to be put to the test. I knew that tone, even from down the long hallway that separated my room from where my parents were hanging out in the den. It was that concerned yet slightly suspicious tone that I'd heard my aunts and uncles use with my cousins.

"Yeah, give me just a sec." I closed the textbook I'd been reading, quickly typing out a message to Kase.

Emmie: It's go time.

Kasen: Holy shit.

Emmie: You backing out?

Kasen: Nope. Never. I'm on my way.

Knowing that Kase was coming gave me the strength I needed to climb off my bed and head toward the firing squad. This was it. This was the moment I let my parents down, by letting them in. I made a detour to the kitchen, buying time by getting myself a drink of water.

"Emmie? Are you coming?"

I put my glass in the sink, allowing myself a few deep breaths before leaving the safety of the dark kitchen and walking into the well-lit den.

"Hey, guys, what's up?"

My parents were sitting side by side on the oversize sectional where we all gathered for family movie nights every Sunday while we were growing up.

"Well, baby, I got a call from Master Degas this afternoon." My mom took off her glasses and sat them and the magazine she'd been reading on the coffee table. "She asked if you were okay. Said you hadn't been to rehearsal in a few days." There was concern in her tone and in her eyes.

"Sweetheart, is everything okay? Are you sick? Hurt? Did something happen?" My dad was perched next to my mom, a worried united front ready to tackle any problem together and head on.

Would Kase and I have that? We'd have to schedule big talks like this with our kid. I'd have to call him and hope that he had cell service, then wait for him to fly home. Whatever, we'd make it work. And hopefully, our kid would never have to sit us down and tell us about an unplanned pregnancy.

"Um, actually, yes, something did happen but—"

"Hold on, baby, I think someone's knocking. Do y'all hear that?" My heart dropped to my stomach when my dad got off the couch to answer door. "Kase? Hey, bud, what are you doing here?"

"I'm here for Emmie."

I could hear them getting closer and closer to the living room with every step. I was shifting on my feet and trying not to vomit all over the priceless handspun Turkish rug.

"Emmie?" My dad sounded a little shocked and a little apprehensive. When the two of them rounded the corner, Kase came over and stood beside me. My dad narrowed his eyes, glancing between us. "What the hell for?"

"Dad." I gulped past the emotion that had formed in my throat, trying to sound as calm as possible. "Can you sit down?"

He didn't take his eyes off us as he sat next to my mother. She grabbed his hand, her gaze switching between my father and myself. "What's going on, Emmie? You're scaring us, sweetheart."

For months, I knew this moment would come. The moment I had to tell them I was pregnant. I wasn't my cousins. I wasn't about to let the whole family find out over the dinner table in some oddly dramatic fashion. Brody had been right. It was unnecessary. And my parents weren't like my aunts and uncles. They wouldn't be able to find humor in any of this. It would take them time to find the silver lining, to find the good in the pile of heartache I was about to lay at their feet.

I blinked rapidly, trying to keep my tears at bay. "I stopped training because it was too hard on my body, and on the baby." I took a small step closer to Kase, liking the way I could feel his warmth against my arm. He was here, right next to us, like he'd promised he would be.

"What baby? There's no baby. Tell me there's no baby and this is some weird joke that little fucker convinced you to play." My dad jabbed a finger in Kase's direction, making sure we all knew he was the *little fucker* he was referring to.

Kasen glanced at me, and then focused on my parents. "I assure you, sir, I don't find pregnancy scares funny." I backhanded his thigh. Like I said, my parents weren't ones to find humor in tense situations. "But, um, no joke. Ems is pregnant."

"No she's not." My dad shook his head.

"I am."

"Emmie doesn't date, she doesn't have sex. You don't know what you're talking about." He put his free hand, the one my mother wasn't clutching on to for dear life, over his mouth, like he couldn't believe he'd had to say those words out loud.

"She is, and she did." Kase nodded, lips pursed. "And I know because I put it in there myself."

Oh for shit's sake.

Chapter Thirty

Kasen

I'm not saying it'd never happened, but it had been a real long time since I'd been punched in the face. And Smith James? He moved fast for a retired rocker, and he had a mean right hook. He didn't knock me on my ass, but I wasn't sure I'd be able to move my jaw tomorrow.

"Dad," Emmie yelled in disbelief as her mom grabbed her father by the back of the shirt and pulled him back to sitting.

"You deserved that, you little fucker, and you know it." He was still steaming, his face red and his chest heaving. He wanted to hit me some more. A lot. I could see it in his eyes.

I held my hands up, even though all I wanted to do was make sure my lower jaw was still attached. "I did." And I always assumed he'd try to shoot me when he found out, so a quick jab to the face wasn't all that bad.

Her mom shook her head, like she still couldn't believe any of this was happening in her living room. "Emmie, baby, tell us how this happened. Kase doesn't even live in this country half the...Cash's wedding? You went to bed early, said you weren't feeling well."

"I did, but—"

"You lied to us." Her mom cut her off, like her dad had earlier. Every time her family spoke over her, it grated on my nerves. "You lied to sneak up to your room with Kasen."

"Sneak?" I didn't like that. It made it seem like we'd done something wrong. And we hadn't. "She's eighteen. She made an excuse and then we went, *consensually*, to her room."

Smith pointed at me again, like he wished he was holding a knife and stabbing me instead. "Why are you even here for this discussion? Why are you talking for her?"

"Because this family has a bad habit of talking *over* her." I put my hand on Ems's stomach, not even really thinking about how intimate my actions must look to her parents. "And I'm here because I'm the baby's father. Where the hell else would I be?"

Where the hell else would I be? I liked that, I liked how true and right it made me feel. I was an idiot to ever think that I would be able to walk away from my child. It needed me. Emmie needed me. And I was glad that I was here, even though its grandfather had jacked me in the fucking face.

"Emmie, dammit, sweetheart." Smith ran his hands through his hair, making it stick up all over the place. "How are we going to deal with this? What are we going to do with you?"

"*Do with me?*" Emmie took a deep breath, then met my eyes.

I tried real fucking hard to give her all my strength, all my snark and sarcasm. I winked at her, hoping she got the message that if she wanted to tell her parents off, I was here for it.

She stood up straighter, her chin lifting and her eyes narrowing as she ticked points off on her elegant fingers. "Evie had a drug addiction, and a whole secret life in Dallas. Halen hid a miscarriage. *For years.* Marley and Jett hid an entire *corporation.* Cash and Crue? You wouldn't even be able to wrap your mind around the messed-up stuff they got into in high school. Yet you've stood by every single one of them. But me? I'm a problem that needs to be *dealt* with?"

"Baby girl, you have to understand, we're shocked." Her dad put his arm around his wife.

I snorted. "Yeah, she doesn't let shocked count as an excuse for bad behavior, trust me."

Smith jerked his attention back to me. "Can you fucking leave? I can't even stand to look at you."

"I'm not going anywhere." I used my thumb to gesture to Emmie's stomach. "I promised my kid."

Her mom wagged a finger between Ems and me, her voice taking on a hopeful note. "Are you two together? Are you dating? In love and having a baby?"

"No." Emmie spoke up, choosing to be the one to rain on her mom's parade. "We're friends. And we'll co-parent the baby together."

"Friends." Her dad nodded, a disgusted look on his face. "You make a habit of having sex with your friends?"

"Dad." Emmie rolled her eyes to the ceiling like she was exasperated. Not that I could blame her. Mr. and Mrs. James were proving to be quite the pieces of work. We weren't high school freshmen experimenting after school. And to be fair we weren't really *friends* before we fucked. But I doubted that would be a helpful add-on, so I kept my mouth shut. "I don't *have* sex, I had sex. The once."

I whispered out the side of my mouth, "Three times. Don't belittle my skills, Ems."

She hit me again, still not appreciating my humor.

"You took my daughter's virginity? *And* got her pregnant?" Smith lunged off the couch only to be jerked back by his shockingly strong wife. "I want to kill him, Dylan. I want to actually harm him. There are images in my head of all the ways I could finish him."

"Were you careful, Emmie?" Mrs. James ignored her husband, making me think speaking over each other was a family-wide bad habit. "And, Kasen, were you? She was so inexperienced. She didn't know what to do, how could you let this happen?"

"*Let* this happen?" My eyebrows rose and I couldn't help but chuckle at their absurdity. "You think I threw caution to the wind? Like, *hey I've avoided fucking up lives so far, but this girl, yeah, I'll put a baby in this one.*"

"Don't say put a baby in her." Emmie's dad shook his head, his face going pale. "I think I might be sick."

"We were careful," Ems said.

I nodded. "Extremely careful."

"And this isn't Kasen's fault. This isn't something he did *to* me. We did this together. And I know I'm the baby of this family, but I'm not a child. I'm not stupid. I'm not naïve." Emmie threw her hands in the air. "Hell, sex comes up at every damn family dinner we have." Her voice got a little softer, like she was losing the energy to deal with this discussion. "And yeah, I planned on learning from everyone else's mistakes. But somewhere along the way, I grew up. I wanted to experience everything life had to offer."

Her dad scoffed. "Well. You got your wish."

"Don't be a dick to her." I knew I shouldn't push him right now, but he was being unnecessarily mean to his daughter and it was pissing me the fuck off.

"Excuse me?" He went to get off the couch again, but this time he stopped himself. "Don't you come into *my* house and talk to me like that, you little shit."

Little shit, little fucker. Emmie said nicknames meant something in her family and I was really loving all my new ones.

"Kase, do your parents know?" Her mom was at least trying to be calm.

"No."

"I bet your sister does though." Smith glared at me, no doubt trying to make my head explode with some laser beam in his mind. "And the rest of the crew? They know, don't they?" He switched his attention and glare over to Emmie. I wanted to step in front of her, shield her from his bullshit. "They've known since the beginning. You told them, and hid it from us. Because that's the way this family works, isn't it? Sneak around, hide your dirty deeds, hide it all."

Dirty deeds? For fuck's sake. I'd heard enough.

"That's the way this family works because you guys are as clueless as it comes. All these things your kids keep from you? They happen right in front of your face." I was gaining speed, saying all the things someone should have said to these people years ago. "Halen and Beau? They hooked up in a tree house on this damn compound. Jett and Marley's empire? There was a tunnel *under your feet*. Hell, my sister lost her virginity while Dash was sleeping two doors away. So don't come down on Emmie, not like that."

Smith's face was turning red again. "You have no fucking right to tell me how to feel, how to speak to my own daughter."

"Ems may be *your* daughter." I reached down and took her hand in mine. "But right now, she's carrying *my* baby. And I'm not going to let you treat her like this. We didn't do anything wrong. This baby was an accident. It wasn't a careless mistake."

I was mad, he was furious. Emmie was crying and so was her mom. This was no good, for any of us. "Come on, Ems, let's get out of here for a bit."

"She's not going anywhere with you." Her dad stood, shaking his head and doing that stabby pointing thing again.

I wrapped my arm around Emmie, almost tearing up myself when she all but collapsed against me. "You need to cool off. I need to try to calm her down." I lifted her into my arms, the fact that she didn't protest telling me all I needed to know. "And what's the worst that could happen, sir? I already got her pregnant."

Chapter Thirty-One

Kasen

I put Ems in my car, buckling her up even though we were only driving a mile down the road back to my sister's house. She was quietly crying, tears streaming down her pretty face. I could almost see the swell of her stomach under the loose t-shirt she was wearing. She'd only stopped training a few days ago, but already her body seemed to be responding. She didn't look so thin, so exhausted. Her cheeks had color and the bags under her eyes had all but disappeared.

Although, at the moment, she looked utterly heartbroken.

"Ems, you doing okay?"

She nodded. But otherwise didn't say anything.

I knew that Smith and Dylan were shocked, thrown for a loop. But their anger and harsh comments were uncalled for. Emmie was their daughter. They'd gone past disappointment, and they'd hurt her. I refused to let anyone make her feel the way they did back there in her living room.

I parked my car, climbing out and moving around to the passenger side. Ems let me pick her up again, which was really starting to worry me. Maybe I should call Landry and have her come check her vitals and shit. Maybe all the stress of the last few months was making her sick.

"What the hell happened to your face?" Cash's eyes went wide when I walked into the living room with Emmie in my arms. "And what's wrong with Em?"

"She's fine, exhausted though, I think." I sat her on the couch, letting her feet rest in my brother-in-law's lap. Then I stood, finally touching my jaw for the first time. Good. It was still there. "We told her parents about the baby tonight and it didn't go well."

"Holy shit, Smith hit you?" Cash winced, standing and carefully putting a pillow under Ems's feet before heading into the kitchen. He came back a few seconds later and passed me an ice pack. He took a seat on the smaller loveseat, letting me sit down beside Ems. "I can't believe he hit you. I didn't think he had it in him. He's old, dude."

Emmie giggled, the sound making me smile despite all the heavy shit we'd gone through this evening. "To be fair, Kase used the term *I put it in there myself* when my dad asked how he knew I was pregnant."

Cash snorted. "You didn't."

"I did." I moved closer to Ems, tossing the pillow into an empty chair and putting her tiny feet in my lap. I needed to touch her. I needed to feel her and know that she was okay.

Katie came into the room, braiding her wet hair over her shoulder. "Where've you been? Wait? Why are you icing your jaw?"

"They told Smith and Dylan about the baby, and Smith punched him." Cash held his arm out, kissing my sister's forehead when she settled next to him. "But I'd hit the guy who knocked up my daughter too."

"Oh my god, Em? Are you okay? Is she okay?" Katie got back to her feet, kneeling beside Emmie and feeling her forehead. "You don't have a fever."

"I'm fine." Emmie crawled down the couch, and laid her head in my lap, tucking her hands under her chin. "Just sleepy."

My heart melted. She needed comfort, and she was asking me for it. This was the first time she was coming to me, asking me to help her. To hold her. I brushed the hair back from her face, then rested my hand on the swell of her hip. "Katie Bug, you mind calling Landry? Let's get Ems checked before we let her pass out."

"Already texted her, she's on her way." Cash tossed his cell on the coffee table, sending me an understanding smile.

That was a first as well, him acting like we were family instead of enemies.

"You going to call Mom and Dad now?" Katie was speaking softly, none of us wanting to disturb Emmie while she rested.

I let my palm slide down, resting it on her stomach, loving that it was no longer flat. "Not a chance. I think one set of parental meltdowns is all either of us can handle in one day."

"They take the news that bad?"

I nodded, my eyes still on Ems. "It was pretty bad."

"They hate me." She whispered her words, the sound breaking my heart.

I used my free hand to wipe a tear from her cheek. "Ems, they don't hate you."

"Yeah, Em, you know your parents don't take shit as well as the other 'rents." Cash put his arm around my sister, kicking his feet up on the coffee table. "They tend to overreact, but they always come around."

They always come around. They had to, right? They couldn't treat her like this forever. They were her parents. They loved her. Or at least, that was the way a parent was supposed to love their children. Wholly, unconditionally, and without fail. That was the way my parents loved me and Katie. And that was the way I'd love my kid.

I kept my hand on Emmie's stomach, trying to push all the love and protection I felt for that tiny growing baby through my palm. I wanted it to feel me, to feel that I was there. If it could feel Emmie's stress, her uncertainty, I wanted to reassure it that all hope wasn't lost and I wouldn't let anyone hurt it. Or its mother.

Fuck me. I was turning into a sappy badass dad.

Landry came in a few minutes later, breaking the silence that had blanketed the room. "What happened?" She knelt beside Ems, opening this fancy-looking duffle bag she brought with her.

"Her dad was a dick when we told them about the baby."

She glanced up at me while she fitted a blood pressure cuff around Ems's wrist. "He the reason your jaw is black and blue?" I nodded and she turned her attention back to Ems. "Her blood pressure is a little low, but not alarmingly or anything. I'm going to set her up with an IV for fluids. And she'll need to eat as soon as she wakes up."

"She can stay with me, that way I can keep an eye on her." I pulled her into my lap, standing with her sleeping body in my arms. I didn't wait for anyone to agree or to protest.

I carried her down the hall and laid her in my bed, dragging her workout pants down her body, then quickly covering her with my blankets. The last thing I needed was her family thinking I was trying to hit on her while she was unconscious. They were finally coming around and not cussing me every time I walked into a damn room. Peeking at her when she had no control would set me back, no doubt.

I stepped back, waiting in the doorway, watching as Landry expertly started an IV drip, hanging the bag from a temporary hook she placed on the wall behind the bed.

"Thank you."

"I'm leaving this cuff." She held up the device she checked Emmie's blood pressure with. "Take her BP again in about an hour, if it's lower than this number," she paused to jot something down on a notepad she'd pulled out of her duffle, "call me."

"I will."

She stopped on her way out the door, resting her hand on my arm. "You're doing a good job, Kase." She smiled, her hold tightening for a moment. "You're taking good care of them, and we all see it."

She left and I climbed in bed beside Ems, careful not to disturb her. I lay down on my side, putting my palm back on the tiny swell of her stomach. Because like I'd said earlier, where the hell else would I be?

Chapter Thirty-Two

Kasen

I checked Emmie's blood pressure again, and she slept through it. Luckily, it wasn't low and we wouldn't need to call Landry back. But now it was late, nearing midnight, and Ems had been asleep for a solid three hours. As I was sitting beside her, unhooking the IV from her arm, she started to stir. The IV bag was empty and it had started to pull blood from her arm a bit. My hands were shaking. I'd never played nurse before. Doctor plenty of times, but never nurse. I smiled at my own joke, the action feeling almost foreign after the night I'd had.

"You're smiling."

"I'm a funny guy." I put a bandage on her arm, using the leftover tape to stick the port to the empty IV bag. "How are you feeling?"

"Better." She stretched her arms over her head, making her shirt ride up and the covers move down. "Where are my pants?"

"I took them off." I winked, chuckling when her eyes went wide. "I wanted to make sure you were comfortable, Ems."

"Thank you." She rolled onto her side, facing me. "I'm sorry about my parents and my dad hitting you, and all the crying and passing out."

I shook my head, grinning. "You don't need to thank me, and you don't need to apologize. We're in this together, and we're doing fine." Other than the fistfight, the dehydration, and IV drip, I suppose. "You hungry? I'm supposed to make you eat."

"Can I have some cookies?" She clasped her hands together, like she wasn't above begging. "Please?"

"Sure, Ems, you earned them today." I kissed her forehead, then got to my feet. "I'll be back in a little bit."

Come hell or high water, I'd find that chick some damn cookies. She'd had one heck of a bad day, and if cookies were all she could stomach at the moment, then cookies it was. I stopped short when I realized Katie and Cash were still awake and lying on the couch. "Hey, I figured you guys went to bed hours ago." I hadn't heard them, hadn't heard the TV. I'd fallen asleep on and off, waking to check on Ems like Landry had instructed.

"I wanted to make sure you guys didn't need anything." Katie sat up, rubbing at her eyes. "I came in there a few times, but you were both asleep."

"You were spooning her." Cash raised an eyebrow. "Are you two together now? I thought this was friends and co-parents."

"It is." I collapsed on one of the two leather chairs opposite them. "But she's carrying my kid, and she had a shit day because of it. The least I can do is watch over her while she takes a damn nap." When Cash didn't say anything else, I turned my attention back to my sister. "You got any cookies around here?"

She nodded, pointing past me and into the kitchen. "Flour is in the pantry, chocolate chips in the freezer."

"You expect me to *make* cookies? Like from scratch?" I stuck out my bottom lip, which always seemed to work when we were kids. "Can't you make them for me? Please, Katie Bug."

"Don't ask your sister to do it for you." Cash jerked his chin, his lips twitching like he was fighting off a smirk. "Come on, dad, step up for your kid."

"You're a real pain in the ass."

"And you're the asshole that knocked up my baby cousin and caused a rift between her and her parents." His eyes narrowed, all humor gone. "Unless you want your eye to match your jaw, I suggest you go make the damn cookies."

***

"Ems? You awake?"

"No." She pulled the covers up over her head. "I'm going to sleep until the baby is born, okay?"

I perched next to her, setting the plate of sugar I'd made myself on the nightstand. "I have fresh-out-of-the-oven chocolate chip cookies."

She peeked her blonde head out, pulling the blankets down to her mouth. "They smell really good."

"I can't promise how they'll taste. I made them myself."

The recipe was printed on the back of the chocolate chip bag, and I'd followed every step carefully. But I'd never baked anything before, so it was really a crapshoot whether they'd be edible. Cash had catalogued the whole process on social media, leaving out the fact that I was baking for my baby momma.

Her eyes filled with tears. "You made me cookies?"

"Uh, yeah?" I scratched the back of my head, not sure what to do about the crying that was seconds away from taking place. There'd been lots of that tonight.

She sniffled, then wiped her cheeks. "That was really nice."

"So cookies are really the only way you turn into a sweet, weepy pregnant chick?" I made room, setting the plate between us. The cookies *did* smell amazing, even if the shape was a bit more triangle than the perfect circles I'd seen Devin create.

She giggled, the sound warming me from the inside out. And then her smile crumbled and she started crying all over again.

"Awe, Ems." I wiped her tears away with my knuckles. "Your parents will come around."

"I know they will." She sat up, taking a deep breath like she was trying to get her emotions under control before she drowned us both. "I've never really fought with them before, though. I'm not used to disappointing them. I hate that they're mad at me. I hate that they reacted the way they did."

"Did you really expect them to take the news well?" I hadn't.

"I didn't expect them to be so hurt, and so angry."

"They're scared for you, Ems." I watched warily as she bit into one of the cookies. When she didn't immediately spit it out, I relaxed. "But what they don't know is that you, me, and this kid? We're going to be okay. I'm here for both of you, and we'll figure this all out. Together."

Because if I could figure out how to make cookies from scratch, I could pretty much do anything I put my fucking mind to.

Chapter Thirty-Three

Emmie

I returned home the morning after I told my parents about the baby. I felt better after a full night's sleep, and the IV boost from Landry had helped almost as much as sleeping cuddled up next to Kase had.

When I'd woken and felt his body against mine, his hand on my stomach, I'd melted. The butterflies I'd banished so long ago had returned full force. I'd slipped out of bed as quietly as possible, needing all the self-preservation I could muster to help me find the strength to leave. I didn't want him to think I was ungrateful, or running away. So I'd made him breakfast in bed, told him it was a thank you for the cookies he'd baked me in the middle of the night.

It was now three days later and my parents still weren't speaking to me. Other than the occasional unsupportive comment, they were either avoiding me, or sending me disappointed looks from across the room. It was like they couldn't bring themselves to kick me out, but the sight of me was making them ill.

It was exhausting and stressful. I didn't tell Kase, though. I didn't want him to worry. These were my parents, and they were my problem. I knew he thought that everything to do with the pregnancy was on both of us, but he shouldn't have to shoulder my parents' hatred. He didn't deserve it, and I refused to let him help me carry it.

It was Friday night, and that meant family dinner. I wanted to stay in my room, buried under my covers, and sleep until it was over. But I wasn't a child, and hiding from my problems would only prove my parents' point. That I was naïve and unprepared for the course I'd set for myself.

Emmie: You coming to family dinner tonight?
Kasen: Would it be easier or harder on you if I came?

Kase had been amazing all week. He texted me constantly, checking on the baby. He made me take my blood pressure every morning. But he kept his distance, not wanting to do anything to cause me any more stress.

Emmie: Harder. My dad will start all his "I told you so" stuff.
Kasen: What "I told you so" stuff?
Emmie: He thinks you'll end up bailing on the baby.

When my dad did speak to me, it was to remind me that I needed to get rid of Kase. *Once a player always a player, Emmie.* This one always made me tear up, even though I never let him know it. *He's here now because it's all new and dramatic, but it'll wear off and he'll be gone.* And then my favorite, the one that hit me in the heart with its truth. *He's never going to settle down, he'll only hurt you both in the end.*

Kasen: I'll be at dinner Ems.

I let out a sigh of relief, lying back on my bed. I needed Kase there beside me if I was going to survive this dinner. I hadn't talked to my aunts and uncles in the last few days either. But they had to know I was pregnant. My dad would have run to his brothers immediately. The parents were as close as all us kids were.

Which was where we got it from.

But that was part of the problem, wasn't it? They chose to lean on each other and away from us, the same way we did to them. There was a clear line drawn down the middle of this compound. There always had been. The more Kase pointed all these things out to me, the more I realized that he was right.

They were clueless. And they didn't deserve the right to reprimand me, to reprimand any of us. The longer they treated me like I was disowned, the easier it was for anger to take place of the hurt inside me.

Chapter Thirty-Four

Kasen

Smith James was starting to piss me the fuck off. Granted, the guy didn't know me, not the real me. He had no way of knowing that when I said I was going to do something, I was going to do it all the way. But that still didn't give him the right to constantly bring Emmie down. His disapproval was weighing on her, making her already heavy load all the more tiresome.

Emmie was exhausted but she was too anxious and on edge to sleep through the night. How did I know this? I moved to the guest room at Cash and Katie's that gave me a clear view of her window. When I asked her why her bedroom light was on in the middle of the night, she told me she was studying. But I knew that wasn't the case. Since she wasn't training anymore, she had plenty of hours in the day to get her schoolwork done.

I wanted her to come stay with Cash and Katie, but I wasn't sure how I was supposed to bring it up. I felt like I was still walking a fine line when it came to my input in her life. I wanted what was best for her and the baby, but I wasn't the boss of her.

She had enough of those hanging around.

"Hey, Katie, can I talk to you about something?" I skidded to a stop when I saw that Landry was there too. "Sorry, I didn't realize you weren't alone, it can wait."

"Nonsense." My sister gave me a toothless manic smile. "Unless you're going to tell me you knocked up another one of my in-laws. If that's the case, let's wait 'til Landry leaves so she's not an accomplice to murder."

"Hilarious."

"I thought so." Katie patted the space next to her on the couch. "Come tell us what's on your mind, punk."

Ems and the baby, they seemed to always be on my mind these days. But that was expected, right? I was on the compound, living in her space. And I couldn't seem to fall asleep at night until her bedroom light went off. It was like my body wouldn't relax until I knew she was resting. Once I was back to my normal routine, my brain would be able to function at full capacity again.

"You sure?" I looked to Landry, making sure that she was cool with my interruption.

"One, Brody has all three boys by himself for the first time in weeks. I'm not leaving this house until it's time to head to family dinner." She patted the same patch of couch Katie had a few seconds earlier. "Two, I love gossip of all kinds. So, let's hear it, little fucker."

Lovely. Smith was sharing his new special name for me with the whole compound.

"You guys should take your comedy act on the road." I sat on the loveseat, choosing not to wedge myself between them.

"If Brody gets me pregnant one more time, I might."

I slouched down, kicking my legs out in front of me. "Smith is still being a dick to Ems."

"Don't you think you should call him Mr. James, you know, at least until he doesn't openly hate the sight of you?" Our mother would be so proud of my sister trying to correct me.

"No." I was raised Southern and I knew my manners. But Smith James lost all my respect the night he made Ems cry. "Emmie's not sleeping well and she's constantly on edge, like she's waiting for the next disappointed comment to come her way. It's not good for her or the baby."

"I've been worried about her too. She lost some weight in the first trimester when she was training all day and I think the stress of the last week has made everything even worse." Landry shook her head. "Stress and anxiety, lack of sleep? You're right, it's not good for either of them."

I kept tabs on her blood pressure, forwarding the texts to Landry every morning to make sure she was okay. But I didn't know she'd lost weight. Maybe I should make her weigh herself every morning too? That was probably pushing it. And Ems would eventually push back.

"I want Emmie to move in here, with Katie." I'd been thinking about it for a few days now, and it seemed like the perfect solution. "Cash leaves for baseball training camp on Tuesday so you'll be here all alone for a couple months. And you're my sister, you won't talk constant shit about me."

Katie raised an eyebrow, grinning. "Oh yeah? What makes you so sure?"

"Fine, you won't talk constant shit about me bailing on my kid."

"Is that what Uncle Smith is saying? That you'll leave Em to do this all on her own?" When I nodded, Landry frowned.

"I may be a lot of things, but I'm not a liar. I'll be there for Ems and for the baby. I fly out in less than a week and I can't go until I know that they're both okay." I looked between the two of them. "So, will you help me?"

"Of course we will. I can get the other guest room ready." Katie hopped to her feet. "And order some healthy yummy groceries and cookie dough so she doesn't riot."

Landry polished off her wine, standing as well. "I'll talk to Em. I'll let her know that I think her being here would be what's best for now, medically."

I got up, crossing my arms over my chest. "And you'll both make sure that all the spawn stop giving her a hard time? Stop eating off her plate. Stop treating her like a baby and talking over her?"

Both girls stopped, staring at me with wide eyes.

"She needs all the food, and she needs to know that you guys believe in her, that you believe in us." I shook my head. "I swear, I will set up camp in front of her bedroom door if this shit doesn't stop."

"Is Brody right? Are you two boning?"

Cash chose that moment to walk into the house with Jett, Talon, and Beau. "What's going on? Kase is banging Em?"

I rolled my eyes. "You guys know that it's possible to truly care about someone without fucking them, right?" They all wrinkled their foreheads, like they were confused by the concept. "No. I'm not boning Emmie."

Jett sighed, shaking his head. "Well, you need to bone someone, because you seem stressed as fuck."

I ignored him, walking out of my sister's place and toward the pool house where this giant Friday family dinner was being held. I seemed stressed as fuck because I *was* stressed as fuck. I was going to be a father, Emmie's parents were treating her like she'd tossed her life in the shitter, and I had to be on a damn plane in three days.

Boning someone else was so far from my mind that it wasn't...Whoa. Since when had sex been a back-burner activity for me? I paused in the middle of the kalachi road, trying to recall the last time I got laid. There was that model I shot with in the Bali. Yeah, we'd spent the night together after our campaign ended. It hadn't been *that* long ago.

But since then I'd been kind of preoccupied. Finding out I got Ems pregnant, deciding I wanted to be a father, coming down here and helping her tell her parents.

But I left soon, in a matter of days. I'd fly out of here and I'd be me again.

Chapter Thirty-Five

Emmie

Dinner was as miserable I thought it would be. The conversation with the 'rents was strained. My father looked like he was going to throw up every time Kase leaned over to talk to me. My aunts and uncles kept shooting worried glances between my parents and me, not sure what to do. And my cousins? Well, I had to assume they were going for distraction.

"I have a video of Kase baking, if anyone wants to see it." Cash held out his cell. Jett immediately snatched it. "He wore his sister's cute *Mrs. Matthews* apron."

Kase groaned, hiding his face behind my back. "You try to do something nice for the chick carrying your child and your own brother-in-law records it." He shook his head, a disappointed yet playful expression on his handsome face. "Is there nothing sacred these days?"

"Apparently not," my dad answered from his spot way down the table.

My cheeks heated, my stomach flipping on itself. Kase and I coming to dinner tonight was to show that we were okay, united. Me shutting down in front of everyone would only add to my parents' opinion that I couldn't handle my life. So I ignored my father. I pretended like I hadn't even heard his backhanded comment.

"Kase, where are you headed next?" I stifled a groan. Beau had a polite smile on his face, thinking he was being nice when all he was actually doing was bringing up the fact that Kase worked out of the country all the time.

Kase put his hand on my knee under the table, comforting me automatically. "Uh, Italy."

"That's got to be pretty awesome, getting to take pictures all over the world." Beau was a photographer, and he sounded genuinely impressed with Kase's career. "I traveled around the US for a while, and the content I got was amazing. I can't imagine the things you get to capture in other countries."

"Yeah, it's beautiful. And humbling in a—"

"Beau traveled because he was hiding from his family, running from his mistakes." My dad was staring down the table, eavesdropping on our conversation. "Is that why you travel, Kasen?"

Halen's eyes narrowed as she adjusted her sleeping baby on her lap.

Beau clenched his jaw.

"Smith, what the fuck?" Uncle Jacks spoke up, coming to his son's rescue. "Don't pull Beau into your shit with Kase."

"You're right. I'm sorry, Beau." My dad rested his head in his hands, like he couldn't believe he'd said those words.

The table was silent. No one knew exactly where to go next.

My dad was harsher than his former bandmates, more emotional when it came to the things that upset him. But outwardly hurting Beau and Halen in order to get to Kase? That was something I'd never seen him do. My fight with my parents was starting to spill over to the rest of my family. And it made me feel terrible.

"Ems, breathe." Kase kissed the side of my head, something he'd been doing more and more often. It was sweet, and it always made me feel a little less like the ground beneath me was about to swallow me whole. "And eat. Take deep breaths and eat your food, but not at the same time. I don't want you to choke." He rubbed my leg. "I don't know how to do the Heimlich on a pregnant chick. I haven't read that book yet."

His words made me feel lighter, and made me laugh.

Which was apparently a major offense to my father.

"You having fun, Emmie? Is this all a good time to you?" My dad tossed his napkin on his plate. "I'm glad you two are enjoying yourselves. Because it's all fun and games until that baby comes, and then what?"

"Dad. Please." Evie leaned forward, intercepting our father's glare with a shocked expression. "Is that really necessary?"

I put my hand to my stomach, the food I'd eaten for dinner sitting heavy and threatening to come back up.

"Yes, Evie, yes it is." He rested his elbow on the table, pointing at Kase and me. "Those two are acting like everything is perfectly fine. But *nothing* is fine. Emmie's ballet career is over. Everything she worked so hard for all these years is gone. She threw it all away for one night with Kasen." He said Kase's name like it was a dirty word. "He's filling her up with all these empty promises. When we all know that he's not going to be around, not when it counts. And then she'll come crying to me and her mother, she'll expect us to—"

"Will you please give it a rest? At least in front of Ems?" Kase slammed his hands on the table, causing all eyes to fly his way. "You can hate me, I don't care. But you're hurting your daughter. You're stressing her out, you're making her lose sleep, lose weight. Can't you see that?

"I don't want to hear another word out of you, little fucker." My dad got to his feet, looking a lot like he did before he hit Kasen the other night.

"Stop it."

I gasped, equal parts terrified and impressed with Cash's tone as he stood, glaring down the table at my dad. "Stop punishing them, stop punishing all of us. You're my uncle, and I love you, but you've been a raging dick since the moment you found out about this baby and I've had enough."

No one spoke to my father that way. No one spoke to any of our parents that way. If we disagreed with something they said or did, we nodded and smiled until their backs were turned and then pocket veto'd that shit.

Beau got up as well, standing beside Cash. "And if Emmie needs anything, the last people she's going to come running to are you guys. You've made damn sure of that." Beau glanced at me, then back to my dad. "You get so pissed that we keep things from you, you plead with us to be honest. But look. Look what that honesty got Emmie. *Emmie.* The sweetest, kindest, most thoughtful person on this whole damn compound." He reached down and helped Halen stand, and the two of them walked away from the table.

"Don't you worry about Em, she has us, and she has Kase." Jett and Devin got up at the same time, a perfect team, always. "It's always been us against the world. Why would this time be any different?"

Cash took Katie by the hand, and then Talon hoisted Marley to her feet. Landry and Brody corralled their boys and they all walked away.

My sister shook her head, disappointment all over her pretty face. "I'm disappointed in you, Dad, because I know you're better than this. I've seen it." Nicky stood, pulling her chair out so she could as well. And then he held his hand out for me, helping me up. Kase put his palm on my lower back, and the four of us left our parents sitting there in the middle of Friday family dinner.

***

"You okay, Ems?" Kase and I were lying in his bed at Katie and Cash's. The rest of my cousins were in the living room, drinking wine and trying to pretend that we hadn't all had an epic fight with our parents. I could hear them, but joining them would take more energy than I possessed at the moment.

I sighed, snuggling down deeper into the blankets that smelled like him. "I'm fine."

And I would be, right? I'd been in the middle of this crap with my parents since I told them about the baby. The only difference tonight brought was that everyone else had been dragged into it as well.

Kase and I were facing each other, his hand resting on my side. He was sexy, don't get me wrong, his every touch sent tingles down my spine. But, at the same time, his hands on me were comforting. He grounded me, and he made it easier to breathe. I wasn't sure when the playboy I'd decided to give my virginity to had become my best friend, but I was glad for it.

We'd decided on co-parents and friends, and I thought we were doing a great job.

"Don't be that girl." He used his hold on my hip to jiggle me. "Tell me how you're actually doing."

I wrinkled my nose. "Do I have to?"

"Yes." He tapped the end of it, refusing to let me out of the truth, the way he'd been doing since I met him.

"I feel guilty for causing drama between my cousins and their parents. I feel sad that my dad is being so mean to everyone. I'm scared because you're leaving soon and I've started to depend on you." I sent him a sad smile to make my next words sting less. "And that was something I told myself I'd never do."

I watched as his face fell and his throat worked to swallow. "You aren't responsible for your father's bad behavior, Ems, that's on him. And although I'm glad that you feel like you can lean on me, you're stronger than anyone gives you credit for, and that includes you." He scooted a little closer, his knees touching mine. "And I'll only be a phone call or a plane ride away."

I nodded.

"As for your cousins? Why don't we let them speak for themselves, huh?" Kase leaned back, calling out toward the doorway. "Hey, you giant group of spawn, get in here." I giggled as Katie's guest room was suddenly taken over by some of my cousins. They filled the space, sitting on the bed, resting against walls and leaning in the doorway. There was barely room for everyone, and this wasn't even all of them.

"Ems here is feeling guilty for causing problems between you guys and the 'rents." Kase sat up, putting his back against the headboard and pulling me to his side. "I figured you guys might want to address that yourselves."

"Of course we would, little fucker." Beau winked, letting me know he was kidding with that nickname. "Em, you have no reason to feel guilty. Uncle Smith was not only a dick to you and Kase, but he decided to bring up shit between Sweets and I that still hurts. He's lashing out, and he doesn't care who's in his path. And that is not okay. *None* of what happened tonight is okay." Halen rested her head against his chest, kissing him softly.

"It's one thing to be shocked, to be sad or disappointed, but the way our parents are acting has moved past that into people I don't even recognize." My sister wrapped her arm around Nicky's waist. "We walked away because we wanted to, because the atmosphere was toxic. That's not on you, not one bit."

"See, Ems?" Kase kissed the top of my head. "No guilt necessary."

"*Are* you two boning?" Brody stood with his arms crossed, his eyes narrowed. "Usually I'm good at this, but I really can't tell."

"I know, right? I can't either." Jett was tapping his finger on his chin, like he was trying to figure out a puzzle. "They're all snuggly and close and he keeps kissing her head, which Turtle tells me is super sweet."

"Em, how would you feel about staying here with me for a few weeks?" Katie ignored her youngest brother-in-law as she perched on the end of the bed. "Cash leaves on Tuesday for training camp, and I could really use the company."

I glanced up at Kase to find him smiling at his sister. "Did you put her up to this?"

His eyes moved to meet mine. "You aren't sleeping at night, Ems, and Landry says you're losing weight again. Your house isn't good for you right now. And Katie is going to be here all alone. It seemed like the perfect solution."

"Because I can't take care of myself? I'm not strong enough to survive my parents' crap? Is that what you think?" My tone was harsh, but I didn't have the energy at the moment to storm out of the room all indignant, so I was stuck resting against Kase's side.

"I'm never having kids." Crue's eyes were wide as he slowly backed away from the bed. "I can't handle these mood swings."

"No one thinks you're weak, Emmie." Landry shook her head, stepping closer and filling the gap Crue left. "But everyone is worried about what this stress is doing to you and the baby."

Kase rested his chin against the top of my head. "I have to work, Ems, and I would feel much better knowing that you two are here." He put his hand back on my stomach. "At least until things blow over with your parents, okay?"

It wasn't like I wanted to go home to be ignored by the two people who were supposed to love me. I liked being here. I liked being with Katie. I didn't want my family to think I couldn't handle my life, but I wasn't stupid. Staying here would be better for me, and I could see that.

"Okay."

"Really?" Kase sounded surprised, which made me smile.

"Really." My gaze darted to Katie where she was standing with Cash, holding his hand. "I'll stay here with Katie until my parents come around."

"And they will, Emmie, they'll come around, I know it." My sister patted my thigh, a hopeful smile plastered on her face.

"Now, everyone out, I need to get these two to sleep." Kase gestured to the door, indicating that my cousins needed to leave the same way they came.

"Putting her to sleep?" Jett's eyes narrowed, his lips pursed. "Is that code for boning?"

"Get out." Kase threw a pillow at him, but he ducked and it whacked Cash in the head.

"Careful, little fucker." Cash closed the door behind him, but not all the way. "Just for that, I want this door open seven inches at all times." He glared at the two of us and backed the rest of the way down the hall.

Chapter Thirty-Six

Kasen

I left Ems this morning, in the nicer, more capable hands of my sister and my brother-in-law. I'd helped her move some of her clothes into their guest room, and spent a couple days helping her get settled. I would lie next to her at night, watching TV or a movie, and then as soon as she fell asleep I'd make my way down the hall to my own room. It's not that I didn't trust myself sleeping next to her or anything. I simply didn't want to blur the lines.

Things were already hard enough, and her cousins kept asking if we were fucking. I needed to keep the snuggles and forehead kisses to the daytime hours since stopping them altogether wasn't going to happen. It was like I couldn't help but touch her. I wanted to make her smile. I wanted to make her feel cared for. I wanted to give her enough strength and support to last her until the next time I saw her. It was hard to leave her, but not nearly as hard as it would have been if she'd been at her parents' house.

I was flying to Italy, but I needed to make a pit stop at my family's ranch. All the crap that went down with Emmie's parents made me realize it was time I tell mine. If that sweet pregnant girl could handle the shit her folks dished out, then I could too.

"Hey, kiddo, we figured you'd fly out of Austin since you were up that way." My dad smiled when I walked into the living room, always so happy to see his kids. "Aren't you supposed to be in Italy already? That's what the family calendar says."

"I pushed my flight back a day." I stopped in front of them, where they were both seated on the living room sofa. I had my first make-out session on that sofa. I was fourteen and my parents were out of town. I'd invited some friends over. Katie had been furious, sure that we were going to get caught. But I'd rounded second base with a girl two years older than me and my parents had never found out. "I wanted to talk to you guys about something before I headed out of town again."

"What's up?" My mom patted the couch, inviting me to come sit.

"I'll stand, but uh, you two should definitely stay seated." I smiled, tight lipped.

"Who did you get pregnant?"

"Mace." My mom backhanded my dad lightly. "Just because our son wants to talk to us doesn't mean he got a girl pregnant. Why does your mind always go to the worst possible scenario? I swear you are—"

"Emmie James."

Both my parents were silent, their jaws hanging open in a way that would be hilarious in any other situation. I'd finally done it. I'd finally shocked them speechless. It'd taken twenty-two years, which was honestly a lot longer than I thought it would. I rocked back on my heels, clapping my hand over my fist, waiting for them to come back to life.

My mom shook her head, like she was clearing the fog my announcement had caused. "Katie's wedding?"

"Yeah." I nodded. "We hung out that weekend and, well, slept together the night of the wedding."

"You had a one-night stand with Emmie James and knocked her up?" My dad hung his head to his chest for a brief moment. "Jesus, Kase." He sighed, then looked back up at me. "Do her parents know?"

"We told them last week." I pointed to my lower jaw and the bruise that had finally faded. "Smith punched me in the face."

My mom gasped. "He hit you?"

"He deserved it." My dad waved away her immediate concern for her child's well-being. "If Cash had gotten Katie pregnant when she was eighteen, I'd have done worse." He shrugged one shoulder casually. "Hell, I still might hit him when the time comes."

I might hit him too. I didn't like the idea of that dude dicking down my sister.

"I saw you two together that weekend. I guess I'd hoped that you knew what you were doing. That you'd remember that Emmie was part of our extended family now, that your actions could blow back on Katie." My mom was using that disappointed tone, her expression sad and defeated. The mom trifecta.

"No one was supposed to get hurt. I was honest, so was she. We were careful."

"Not careful enough." My dad stared pointedly at my crotch, like my dick was the one that had fucked up. "How is she doing with all this? Where did you two leave things? She keeping the baby? Are you together? Are—"

"Whoa, slow down." I held my hands out, placating style. "Ems is doing okay, all things considered. She does want to keep the baby. She gave me a few weeks to figure out what I wanted to do, and I decided that I want to be in the kid's life, that I want to be its dad."

My mom's eyes went wide. "Was not being its dad an option? Were you thinking of bowing out?"

"I was shocked when she told me. And I never wanted to be a father. I never wanted that life. Or at least, I'd never given it much thought, I guess." I licked my lips, thinking about the tiny swell of Emmie's belly. "But. It's happening."

"You travel so much. How are you supposed to be there for this baby?" My dad threw that wrenched-up question out there, triggering automatic annoyance because it reminded me of Smith James.

"I'll figure it out."

"Kids need consistency, Kase. There was a reason I didn't go on the road for years." He dipped his chin in my direction.

I nodded, not wanting to start an argument with my dad before I had to fly to another country. "Kids also need loving parents, and this kid will have two."

My mom volleyed back, "What about Emmie?"

"What about her?"

This back-and-forth must be like watching a ping-pong match for my parents. "Are you two together?"

"No. We're friends, we'll co-parent. That's it."

"And what happens when she meets someone?" She crossed her arms over her chest. "When you do?"

"We both know it'll be her meeting someone to settle down with and not the other way around." I grinned. "I'll be happy for her. She deserves a good guy."

"A good guy who will be around all the time, when you won't be." She raised an eyebrow, refusing to back down. That was my mother, kind but deadly. "A good guy who'll be helping raise your child."

"Well, it takes a village, right?"

She shook her head. "I think you're being entirely too blasé about this."

"And I think you're heaping on unnecessary stress where it's not currently needed."

"Kase." My dad finally spoke up. "We want to make sure you've thought this through, from all angles."

"I have. And now I have a flight to catch." I leaned down, hugging and kissing them both good-bye before walking out of the house as quickly as possible.

Once I was safely in my car and on the road, I let out a big deep breath. Well, we'd all survived and no one had gotten punched in the face.

I'd take that as a motherfucking win.

Chapter Thirty-Seven

Emmie

I re-read our last text conversation again, making sure I hadn't missed something.

Kasen: Nineteen weeks.

Emmie: At my twenty-week appointment they'll be able to tell if it's a boy or a girl.

Kasen: Isn't there some kind of test you can do to find out sooner?

Emmie: Yeah. But things were so chaotic then. I wasn't ready to know anything past the fact that it was in there, and I was keeping it.

Kasen: You aren't going alone are you? You taking one of your million cousin/siblings, right?

Emmie: Nope. Only me.

Kasen: Why?

Emmie: I don't know. It feels like a cool moment, and I didn't want to share it with any of them.

Kasen: What about me? Would you be okay sharing it with me?

Emmie: You're in Italy.

Kasen: You could video call me.

Emmie: It'll be late your time.

Kasen: I think I can stay up past 11 Ems.

Emmie: Okay, sure.

But I'd tried calling Kase four times from the waiting room, and then once again after the sonogram tech brought me back. Now I was on the table, my pants pushed down and my shirt pushed up, belly full of cold gel and no baby daddy. I didn't want to be disappointed that he hadn't answered, but I was. And this sort of thing was exactly what I'd been worried about from the beginning. I'd been fine with being alone when I found out the baby's gender.

But then Kase had wanted to be part of it and I'd gotten my hopes up, excited to share this moment with him. He let me down, and I hated this feeling.

"You ready?"

"Yeah." I couldn't very well ask her to wait while I tried to call him again. She'd already watched my last attempt go unanswered. I had pride, and she had other patients to see. "I guess something came up. Let's get started."

The door opened, flooding the dimly lit room with the light from the hallway. "Wait." Kase stumbled in, knocking into a plastic display of a pregnant woman, making the fetus fall out of the uterus. "Sorry, I'm late. This place is a fucking maze." He bent down and picked up the baby, holding it by the head and using it to gesture as he talked. "I ended up walking into the wrong office and I didn't realize it until they asked if I was there to give them my sperm sample and—"

"You're here." I was smiling, too big, but I couldn't seem to help it. Kase was here. He'd showed up for the baby.

"I'm here." He grinned, leaning down and placing a quick kiss on my cheek, and I swear the baby did a somersault. "You were right, it felt like a cool moment. I didn't want to miss it."

I almost didn't know what to do with the fact that he'd flown in from Italy to be here for this appointment. It was a big move, a big gesture. My dad was wrong. Kase wouldn't bail on us. And if Smith James ever decided to speak to me again, I'd be sure to tell him.

"Is this Dad?"

I wiped at a tear, refusing to let it fall. "Yeah, this is Dad."

Kase came and sat in the chair next to the exam table I was on, his eyes on the TV mounted on the ceiling, his hand reaching for mine.

"Okay, let's see your baby."

She placed the wand on my belly and the sound of the baby's heartbeat filled the room.

Kase whispered, "Wow." And then he squeezed my hand in his.

"I know."

"It looks like a real baby." He glanced at me, then back to the screen like he was afraid to miss anything. "In the ultrasound pics I've seen, it looked more like a chicken nugget."

I smiled, remembering the few times he'd referred to the baby as a little nugget.

"Mom? Dad? You want to know the sex?"

Kase looked to me, his eyebrows raised in question. I nodded, knowing that he'd come all the way for this moment right here. To be with me when we found out if we were having a boy or a girl. "Yeah, yes, we want to know."

She moved the wand a few inches to the left, pressing in harder. "And it's a…. It's a girl."

"Holy shit." Kase rested his forehead against our hands, chuckling quietly.

The tech started pressing a series of buttons, taking measurements of our daughter. I was crying, and I wasn't even sure why. Kase was laughing. His head had moved to my shoulder.

"You know, my uncles say that fuck-boys always have daughters. It's karmic balance." I put my hand on his hair, ruffling it playfully. "So, thanks for my little girl."

He pulled back, his eyes still dancing with humor and un-shed tears. "If fuck-boys need daughters for karmic balance, then I'm afraid we're going to end up with a whole softball team full of them."

I gasped, my lips parting.

His eyes got rounder, my reaction to his words alerting him to what he'd actually said. "Oh, um, yeah, I'm sorry. I don't even know…I'm sorry, Ems, I didn't mean it like that. It, uh, it was a joke."

I nodded, my heart pounding in my chest like the silly foolish girl I was when it came to Kasen Cadence. It was a joke. He didn't mean *us*. He meant whatever gorgeous carefree woman he settled down with, not the chick he accidentally knocked up after a wedding.

He didn't mean me.

I smiled, laughing lightly and trying like hell to play it off as nothing.

"We're having a girl, Ems." He helped me sit up when the sonogram tech left the room, a stack of small black-and-white pictures on the counter for us. "That was…that was a moment I don't think I'll ever forget. Thanks for letting me be here."

"Thank you, for flying all this way for a thirty-minute appointment." I hopped off the table, letting him help me down. "I'm glad I got to share it with you." I wanted to take a picture. I wanted to capture this moment. I wanted to run to my parents and show them that Kase had shown up for his kid.

I wanted the whole world to see that he was keeping his word and shocking us all.

"I have to get back to the airport, I shoot tomorrow." He dropped down to his knees, glancing at me pointedly before putting his hands on my small bump. I closed my eyes, like I knew he wanted me too. "All right, little girl, I've got to go to work, but I'll see you soon." I bit my lips together to keep my smile in check when I felt him lift my shirt and place a soft kiss on my belly. "Be good for your mom, okay?"

Once he got back to his feet, I opened my eyes but avoided his gaze. I didn't want him to see the emotion swimming in mine, the sweet tears that were threatening to fall.

Kase was proving to be a better man than I ever thought possible. And that?

That was something I wasn't sure I could survive.

Chapter Thirty-Eight

Kasen

Flying to see Ems for the sonogram appointment had been a last-second decision. I woke up that morning, set alarms on my phone so I wouldn't get distracted and miss it when she called that night. The time difference between Italy and Texas was pretty intense. But then I hadn't been able to stop thinking about it. And the more I tried to go about my day, the more distracted I'd become.

It was all I could think about, how much I wanted to be part of that cool moment. I mean, finding out if we were having a boy or a girl? That was huge. I didn't want to miss it. So I'd chartered a private plane and got my happy sappy ass back to Texas.

That was a week ago, and the sonogram picture was taped to the mirror in my bathroom. The Italy trip got extended. A company hired me to get content of a big festival. I loved to travel, I loved to see the world and experience everything I possibly could. But even I had my threshold, and I was starting to miss home.

And Ems. I was missing Ems. Not in a I-want-to-date-her kind of way, but in a she'd-become-my-best-friend kind of way.

I pulled out my cell, texting her to check in.

Kasen: Twenty-one weeks.

Emmie: She's kicking like crazy now. I'm the only one that can feel it, but she moves in there like a racoon on crack.

Kasen: A racoon on crack?

Emmie: She's nocturnal.

Kasen: Are you still not sleeping well?

Katie promised me that Ems was doing great. She said she was sleeping and eating more than sugar.

Emmie: I fall asleep fine, but then she starts scurrying around once the clock strikes two.

Kasen: Maybe she's a late night party animal like her dad.

Emmie: Does it freak you out to call yourself her dad? I still feel weird when I call myself her mom, even if it's just in my head.

I had to laugh, because it did still freak me out to call myself her dad. It was surreal. And I wasn't sure what was more unreal: the fact that I was having a kid or the fact I wanted her to be like me. Even if it was something as silly as her sleeping habits.

Kasen: I think it's easier to call myself her dad when I'm talking to you. I don't tell strangers I have a daughter on the way. I don't tell people I'm going to be a dad soon.

Emmie: We're going to be parents.

Kasen: Holy shit.

Emmie: Right?

Kasen: At least we're both freaked.

Emmie: Co-parents, friends, and freaking out.

Kasen: We should make shirts.

Emmie: We should.

I glanced at the clock, doing the math easily in my head. At this point, I was used to calculating our time difference.

Kasen: Have a good day, Ems.

Emmie: Have a good evening Kase.

Texts while I was in Italy

Emmie: Marley and Talon had their baby.

Kasen: Oh cool! They were having a boy right?

Emmie: Yeah, Caspian Owen, they want to call him Co for short.

Kasen: Why Co? Because Caspian is a fucking mouthful for a toddler?

Emmie: Idk, they have some weird thing with Kurt Cobain, but didn't want to name their kid after someone who overdosed more than once.

Kasen: Makes sense. How's she doing? Did you get to go see her?

Emmie: Yes. Yes I did. And it was a terrible mistake.

Kasen: What? Why?

Emmie: I asked her what delivery was like, what everything was like. I told her to not hold back, I told her I could take it.

Kasen: Ems. Why? She'd shot a kid out of her vag and you wanted her to be honest?

Emmie: She said her "vag" felt swollen and bruised and engorged. And then she showed me her nipples, Kase.

Kasen: I don't want to know.

Emmie: Too bad. They looked like hamburger meat. They were cracked and bloody. There was BLOOD, KASEN.

Kasen: You know, they say every experience is different for every person.

Emmie: I'm going to hate you so bad if our daughter makes my nipples bleed.

Kasen: Can I preemptively tell you how sorry I am?

Emmie: No.

Kasen: Did she say anything else? Anything remotely uplifting?

Emmie: She said, "It's the worst and the best at the same time. I know that doesn't make sense. But it's the most terrifying, painful, exciting experience of my entire life. And I'd do it all over again in a heartbeat if it meant I'd get him afterward."

Kasen: Aw, see there Ems? It's not all bad.

Emmie: Fuck off.
Kasen: Fair enough.

Kasen: You know, Marley and Tal having their baby reminded me. We need to pick out a name.

Emmie: You have any in mind?

Kasen: Mercedes.

Emmie: No.

Kasen: Cayenne.

Emmie: No.

Kasen: Mandy.

Emmie: Did you pick up a book of stripper names for baby girls?

Kasen: Those aren't...well shit. I think I did know a stripper named Mercedes.

Emmie: I have no doubt.

Kasen: Okay, first names on the back burner, what's her last name going to be? Cadence? James? James-Cadence? We could hyphenate.

Emmie: If we're going to hyphenate, then why not Cadence-James?

Kasen: Because your dad hates me and treats our daughter like a disease?

Emmie: Point taken.

Kasen: Never mind, names are stressful.

Emmie: We'll figure it out.

Kasen: We always do.

Kasen: What are you doing?

Emmie: Watching a movie with Katie and Benson.

Kasen: Why is Benson there?

Emmie: He comes by every once in a while, checking on us since Cash is gone.

Kasen: There are like four other dudes that live within walking distance of Katie's house that can check on you two.

Emmie: Oh you're right, I'll tell him to stop coming over to his best friend's house to make sure his new wife doesn't need anything.

Kasen: You feeling feisty tonight, Ems?

Emmie: Apparently.

Kasen: How's our girl?

Emmie: Growing. She's also developed an addiction to whipped cream in a can.

Kasen: No whippets.

Emmie: What's a whippet?

Kasen: You really are a good girl, aren't you?

Emmie: I was. Until I gave my virginity to a model I met at a wedding.

Kasen: When I first saw you, I immediately wanted to corrupt you.

Emmie: Well, you got your wish little fucker.

Kasen: Funny. Have you talked to your parents?

Emmie: Nope. They don't seem to want anything to do with me.

Kasen: They'll get over it Ems, I promise.

Emmie: Have a good day.

Kasen: Sweet dreams.

Chapter Thirty-Nine

Kase

I was home.

I plopped on my bed at my parents' house, breathing in the scent of fresh laundry and my dad grilling out on the patio as I pulled my phone out of my pocket.

Kasen: Twenty-two weeks.

Emmie: How does it feel to be back in the States?

Kasen: Other countries give Texas a bad hick Republican rap, but it's always nice to be home. How's the nugget?

I knew it looked like a real human baby now, and not a chicken nugget. But I was afraid the nickname was going to stick.

Emmie: It's official. I popped. Nothing fits except for yoga pants.

Kasen: Let me see that belly.

I smiled when my phone rang in my hand. Emmie and I didn't Face-time call, ever. The one time she'd suggested it, I'd gotten on a plane and flew to see the ultrasound in person. But I was excited to see her, to see the evidence of our daughter growing inside her.

I clicked accept and laughed when Emmie pulled her shirt up and turned to the side. "Here she is." She rubbed her hands on her belly. Her phone seemed to be propped up in the kitchen at my sister's house.

"She *is* growing." Emmie was beautiful, and even pregnant she looked like a fairytale princess. "You make one hot pregnant chick, Ems." That was part of a co-parent's job right? Making sure that Ems knew she was still sexy, even carrying my kid.

"Thanks." She came closer to the phone, her shirt still tucked over the top of her rounded stomach.

"Can anyone else feel her move yet?"

She picked her phone up and carried me into the living room. "Katie's felt her a few times, but no one else has asked."

I was glad Katie got to be there for those moments, and more than that, I couldn't possibly be jealous of my big sister getting to feel her niece move in her mother's stomach. But I wanted to feel her move too, and I felt like a bit of a sap for it. But the more I read in those baby books Emmie didn't have time for, the more I realized how freaking amazing it all was.

"Hey, how would you feel about coming to the ranch this weekend? My parents haven't seen you since I told them about the baby. And I want to see my unborn kid because I'm becoming increasingly obsessed with her."

"Yeah, I guess I could drive down for a few days."

I shook my head. "Drive? No way." The highway that stretched between Austin and my family's ranch in south Texas wasn't the safest stretch of pavement. "I'll send a plane. I don't want you two on the road by yourself for four hours."

"I have my own plane." She rolled her eyes as she plopped down on the couch, kicking her feet up on the armrest.

"Yours or mine, either way, no driving. Okay?"

"Okay." She grinned, tilting the phone down so I could see her stomach again. "Kid? Good luck, your dad is proving to be a bit overprotective."

Chapter Forty

Emmie

In the end I took Kase's plane because I didn't want to have to communicate with my parents about taking ours. The flight was quick and he'd been there to pick me up from the small private airport. When he saw me, his hands went to my stomach and his lips went to the top of my head. My heart was pounding and I couldn't stop smiling. It'd been a couple weeks since we'd been together. And I'd missed him. And I hated that I'd missed him.

We were friends, and we were making this work. But every time he touched me, every time he was sweet to me... It was dangerous. And hazardous to my health.

I could not fall for the father of my child. I couldn't.

"You ready?"

I smiled, letting him help me out of the car. "Do they hate me like my parents do?"

Kase wrapped his arms around my neck, letting me rest my forehead against his chest. "Your parents do not hate you, Ems." He put his hands on my shoulders and pushed me back so we could look at each other. Damn he was handsome. "And my parents are going to *love you*. I promise, you have nothing to worry about with them, okay?"

I nodded, letting him take my hand and lead me into the home he'd grown up in. I was a ball of nerves, despite his motivating speech. This tiny baby girl was already down one set of grandparents. I'd hate for Kase's parents to be angry with us too.

"Hey, guys, we're back." Kase dropped my bag by the front door, helping me down the step that separated the entryway to the living room. He treated me like every step I took might be the one that took me out. I was a freaking ballerina. I could walk a tight rope, pregnant belly or not.

"Emmie, sweetheart, it's so good to see you again." Kase's mom, Payton, came into the living room wiping her hands on a checkered dishtowel before pulling me in for a warm hug. There was nothing like a mom's hug, and I hadn't had one in a really long time. "Let me look at that baby."

I tried to hide my tears as she took my hands.

"Ems? Are you crying?" Kase rested his palm on my back, concern in his gaze.

I shook my head, smiling. "I'm fine. I'm fine." I waved away his concern, choking back my emotions. "It's…it's really great to be here."

I hadn't realized until that moment how much I missed my mom, how much I missed my parents. Payton Cadence was welcoming and kind, excited to see me, excited to see her granddaughter growing in my stomach. And it made all the hurt I'd been feeling bubble to the surface.

"Kase, why don't you go down to the stables and get your dad for me?" His mom wrapped her arm around my shoulders, steering me onto the large leather sectional. "He'd want to know that you guys are back."

Kase glanced at me, his eyes narrowed. "You sure? You sure you're okay?"

I nodded, teeth clenched and smile firmly in place.

"Stop hovering." His mom shooed him away.

"I'll be *right* back."

"He's very attuned to you, that son of mine." Mrs. Cadence sat down next to me, mischief in her eyes. I didn't say anything because I wasn't sure what she wanted to hear. Kase wasn't in love with me. He was in love with his daughter. "Are you really okay, Emmie?"

I wanted to lay my head in her lap. I wanted to be taken care of. I wanted my mom. "It's been hard with my parents."

"Kase told us that they weren't taking the news well." Her kind smile turned sad, like she was hurting for me. "I'm sorry to hear that, sweetheart." She reached out, putting her hand on mine where it rested on my bump. "Mace and I are always here if you need us."

"Emmie, sweetheart, I'm so glad you could come see us." Kase's dad came into the house through a back door wearing worn jeans and a thin t-shirt. He was handsome, like his son. And his smile was warm, like his wife's.

I stood, holding out my hand to shake his, but instead he used it to pull me in for a warm hug. Kase's parents were the complete opposite of mine, that was for sure.

Chapter Forty-One

Emmie

"Emmie, sweetheart, you okay?"

We were all in the Cadences' living room watching a movie. I'd been fighting to keep my eyes open for the last twenty minutes.

"Yeah, sorry, I guess it's been a longer day than I'm used to." I held my hand over my mouth, doing my best to stifle another huge yawn. "I feel like I'm borderline narcoleptic after eight o'clock."

"Oh I remember those days." Kase's mom chuckled as she leaned forward and rubbed her hand on my thigh. "Don't feel like you need to stay up for us though. We have all day tomorrow to hang out."

I enjoyed Kasen's parents, both of them. They were kind and sweet. They didn't treat me or Kase like we were a disappointment to them both, which was a real nice change of pace from life back at the compound.

"Come on, Ems." Kase took my hand, pulling me to my feet. "Let's get that baby in bed."

"I fixed up the guest room at the end of the hall." His mom blew us kisses. "Good night, loves."

We both blew a kiss back and I let Kase guide me down the long hallway, pausing in front of a door. "Your bathroom stuff is in there, get ready for bed and then I'll tuck my girl in."

He closed the door behind me, and I tried real hard to tamp down the smile on my face when I saw it in the mirror. His kindness, his words, they were all directed at our baby. But I couldn't help but swoon a little. Kase wasn't anything like the guy I'd thought he was. I assumed he wouldn't want anything to do with me, or with the baby. I thought a child would harsh his player vibe, I thought he'd choose his lifestyle over having a daughter. I'd been wrong. Kase was in love with our baby, and he was a good man. He cared.

And he was making it so damn hard for me not to fall for him.

Pregnancy hormones. I'd blame it on my pregnancy hormones. Of course I'd think a hot dude being nice to me and my unborn child would be the perfect mixture of sexy and sweet. Right? Right. And being here with his parents, who were everything I'd been craving, everything I'd been missing from my own family? That was all adding to the problem.

I brushed my teeth and washed my face, taking deep breaths and willing my heart to stop its dumb fluttering act. I wasn't falling in love. I was falling into my third trimester.

When I opened the bathroom door, fully prepared to tuck my own damn self into bed, my mouth went dry at the sight of Kase walking toward me, using a towel to dry his hair. Shirtless. He was shirtless and there were droplets of water trailing between his pecs and down to his belly button. And worse? He was smirking at me. He needed to stop smirking at me right the hell now.

"You've got to be the cutest pregnant chick of all time, you know that?"

Jesus H. Christ.

"I doubt that's true." I waved away his compliment as I stepped past him, peeking into two empty rooms before I found the one with my suitcase in it. "You're being nice because your kid is probably about to wreck my body."

Marley's terrible description of post labor was never far from my mind.

I picked up my bag, about to swing it around to land on the bed so I could change into my pajamas. But, Kase came and took it out of my hand, placing it on the mattress and shooting me a stern look. "Don't lift heavy shit while I'm here to help you."

"Heavy shit? Kase, it's a weekend bag, not a suitcase full of bricks." I rolled my eyes, laughing lightly when really, in my mind, I was fainting onto a pretty pink velvet couch from his sweetness and attention.

"Doesn't matter." He unzipped the suitcase and tossed the lid back before jumping onto the bed and lying on his side. "I don't get to be there for you often, so while I am, let me help, okay?"

I nodded, keeping my lips firmly shut so I didn't whimper and beg him to kiss me. I pulled out a stretchy tank top and some soft maternity pants I'd gotten from Halen. I refused to go buy maternity clothes when three people who lived within walking distance of my house had closets full.

"Um, I'm going to change." I shifted on my feet, glancing at the door he'd shut behind us.

"I've seen you naked, Ems." Kase wagged his eyebrows. "Change."

I took a deep breath, not liking the way his words made my core clench. Pregnancy hormones. Yep. I wasn't in my right mind. Not my fault. It was the baby's fault.

"You haven't seen me naked and knocked up though." I rubbed my belly. "Not the same experience, I can assure you." I expected him to make some joke, or to tell me I was crazy, or to close his eyes with a smile so I could change in peace.

I knew he'd never actually get up and leave the room.

But what I didn't expect was for him to sit up and reach for my hands, and to drag me closer to the bed, to pull my shirt up and off my body, and to push my jeans down to my ankles. He sat back when I was standing in front of him in my bra and panties, a smile on his face.

"You're right, it's not the same experience." He leaned down and placed a soft kiss on my stomach. "It's better." Then his gaze met mine and I hoped like hell he didn't see the brimming tears. "You're gorgeous, Ems."

I took another deep breath, turning my back on him as quickly as I could. I tugged on my shirt and put on my pants, then wiped at my eyes to make sure that all traces of the tears that had almost spilled over were gone.

When I finally felt strong enough to face him, he was lying back on the bed again, cool and casual. Like he hadn't rocked my whole world with nothing but a soft sweet kiss to our daughter.

"Your parents are great."

He wrinkled his nose. "Yeah, they're okay." He closed my suitcase and moved it down to the floor, making room for me on the bed.

"They're handling all this so much better than mine. They're being so kind to me."

Kase lifted the covers and then patted the mattress. "Come on, I'll tuck you in and tell you a bedtime story."

I climbed into bed beside my friend and co-parent and was instantly surrounded by his spicy scent. Dammit. Why did he have to smell good too? I needed to find his cologne and pour it down the drain.

"Did you know that me and Katie have different parents?"

I gave myself a mental headshake, remembering that I was lying next to him for a reason. He'd tell me a story and then he'd leave. I needed to keep my chill for like ten more minutes. I could do that. Anyone could do anything for ten minutes, right?

"Uh, I vaguely remember hearing my dad and Uncle Luke talking about it one day."

"Katie's bio parents died the night she was born. Her mom lived long enough for them to get Katie out, but that was it." He folded the pillow behind his head. "My dad was this young rocker, traveling the world and hooking up with a new girl at every stop."

I snorted. "Like father like son."

"Funny." He sent me a toothless smile and then continued, "He lost his parents and gained a little sister all at the same time. He said it was such an odd and inexplicable feeling, happiness that Katie had survived, and overwhelming sadness that his dad and stepmom were gone." He rested his palm on my stomach, like it was the most natural thing in the world for him to do. "He had no clue what he was doing. He'd never even held a baby before. And Katie was so tiny, a preemie. My mom was a nurse in the NICU. She moved in here to help my dad once he brought Katie home."

"And they lived happily ever after?" I tucked my hands under my chin, liking that we were getting to the sweet ending where two people fell in love.

"Nope." Kasen wrinkled his nose. "My dad kind of lost his shit at one point. He said he went back on tour, but the reality was, he ran away. He left my mom here to raise Katie on her own for a few months."

He up and left the girl who had been kind enough to help him? That was shitty, and it made me admire Kase's mother even more. "Your mom sounds like a pretty spectacular person."

"She is." His palm started to rub big circles on my bump. "Anyway, my dad came home and groveled at my mom's feet and begged her forgiveness. It all worked out in the end." His hand stopped and he used it to run his fingers through his hair. I had to bite my lips together to keep from begging him to put it back on me. "My parents are great, but I think that's because they know a little bit about what we're going through: the uncertainty, the fear, and the excitement. They understand that it's not all black and white, and that people can thrive in the shades of gray."

I turned on my side, my belly resting between us, one of the words he used standing out from the others. "*Are* you excited?"

"Yeah, I think I am." He rested his cheek on his pillow, his face level with mine. "I'm a lot of things, but excited is definitely one of them. What about you?"

"Excited, nervous, and terrified." My hand went to my stomach, pushing at our daughter's tiny butt when she tried to float it under my ribs. "I run the full range about thirty times a day."

"You're doing great, Ems." His hand reached out and grabbed my shoulder, massaging the knots that had been growing ever since we told my dad about the baby.

"That feels so good, my neck and my are back killing me. My body is used to constant stretching and exercise, and all it's been getting lately is—"

"Stress?"

I nodded. "Stress, two a.m. wake-up calls, and hours of watching lectures on my laptop." I'd doubled down on school, adding more classes to my course load now that I wasn't in rehearsal most of the day. I wanted to get as much accomplished as possible before the baby came.

Kase wanted to be in our daughter's life, and I knew he'd try his best. But I wasn't delusional. I knew what his career was like, how much traveling he did. I knew the majority of parenting would fall to me. Which meant it'd be a couple years before I could focus this much time and energy into getting my degree again.

"Like I said, I'm here now, let me help." He made a roll-over motion with his finger, waiting until I got comfortable on my other side. "Close your eyes, I'll rub you until you fall asleep."

I snorted, pulling an extra pillow from behind me and wedging it between my legs. "Isn't that what got us into this mess?"

"You got jokes tonight?" He tickled my ribs, making me laugh. "I promise not to get you double pregnant from this massage."

As Kase rubbed at the knots in my shoulders and my neck, his words kept repeating in my head. *Double pregnant.* If anyone had the power to get someone double pregnant, it was Kasen Cadence.

The fuck-boy who'd done a one-eighty when he'd decided to be a dad.

Chapter Forty-Two

Kasen

I opened my eyes, blinking into the darkness. I was in my room, but I wasn't alone. *Ems*. I glanced to my right, everything from tonight coming back to me. I'd dropped her bag in my room after she'd gotten to the ranch. I hadn't been sure which guest room my mom wanted her in. Then after she changed in here, I'd decided she could have my bed and I'd bunk in a guest room. But then I'd fallen asleep giving her a massage.

And she was lucky that was all I'd tried to give her. Holy hell. When I told her to get changed, it had really started as me simply wanting her to know that she was beautiful. But then her perfect little bump had been right there and I'd started to get a bit choked up. So I'd kissed her stomach. When her eyes welled with tears, I'd wanted to pull her into my lap. I'd wanted to wipe those tears away and kiss her lips. I'd wanted to move those tiny lace panties to the side and taste her again.

But. That wasn't part of being friends. Or co-parents for that matter. I'd already fucked her life up enough. I didn't need to add my dick roaring back into the mix again and making anything worse.

"Kase?" Emmie's voice was sleepy, soft. "What time is it?"

I held my wrist in front of my face, squinting. "It's almost two."

She groaned, rolling onto her back and sitting up a bit. "Well, that makes perfect sense." Her hands went to her belly, rubbing soothing circles as she let out a tired sigh. "It's her witching hour."

"She's moving?"

"Like a racoon on crack." She turned to me, wincing. "You should go back to your room so you can sleep."

I grinned. "This is my room."

Her eyes got wide. "Oh, I'm sorry." She looked around, trying to see her surroundings in the dark. But it would be no use. I had blackout curtains. The only reason I could see her was from the light on my watch. She threw the covers off, pushing herself up. "Which room is mine? I'll go there and sleep."

"Don't go." My words came out fast, louder than I'd meant. "I, uh, can I…" I pointed at her stomach. "Can I feel her?"

She was silent for a few seconds, still as a statue. I was almost afraid that she was going to tell me no and leave. If she did, I'd get on my knees and beg her to stay, which would have been embarrassing as fuck, but I wasn't above it. I'd never felt my daughter move before. I wanted to more than I'd wanted anything in a long time.

Luckily, Ems lay back down and pulled her tank top up, exposing her belly. "Yeah, of course you can."

I placed my palm on her stomach, which was harder than it'd been earlier when I was telling her about my parents. She took my hand and moved it lower and to the side. In a matter of seconds, I felt it. It was more alien-like than I'd thought it would be. But I sort of loved it. And I couldn't stop smiling. "That's so weird."

Emmie snorted. "You're telling me." She took my hand and switched it to the other side. "She has a lot of room in there right now, she does laps from one side to the other."

I sat up, putting both my palms on the bottom section of her rounded bump, enamored with the fact that my kid was alive in there. Growing and thriving, and from what it felt like, she was having a hell of a lot of fun.

"Thank you." I whispered the words softly, not wanting to disturb the silence between us in case Emmie had fallen back asleep.

"What for?" She was whispering too, matching my tone.

I dipped down and placed another kiss on her stomach, moving slowly this time, letting my lips linger on my daughter. "For giving me a choice, and a chance."

Her hand went to my hair, her fingers running through it twice before stopping. She didn't say anything, but the silence between us wasn't uncomfortable. I kept my hands on her, laughing as our daughter moved back and forth, kicking and elbowing my hands.

"See what I mean? Racoon on crack." Emmie sighed. "She'll do this for at least an hour, keeping me up all night."

"Hm." I felt around at the end of my bed, snagging my dad's old acoustic guitar and strumming a few notes. "Maybe some music will get her back to sleep."

"You want to sing our unborn baby back to sleep?"

I winced, even though it was dark and she most likely couldn't see me. "You think it's stupid?"

"Stupid hot." She gasped, her hand flying her mouth like she was trying to stuff the words back in.

I chuckled. "Did you call me stupid hot?"

"No."

I knew I was grinning from ear to ear, but like I said it was too dark for her to see it so it was okay. "Well, you ain't seen nothing yet, Ems." I balanced the guitar in my lap, reaching out to rub the bump one more time. "Okay, kid, your mom is so exhausted her brain-to-mouth filter is on the fritz, so how 'bout we let her get some sleep?"

I strummed a few notes, humming softly. I never played or sang in front of anyone besides my parents. I wasn't a musician, and I didn't want to be. But my father insisted we each try our hand at a musical instrument. Katie was hopeless, but I ended up being not half bad on a guitar.

I started cataloguing songs in my head, trying to find the perfect one for my restless daughter. I couldn't help but smile when the perfect lyrics came to mind from an old Bob Dylan tune and then I started to sing about growing up and staying forever young.

Ems whispered, "It's totally working. Tiny traitor, I've tried singing to her. I've even tried freaking rocking her back to sleep in there. Nothing worked." Emmie adjusted the pillow behind her head and closed her eyes. "If I fall back asleep, wake me up and I'll go get in the other bed."

Like hell I was going to wake up my sleeping baby momma and make her walk down the hall to a cold, empty bed. But she didn't need to know that. She'd figure it out in the morning when she woke up and we were still here, side by side. Which was totally acceptable since we were co-parenting.

Chapter Forty-Three

Kasen

Ems and I did wake up together. My mom had come to tell me breakfast was ready. I opened my eyes to her smiling at us like a maniacal person. I shook my head, slowly, trying to silently convey that this wasn't what it looked like. I hadn't touched Ems, other than the kisses to her belly and the massage. We were still friends, still co-parents. Nothing more.

After breakfast, we spent the day exploring the ranch with my parents. We took a long walk, showing Ems the stables and the woods I'd played in as a child. We had lunch and Ems took a nap on the couch, her head resting in my mom's lap while she slept. I'd grabbed my camera from my bag, snapping a few pictures of how peaceful and happy Emmie looked, how sweet the moment was.

Now the sun was setting, and my dad was preparing to grill us some burgers out on the back patio. Ems was on the floor, doing prenatal yoga with my mom. It was hot as hell, and I was plenty content to sit my ass on the couch and watch. Ems. Not my mom.

"Hey, kid, why don't you come outside and help me get the grill started?"

"Uh, because it's a gas grill and all you do is turn the knob?" And I wasn't about to miss Ems's perfect long legs in the air.

"Okay, how 'bout get your ass outside so I can talk to you for a bit? Now."

I tore my eyes away from the mother of my child, glaring at my father. "Sure, Dad."

Reluctantly, I followed him out back, starting the grill with the flick of a switch. Maybe if I could get this little chat over with, I could make it back inside to see the end of that yoga session. I couldn't fuck her, but that didn't mean I couldn't *visually* enjoy her stellar body. Ems. Not my mom.

"Did you and Emmie stay together last night?" My dad held his hand over the grill, checking the temperature.

That's what the talk was about? My mom had narc'd on the fact that I'd been in bed with Ems this morning? This could have definitely waited until yoga was over. "We slept in the same bed if that's what you're asking."

He used the spatula to place the patties on the grill, closing the lid. "I thought you two were friends and co-parents, not bed buddies."

"Bed buddies? Are you asking me if I'm having sex with the mother of my child?"

He turned to me, his hands on his hips. "Are you?"

"Not since the night I put that kid in there." I grinned, blinking at him innocently.

"I know that when babies get involved, emotions run high." He chose to ignore my inappropriate humor, something he'd been doing for most of my life. "Emmie is a beautiful girl and…"

"Right?" He wasn't wrong, and there was no use denying it. He'd only call me out on it, prolonging this father/son talk. "And it's like being pregnant has made her even hotter. I didn't even know that was possible."

"Well of course you'd think so, that's your baby she's carrying. There's something acutely visceral about it. But because your hormones are running high doesn't mean—"

"My hormones?" I cut him off, wincing when I realized I'd picked up a bad habit from all those Devil's Spawn fuckers. "I don't think that's how that works, old man."

"Okay fine, your *libido* and her hormones." He lifted the lid, flipping the burgers. "Pregnant chicks can get, well, sometimes their hormones can make them want, um, companionship?"

Companionship? For crying out loud. This was getting embarrassing for him. "Are you talking about sex again? If you're talking about sex, why don't you come right out and say it?"

"Emmie is an eighteen-year-old ballerina who's carrying my granddaughter. It seems inappropriate to put it so bluntly." He closed the lid again, waving away my question with the spatula in his hand.

"She's not a virgin." I licked my lips, fucking with him for the hell of it. "And to be honest, even when she was that girl, she had a bit of kink hiding behind that proper bun of hers."

"I can't believe you're going to be a father."

I nodded. "I know, right?"

"Anyway." He sighed, rubbing his temples like I was giving him a headache. "If Emmie asks for more, I hope you'll keep a level head because she may not be thinking clearly. This situation between you two is already complicated enough without throwing sex into the mix."

"So you're saying that the pregnancy hormones are going to make Ems want my dick? And you want to make sure that I plan on keeping it in my pants?" Would I be able to keep it in my pants if Ems jumped me? I snorted out a laugh at the notion. Ems was not going to demand I fuck her. Both of us were in this for the long haul, and we both understood what it would take for our unconventional little family to work.

"I feel like you're being difficult on purpose," he grumbled.

"I am." I clapped a hand on his back. "Dad, you don't have anything to worry about, okay? I care about Ems, and I care about our baby. I'm not stupid. I know that blurring the lines we've established would be a terrible decision. I promise I'm going to go out of my way not to mess this up."

And that was the truth.

"That helps." He smiled, looking incredibly relieved. "I'm glad we had this talk."

"And it's not like pregnancy hormones are going to turn her into a sex addict or anything. I mean, come on."

He opened the lid one more time, removing the hamburger patties and placing them on the clean plate he'd brought out with him. "You'd be surprised, kid. When your mom was pregnant with you, I could barely keep up."

I put my fingers in my ears, not caring how immature I was being. "Ew. Dad. Stop. No. No sir. Not okay."

He held one hand out, the other holding the platter of our dinner. "Fine. Fine. All I'm saying is that hormones make you do crazy things. You know her emotions are all over the place."

"Wait." He wasn't wrong. She cried a lot. And last night she'd called me stupid hot. "What if Ems does get like that? What if she wants some dick? If I don't give her mine, will she look for someone else? Benson? I bet Benson would bang her in a fucking heartbeat." And Cash would love that, wouldn't he? His best friend dating his cousin. It would be a dream come true for that asshole brother-in-law of mine. "That stupid backwoods hick. He'd hang his cowboy hat on her bed and... No. She can't have sex with Benson."

"Who is Benson?" My dad paused on his way to the back door.

"This friend of Cash's who wanted her number and checks up on her all the time."

His eyebrows rose to his hairline. Geez, when had he gotten so many wrinkles? "Does he know she's pregnant?"

"Yeah." I nodded, my stomach in knots thinking about Ems and Benson getting married this summer. "They grew up together. He doesn't see the baby as a reason to stay away. He cares about her. Holy shit. Emmie is going to have sex with Benson. Benson's sperm is going to go whizzing by my kid's head."

"I don't think that's the way that works, son."

"That stupid motherfucker."

Chapter Forty-Four

Emmie

I was living with Katie, taking a heavy course load of online classes, my belly was growing, and so was my appetite. I ate nonstop, always hungry. But I felt better than I had in months. I did yoga every day, the way Kase's mom had showed me. Sometimes she Face-timed me and we did a session together.

Visiting Kase's parents had made everything a little more...bearable. I didn't feel so weighted down by my own parents' disappointment. For the first time in a long time, I felt capable. I felt like I was going to be okay, and so was my daughter.

I smiled when my cell dinged from its place on the coffee table. I knew it was Kase. It was always Kase. He checked on us every day.

Kasen: Twenty-four weeks.

Emmie: Twenty-four weeks and three finals to study for.

I adjusted the laptop on my thighs, the heat from it making me want to toss it across the room.

Kasen: Sleeping any better?

Emmie: Until two am hits and she starts doing laps.

Kasen: You want to hear the sappiest most ridiculous thing you've ever heard?

Emmie: Of course I do.

Kasen: I recorded the song. And I emailed it to you.

Emmie: Are you telling me you recorded yourself singing and playing the guitar so that I can play it for our unborn daughter when she wakes up in the middle of the night?

Kasen: Yes. Told you it was the sappiest.

Emmie: And by sappy you mean sexy right?

Oh wow. Did I actually send those words? Pregnancy was frying my brain. I'd called him stupid hot when we were lying in his bed. And now I'd called him sexy. Fantastic.

Kasen: Did you just call me sexy? Stupid hot, and sexy.

Might as well own it, and try like hell to deflect.

Emmie: Kase. You are an actual male model, who plays the guitar and sings like a fallen angel. And you made a recording of it for your unborn baby girl. ARE YOU KIDDING ME? People write romance novels about guys like you.

Kasen: Thanks? I think. I'm not there for her, or for you. And since, you know, you're carrying her, I wanted to help.

Emmie: I'll try it tonight. Thank you Kase.

Kasen: You're welcome.

Emmie: No, I mean it. Thank you, for the song, for wanting to help. For all of it.

Kasen: It's the least I can do. After all, I'm the one that put her in there.

Emmie: If only my dad could punch through text.

Kasen: He still being a dick?

Emmie: He pretty much ignores me. My mom has come around a bit though. She asked if I wanted to go to lunch together tomorrow.

Kasen: Progress, huh?

Emmie: Progress.

I was nervous to have lunch with my mom, but I was excited as well. I wanted things between us to be better. I wanted her to know her granddaughter. I wanted her to be proud of me. I wanted her to see that I could do this.

Having a baby before my nineteenth birthday was never how I saw my life turning out. But Kase, his parents, my cousins…they'd all made me see that I didn't do anything wrong. I didn't deserve to be punished by my parents, not like this.

Chapter Forty-Five

Kase

Emmie: You want to hear the sappiest most ridiculous thing you've ever heard.

   Kasen: Very much.

   Emmie: The song worked.

   Kasen: Are you serious?

   Emmie: Yeah, I grabbed some headphones, put them on my belly and played it on repeat. She fell back asleep like three minutes later.

   Kasen: Daddy's girl already,

   Emmie: Looks that way, the tiny traitor.

   Kasen: You have lunch with your mom today?

   Emmie: Wish me luck.

   Kasen: Luck.

I was wishing Ems more than luck. I spent all morning throwing it out there to the universe, sending good vibes and everything else I could think of. Emmie didn't need her parents to hold her up or pay for anything. It wasn't like that. But I knew that she wanted them to be there for her, wanted their love and approval.

And I wanted it for her.

***

I threw the pile of clothes I was packing to the floor, searching for my cell phone. It'd been ringing for the last three minutes and I couldn't find it anywhere. I was preparing for a two-week trip to the northeast, and I had shit scattered all over my room.

Dammit.

I pulled the covers off my bed, finally spotting it under my pillow.

"Hey, Katie Bug, what's up?" I paused, trying to get my breathing under control while looking for my phone had been like running sprints. "Cash comes home in a few days. You two keep it down while you're…reuniting."

"Kase."

Her tone wasn't right. "What's wrong?"

"Emmie has been crying in her room for like an hour. Did you do something? Did you, like, change your mind about the baby or, like, I don't know, hurt her somehow?"

"What? Of course not." I put my phone on speaker, checking to make sure I hadn't missed any text from her while my cell had been buried under a mound of clothes and pillows. "I talked to her this morning, she said she was having lunch with her mom."

"Oh. Okay. Then maybe it's hormones or something?"

I sat on the edge of my bed, worry churning in my gut. "Did you try to go in there and check on her?"

"I knocked, but she said she was fine."

"And you believed her?" When Ems said she was fine, it meant that she didn't want to bother anyone else with her shit. "She's fucking six months pregnant and crying loud enough for you to hear her. Go in there."

"You're right. I'll go check on her and then call you back."

"No. Do it now. I'll stay on the phone."

"Em?" There was a pause, and then the sound of her bedroom door squeaking open. "Oh Emmie, what's wrong?" My heart dropped down through my stomach and landed at my feet. My sister's tone went from concerned to distraught.

"I'm fine."

Ems. At least she was able to talk, able to lie. Silently, I urged my sister to call bullshit, to dig deeper and find out what the hell happened.

"Your eyes are all red and puffy, and you're crying so hard you're hiccupping. You're not fine. Tell me what's going on. Do you want me to call Evie? Or your mom?"

"No. Not my mom." There was a brief moment of silence and I strained to hear everything that was happening hundreds of miles away. "We had lunch today, and I thought maybe she was coming around about the baby. I thought maybe… It doesn't matter. I was wrong."

Her mom. Her own mother had made her that upset? What the hell was wrong with her fucking parents?

"What happened?"

"She brought a friend of hers, someone who runs an adoption agency. She said she wanted me to understand my options." Her words kind of cut off at the end, the sound of her crying coming through the line, shattering the heart that was already lying at my feet.

"Sit tight. I'm going to go get you some water. I'll be right back and we can talk this out." I waited while Katie left the room, shutting the door behind her. I was already making moves in my mind. I'd had enough. "Did you hear all that?'

"Yep. I'm on my way." I started tossing all my clothes into my giant suitcase.

"What? Aren't you headed to like, Maine, for some watch shoot or something?"

"Doesn't matter." I grabbed my toiletry bag off the top of my dresser, throwing it into the pile of stuff I hadn't bothered to re-fold. "I'm tired of her parents' bullshit. I thought moving her into your house would give them the time and space they needed. But what her mom pulled today? Is not okay. Keep Ems calm. I'll be there soon."

"Kase, do you really think that's necessary? I can take care of her, and like you said, Cash will be home soon. I'm sure he'll know what to do and he can get Beau over—"

I cut my sister off, not having dropped that bad habit I'd picked up from the Devils. "That's not Cash's baby her mom is trying to make her give up. It's not Beau's. It's not yours. That's *my* kid, and that's my…Ems. Don't let her go anywhere. And stop fucking trying to stop me."

Chapter Forty-Six

Kase

I took the plane, and I was pulling up in front of Emmie's parents' house ninety minutes later. I'd cancelled my watch campaign, tarnishing my record for the first time in my career. I never cancelled. But then again, I'd never had a reason to before.

I slammed the door on my rental car, tugging my jacket tighter around me when the wind whipped across the Jameses' front walk. I took a deep, fortifying breath, then banged on their door. It wasn't a nice knock. I wasn't in a nice fucking mood.

Smith opened the door, jerking back in shock. "Kasen? What the flying fuck are you doing here?"

"I need to speak with you and your wife now."

He scoffed, going to shut the door in my face. "Too bad."

I put my hand out, stopping him. "I'm not fucking around, Smith." I met his eyes, letting him see the anger in mine. "And I'm not leaving until you both hear what I have to say. I'll call my dad. I'll call Dash. I'll get the whole fucking RiffRaff family involved in this bullshit if I have to."

"Smith? What's going on? Who was at the door?" Dylan, Emmie's mom, came to stand beside her husband, her face paling when she realized it was me. "Kasen?"

"He says he needs to talk to us, and he's not leaving until we hear him out." Smith opened the door wider, not to invite me in, but to gain momentum so he could slam it shut. "But I say, who the hell cares what he has to say."

"Let him speak, Smith."

"Seriously?" Smith glanced down at his wife, but when she didn't back down, he sighed, checking his watch. "Fine. You have three minutes, asshole."

Three minutes? Perfect. I didn't want to be in their presence any longer than that anyway.

"I never intended to fuck up Emmie's life, or to fuck up your happy little family. This baby threw me for a loop too, you know? This wasn't the way I saw my future panning out, but I'm here, and I'm in it, and I would do just about anything for my daughter. And right now, that includes taking care of her mom."

I pointed at them. "You two are stressing Ems the fuck out. Why the hell do you think she moved out of here? She wasn't sleeping. She was losing weight, and she felt abandoned. It's one thing to ignore her, it's one thing to be disappointed in her choices." I shook my head, my eyes zeroing in on her mom. "But what you did today? That's something altogether different."

"What are you talking about?" Smith looked to his wife, like he was truly lost. "*Cher*, what's he talking about?"

"I had lunch with Emmie today. And I had my friend Angie who runs the adoption agency come meet us," Dylan spoke softly, like she was ashamed to admit what she'd done.

I didn't give two shits if she was feeling remorseful. The damage was done. "You had no right to ambush her. And more than that, you have no fucking say over what happens to that baby. *My* baby. That kid already has two parents who love it."

Smith crossed his arms over his chest, widening his stance. "Two parents? You're never around. You really expect us to believe that's going to change once the baby comes?"

"Believe it, because it's changing right fucking now."

"What's that supposed to mean?"

I'd thought about this the whole plane ride over. And I knew that I was making the right choice, the right choice for *my* family. "Until I know Ems is okay, I'm not going anywhere."

Smith narrowed his eyes. "Oh yes you are. This is *my* land."

"No problem, we'll move across the street to Jett and Marley's land. You know, the land you looked at every day but still had no clue your niece and nephew were running an empire on." I gestured across the street in the direction of the office building and grow operation that was visible from the Jameses' front porch. "And if you keep pissing me off by hurting your daughter, I'll move her to south Texas. My parents are excited about their grandchild. They'd be thrilled to have us."

I turned on my heel, more than done with the two of them.

"Where the hell you think you're going?"

I didn't bother facing Smith to answer him, calling over my shoulder instead. "My three minutes are up and so is my patience with the two of you."

***

My sister let me in then quietly told me that Emmie was still in her room. She'd cried herself to sleep sometime while I was in the air, changing my whole life for my daughter. I stood in the doorway, watching Ems rest. Even with her eyes closed, she seemed consumed by stress. Her jaw was clenched, her brow furrowed, her elegant hands in tight fists under her chin.

I already loved my kid. I knew there was no other explanation for the feeling in my chest every time I looked at her mother. Even now, I wanted nothing more than to crawl in bed beside Emmie and rest my hand on her stomach. I wanted my baby to know that I was here, and that I would do anything and everything to make sure that they were both safe and healthy.

I'd never wanted to be a dad, but somewhere along the way, I'd become one. And to my shock, it was so easy, so effortless. Loving my child was as easy as existing. So why in the flying fuck were Emmie's parents having such a hard time loving her? Taking care of her?

"Kase?" Ems woke up slowly, confused as to why I was standing in her bedroom, watching her sleep like a creeper. "What are you doing here?" She pushed herself up, her rounded bump almost sitting in her tiny lap. "I thought you were flying to Maine today." She gathered her long blonde hair, piling it up neatly on her head.

I stepped farther into her room, taking in the framed sonogram picture on her nightstand. "Katie called me." My gaze moved to the one I'd taken of her and my mom back at the ranch, and next the one of us in my bedroom mirror, her bump out and my hands on it.

"Oh, I'm so sorry, I didn't ask her to do that." She rubbed at her eyes, like she was checking to see if the evidence of her tears were visible to me. "You didn't need to come. I'm fine. Lunch with my mom didn't go so great, but I didn't mean for anyone to worry or anything."

"Ems, you're not fine." I sat on the bed, my hand going to her knee. "And stop apologizing. *You* should have called me. We're in this together, right?"

"Co-parents and friends, Kase. Not call-every-time-one-of-us-has-a-shit-day besties."

I put my other hand on her cheek, wanting to catch all her sadness and low expectations and throw them out the window. "Your mom trying to make you give our kid up for adoption is more than a shit day."

Her face crumbled, fresh tears spilling out of her eyes and onto my thumb. "I don't know why I keep crying. I'm not going to do it. And it's not like she can actually make me."

My heart continued to ache for the sweet girl sitting in front of me trying to tuck into a ball and make herself as small as possible. "Because she hurt you. You thought she was coming around, you thought she wanted to spend time with you. And she let you down. Hard. She betrayed you." But Emmie wasn't small, she was never meant to be. She was stunning and bright, like a star, beautifully blinding. "But that won't happen again, Ems, I promise."

"You're sweet, but you can't control my parents, Kase." She shook her head, took a deep breath, and tried like hell to make her tears go away. "I'm going to have to give up on them ever being supportive, that's all."

"No, that's not all." Now here was the part I wasn't sure of, the part where I butted fully into her life and took over a bit. "I went to their house and talked to them first. If they didn't fully hate me before, they do now."

She gasped. "You talked to my parents?"

"Your dad treats you like shit and your mom tried to ambush you into an adoption." And it made me see fucking red. "It's one thing for them to be disappointed, it's another to try to make you give up our kid. Or stress you out so badly that your health is compromised. You're their daughter." I put my palm on her belly. "But that's mine. And I will protect her, always."

Chapter Forty-Seven

Emmie

Kase moved into his sister's house, temporarily, and Cash was back from training camp. It had been Katie and I for so many weeks, having a house full was almost alarming. Cash and Kase had reached an understanding: mutual disgust with my parents. My cousins came over a lot, taking turns to check on me and hang out with the four of us. Five if you counted my ever-growing baby bump.

I was twenty-eight weeks now, in my third trimester. And this was our new normal. Kase put his life on hold to come here and take care of me. He loved our daughter, and that was admirable. But part of me felt so damn guilty, like I wasn't strong enough to be on my own. Like he didn't trust me to take care of myself and our baby. He was pissed way the hell off about the way my family treated me like a child, but he was doing the same thing.

When there was a knock at the door, I sighed, glancing around, hoping someone else would run in to get it. I'd peed four times in the last hour and getting up again seemed like the worst. Luckily Kase came from the back of the house, shaking his head and laughing when I waved from my comfy spot on the couch.

"What the hell are you doing here?"

I sat up at Kase's harsh tone, my stomach twisting when I heard my dad reply, "I want to talk to my daughter."

"No." Kase's hold on the door was turning his knuckles white.

"I will fucking hit you again."

Kase shrugged, like the threat was idle and not at all worrisome. "So hit me. But I'm still not letting you in." I scooted closer to the edge of the couch, not sure what I should do. "This isn't good for her. You aren't good for her. The way you and her mom have been acting, fuck, I can't even wrap my brain around it."

"You're right," my dad barked out. I covered my mouth, stifling the gasp that came flying out. "The way we've been responding to this news…it's deplorable. Her mom was trying to help. She was trying to give Emmie back the life she worked so hard for. But she missed the mark, and it was taking things too far."

Kase sighed, some of the fight seeming to leave his body. "And you don't think screaming at her across the dinner table was taking things too far?"

"Look, fucker, you're going to be a dad. And one day your kid is going to rip your heart clean out of your chest. And maybe you'll handle it well, maybe you'll learn from my mistakes. But then again, maybe you won't. Maybe you'll be standing in her doorway, hoping like hell that she'll forgive you."

Kase was silent, standing guard at the door. I was, dammit, once again crying. My dad sounded broken, and even though he didn't deserve it, my heart ached for him. I got to my feet, shuffling forward, unsure of what should come next. They'd hurt me over and over. But they were my parents, and I missed them.

Eventually Kase stepped back, opening the door wider so my father could see me standing there. I was wearing yoga pants and a sports bra, my belly on full display.

He moved past Kase and crumpled to his knees in front of me. He wrapped his arms around my waist, his shoulders shaking as he cried. "I'm so sorry, baby girl. I'm so sorry."

I rested my hands on his shoulder, tears streaming down my face as I met Kase's dark gaze.

He shut the front door, pausing to kiss the side of my head on his way out of the room.

Chapter Forty-Eight

Kase

Emmie had a doctor's appointment this morning, and her mom took her this time. Both of her parents were trying really hard to redeem themselves in all our eyes. The words Smith had spoken to me while I stood guard at the front door last week were never far from my mind. He was right. I was going to be a dad, and I hoped I'd learn from his and Dylan's mistakes. He'd cried in the living room for a solid hour, clutching on to Emmie like she was a lifeline. Then Dylan had come over, apologizing to both of us. Things still felt a little strained when the four of us were together, but we were on the mend. And I was glad.

Ems told me I should go back to work, that I didn't need to guard our kid anymore. But I didn't want to leave. I wouldn't always be around. I knew that. I wasn't putting my life on hold, not like she thought I was. I'd been working and traveling nonstop since the day I turned eighteen. I considered this a well-deserved vacation.

I put the plate of fresh cookies on the coffee table, going to the front door when I heard a knock. Typically, all the cousins walked in without bothering to wait for permission, so I was almost nervous to see who was on the other side. Hell, the last person who'd knocked was Smith.

Well. Fuck. It was Benson, the cowboy who wanted to fuck my baby momma. "Can I help you?" I frowned, looking past him, like I was confused as to who the hell he was and why he was standing on my brother-in-law's front porch.

"Hey, man, how's it going?" He held his hand out to shake mine.

Great, now I'd be labeled a rude fuck if I chose to ignore it. "Uh, good?" I shook it, warily, continuing to play the confused part. "Are you here for Katie or Cash? Are they expecting you?"

His smile fell. "I'm Benson. We've met a few times."

"Benson?"

His eyebrows rose. "I was a groomsman in Cash's wedding."

"Oh." I chuckled good-naturedly. "Benson, sorry, bro, didn't recognize you without your big cowboy hat." I stepped back, opening the door wider and gesturing him inside the house when all I really wanted to do was slam the door in his smiling face. "Come on in."

I'd been here for almost two weeks, and I hadn't seen this fucker once. I knew he traveled some for work, hauling bulls to rodeos or some shit.

"Hey, sweet girl." His stupid face lit up when Ems came waltzing into the room. I always thought pregnant chicks waddled. But not Emmie James. She floated gracefully everywhere she went. "How're you feeling?"

"I'm good, thanks." She let him hug her, both of them laughing when her belly stopped them from getting too close. "Are you staying for dinner tonight? I think Katie is making that chicken soup you like."

"Well then, I'm staying." How the hell does Ems know he likes my sister's chicken soup? That soup was mine. Katie was mine, and that bump getting in his way was mine. "Come here and let me work on that knot for you." He sat on the couch, patting the space in front of him.

"What knot?" I'd rubbed Emmie's shoulders when she'd stayed at the ranch, but she hadn't complained about anything since then. "You have a knot?"

"Em gets these tension knots in her shoulders," Benson spoke over her head, informing me of this like I knew nothing about my own pregnant...Ems. "I rub her shoulders when I come over."

"Benson majored in sports medicine. He's been helping me stay loose." Ems dropped her head, letting it hang while Benson dug his fingers into her neck.

What the actual fuck? How often did he rub her down? Was he dicking her down while he was at it? Exactly how loose was this motherfucker making her? I knew, logically, it was none of my goddamn business.

But that didn't mean I was going to act rationally.

I joined them on the couch, sitting closer than socially acceptable. "Well, I'm here now, so why don't you show me how to do it and I can help her stay loose."

"Uh, yeah, sure, I can show you."

He was either a pushover or a nice guy. Either way, Benson showed me how to rub all the knots out of Emmie's shoulders and neck. And then the two of them posted up on the couch to watch a movie, eating the cookies *I'd* made.

I wanted to wedge myself between them.

So I sent myself to my room.

***

I skipped dinner, too afraid to sit across from Emmie and Benson and watch them fall in love. She let him put his hands all over her. They ate together and shared plates of cookies and had favorite movies.

When the hell had she become so close with that kind, friendly fucker? I was pacing in my room, not sure why I was feeling so close to jumping out of my skin. I needed to talk this out. I needed some solid advice.

I grabbed my cell from my back pocket, dialing my uncle, putting it on speakerphone.

Pax answered after the first ring. "Hey, kid, what's up?"

"I need to talk, but I can't do it with my dad because he'll tell me he told me so. And I can't talk about it with my mom because she'll get hearts in her eyes." My parents were great, but Uncle Pax knew me. He knew me because he was me. Or I was him, I guess.

"You falling for your baby momma?"

"No." I wasn't, right? Nah. "I'm extremely jealous of the dude that is."

"What dude?"

"Benson, the tool in the cowboy hat from Cash and Katie's wedding." Except he wasn't a tool, he was actually a really nice guy. Which sucked.

"Why is he making moves on your girl?"

"Right?" No. Wait. "But, I mean, she's not my girl."

"The baby in her belly is."

Damn straight it is. I sighed, knowing that I was being unfair. "He's into Ems. He's not trying to ice me out as a father." *Well shit.* He wasn't trying to lay claim to my daughter. He was into her mother. And for that, I couldn't blame him. "Oh. I see what you did there."

Uncle Pax chuckled. "If he's a nice guy and he likes Emmie, then don't stand in their way."

"But she's pregnant with my child. It seems, I don't know, weird or something." And by it seems weird, I meant it made me feel irrationally irritated.

"Are you in love with Emmie?"

"No?" *Did I end that with a question mark?*

"Kase."

I was in love with my daughter, and those emotions got skewed sometimes when I looked at her mom. Even I could admit that. "I care about her, a lot."

"That's not love, Kase, not the kind she deserves."

He was right. Emmie deserved someone to be consumed by her. To fall for her so hard there was never any chance of stopping it. But. "Can't she wait 'til the baby comes out before she starts dating?"

"Are you waiting? Are you seriously telling me that you've been celibate while you've been traveling? I've been with you in Italy before, bro, I know how it goes."

I snorted, recalling the week Uncle Pax and I had spent in Italy during fashion week after my twenty-first birthday. Although the last time I was there, nothing like that happened, not even close. "I haven't been with anyone in a few months."

"No shit?"

I nodded, sighing as I sat on the edge of my bed. "No shit. And all I'm asking is, is it too much to ask that she do the same?"

"Yes." Well that was a fast, definitive answer.

"Really? But I'm here."

"Yeah, you are there, which makes me so proud of you. But after that baby comes, you'll go back to your job, to traveling, to sleeping around. Anytime you're not with your daughter, you'll be the same old Kase, living large, doing what you want to do with whomever you want to do it. Emmie won't. She'll be there day in and day out, a mother twenty-four seven. You can't ask her to put her life on hold because it makes you uncomfortable." He paused, letting all that settle in my mind. "And wouldn't you feel better knowing that Emmie and your daughter are being taken care of by a good guy while you're not there? Think of the alternative: she dates a string of losers who don't care about either of them."

"I don't want her to date Benson." Oh. That came out harsher than I thought it would.

"Then you need to look real fucking hard at why."

"You think I'm being selfish?" Was I being selfish? Was I allowed to be selfish? Something told me Uncle Pax, and anyone else I asked, would say fuck no.

"I think putting a wedge between Emmie and a nice guy because it bugs you to see them together is selfish, yes." He paused again. "Being a parent means putting your kid first, even if it means letting someone else love them."

I hated what he was saying to me. I hated how true those words were. "You give serious fatherly advice for a fun uncle. How'd you get so smart?"

"My baby sister fell for some idiot rock star, and they gave me two kids who I love more than anything. More than myself, that's for sure."

Well fuck. Tears pricked the back of my eyes at my uncle's declaration. I knew he loved my sister and me, but he and I didn't do this sappy shit together. Maybe pregnancy hormones were catching because I felt real fucking close to crying at the moment. "I love you too, Uncle Pax."

"Kase, kid, if you're falling for Emmie, that's okay. But if you're not sure, let her be."

"I know. I will."

The last thing I wanted to do was cause her any more heartache than I already had.

Chapter Forty-Nine

Emmie

I rolled over, hoisting my belly up and onto the other side, reaching for my phone when it chimed loudly.

Kasen: Do you like Benson?

Kase. He was in his room next door.

Emmie: Why are you texting me? We're one wall away from each other.

Kasen: I didn't want to wake you in case you were sleeping.

Emmie: I'm studying.

Or I was trying to, but I'd been nodding off when I heard my text alert.

Kasen: Do you like Benson?

Where was this coming from? Was he jealous? No. Kase couldn't be jealous of Benson because Kase didn't want me. Not like that.

Emmie: He's okay, I guess.

Kasen: Don't be that girl.

It'd be nice if just once he'd let me get away with a bullshit answer.

Emmie: I like that he's nice to me. I like that he doesn't see me as a pregnant teenager. I like that he doesn't pressure me for more. And I really like the way he keeps me loose.

I covered my mouth, laughing when I hit send.

Kasen: Stop it.

Emmie: You acted like a caveman earlier.

He'd basically shoved Benson's hands off my shoulders and told us he was more of a verbal learner, not visual.

Kasen: I'm not proud.

Emmie: He's a good guy, Kase.

Kasen: Are you in love with him?

No. How could I possibly be in love with Benson when Kase consumed so much of my heart, despite my best efforts?

Emmie: No.

Kasen: Could you be? Someday?

Emmie: I don't know. Falling in love is the furthest thing from my mind right now.

Kasen: Fair enough.

Emmie: You can always come talk to me, Kase. You don't have to text.

I wanted to see him. I wanted him to sit next to me and rub sweet circles on my belly. I wanted his hands any way I could get them

Kasen: Are your pregnancy hormones making you horny?

Emmie: Never mind. Stay in your room.

Kasen: My dad said pregnant chicks like the dick.

Emmie: I have a hard time believing he said that.

There was no way Mr. Cadence would use those words.

Kasen: I'm paraphrasing. But still.

Emmie: I'm fine.

"That's not an answer, Ems."

I looked up. Kase was leaning against my doorjamb, refusing once again to let a bullshit answer fly. His hair was a mess, like he'd been running his fingers through it. He wasn't wearing a shirt and his sweatpants were riding low on his hips. He was the most attractive man I'd ever seen. And he was the father of my child.

"I don't think it's sex I want." At least not with Benson. No, my hormones were all geared toward Kase.

"What is it then?"

I took a moment, trying to find the right words, trying to tell him why I enjoyed my time with Benson. Trying to explain what I missed most, and what I needed. "I want someone to hold me. Someone to kiss my forehead and tell me that everything is going to be okay."

"Do you let Benson hold you?"

"We cuddle sometimes."

Kase licked his lips, standing up straight and taking a step closer to my bed. "Do you like it when he touches you?"

My breath caught in my throat, my heart pounding. His words, they'd had the ability to turn me on from day one, and it seemed not much had changed. "I don't hate it, but I can't say I crave him or anything." I've only ever craved one man in my entire life.

"Can *I* hold you?"

It's not like he hadn't held me before. We'd slept next to each other. We'd napped on the couch. He touched my belly all the time. He kissed the top of my head. He guided me into every room with his hand on the small of my back.

I nodded.

"We can't have sex, Ems, we can't blur the lines, but I'd like to give you what you need if you'll let me." He crawled on my bed, wrapping his arm around my middle and pulling my back against his chest.

I sniffled, wiping at my eyes, trying to hide my tears before he could see them.

"Why are you crying?"

Oh let me count the ways. "I guess I've been so lonely lately." That was what it boiled down to, right? My life was different, and I felt a little lost.

"I'm here now, Ems." Kase kissed my shoulder, and chills traveled down the length of my spine. "I should have been here all along."

"I don't expect you to put your life on hold, Kase." And I hated that he felt like he needed to.

"Why not? You are." His palm rested on my stomach. "Co-parents and friends." He slipped it under my shirt, rubbing soothing circles. "You take care of the baby, and I'll take care of you. And then once she's here, we'll find our new normal. Together."

Chapter Fifty

Kase

I slept in Emmie's room now. I knew it wasn't the smartest move, but I couldn't seem to stay away. Every time I thought about going back to my own bed, I remembered her telling me that she felt lonely. And instead of walking away, I pulled her closer.

It'd been a week or so, and no one in the house had mentioned it. Either they hadn't noticed, or for once, her family wanted to stay out of our business. I went for a run every night. Usually Emmie and her mom came with me. They'd walk, and I'd do laps around them. Ems wanted to run. She said she felt like her muscles were atrophying. But Landry came over and argued my point alongside me. She told Emmie that if she would've started running at the beginning of her pregnancy, then she would have still been able to. But since all she'd been doing the last few months was yoga, she had to stick to that as we got closer to the end.

And that yoga? I was a big fan. We'd go on our walk/run and then she'd come inside and pull out the mat my mom had sent her. I'd sit on the couch and watch, you know, in case she needed me. Emmie was gorgeous, her body slender, until she turned to the side. And then she looked like she'd swallowed a bowling ball.

But tonight, she was in her room taking a test for one of her online classes, so I was running alone. The compound was sort of spooky after the sun went down, but I refused to use a flashlight like I was scared of the dark.

"Boo."

Shitfuckdamn. I skidded to a stop, my hand flying to my chest as I slipped on the loose gravel. "What the fuck, Brody?" I regained my balance, leaning forward with my palms on my knees. "You about gave me heart attack." I glared at him. "Why are you hiding in the dark, jumping out at people? If Ems had been with me, you'd have sent her into labor."

He was laughing, hard, gasping while he tried to catch his breath. "If Em was with you, I wouldn't have done it." He erupted into another fit of hardy ha-ha, the bastard. "I wish I would have videoed that shit."

"Is there something you need? Or is this a new hobby I should alert the rest of the compound about?" I had my hands on my hips, taking big gulps of fresh air, willing my pulse to return to a more normal rhythm.

"I wanted to talk to you." He snorted, trying and failing to quell his laughter. "Sorry, I'm sorry. I'll stop. I promise." He bit his lips together, turning around for a moment. "Okay. Yeah. I'm good."

I started walking, knowing that if he really wanted to talk to me, he'd catch up.

Which he did.

"I wanted to see how you were doing."

"With what?" I liked Brody, but it wasn't like we were best friends or anything.

"With the baby. With Em." When I didn't answer, he continued, "I know what it's like to have your whole life turned upside down. Wyatt wasn't planned, and finding out Landry was pregnant shocked the shit out of me. She and I were only fucking around, you know? I was about to leave on my first stadium tour and she was deep into her surgical residency."

"I thought you guys were dating when you knocked her up." I knew that Wyatt wasn't planned, but I'd always assumed that they'd been together from the start.

"No." He chuckled, rubbing at his blond curls. "We were banging, a lot. Like nonstop. But we weren't dating." He cleared his throat, keeping pace beside me as we walked toward Katie and Cash's house. "I knew I wanted to be a dad, that part was easy. I loved Wyatt almost instantly. But I wasn't sure how I felt about Landry for a bit." I glanced at him, surprised to hear that. "I fell for Landry slowly, and then hard. Hell, maybe I was always in love with her and refused to realize it. It's hard to know, it seems so long ago now."

"Why are you sharing all this with me?" I wasn't being mean, my tone wasn't rude, but I honestly wanted to know what he was getting at, if there was a point he was trying to make.

"You're in love with your kid, we can all see it. But I think you're in love with Emmie too."

Bold. That was a bold-ass statement. "I care about Ems, Brody, I do. But there can't be more between us. We have a good thing going here, and we don't have the luxury of fucking it up." It wasn't about only the two of us. There would always be someone else's heart we needed to protect.

"If you could invent a time machine, if you could go back in time, would you have not touched Emmie at all, or would you have just kept your dick in your pants?"

I'd thought about that very thing, I'd even asked Ems what she would do if we could go back in time to that weekend. But it seemed like a lifetime ago.

"I can't answer that. Not now." I shot him an irritated scowl. "That would be me saying I don't want my daughter to exist."

He rolled his eyes, gently shoving me to the side. "Come on, dude, we all know you're head over heels for your kid. Go along with me here. Play the game."

I sighed, closing my eyes, remembering that first weekend I'd spent with Emmie. I was like a man possessed. I had to have her. My uncles had warned me away, both of them. But I'd refused to listen. I wanted her too badly. The way she came apart from my touch beside the pool, the way she felt in my arms while we danced. The way she'd tasted, the sound of her orgasm while I feasted on her. No. I wouldn't have given that up, not a single second of it. And I wouldn't give up anything that happened since then. It wasn't always easy, and we'd both been through so fucking much, but not knowing Ems? The notion alone made me queasy. She was my best friend.

"I would have kept my dick in my pants. What's your point?"

"My point is that if magic existed and you could travel back to that long-as-fuck wedding weekend, you'd *still* touch her. You'd kiss her and hold her and dance with her. You wouldn't give Emmie up, not completely, no matter what." Brody kicked a rock, sending it sailing into the woods.

"Why are you doing this?" *Why are you making everything so fucking hard? Why are you saying these things to me? Why are you trying to throw us off balance?*

"Because I know what it feels like to fall in love with the mother of your child." He veered off, heading back the way we'd come while calling over his shoulder, "What's better for a little girl than two parents who are as obsessed with each other as they are with her? If there's a chance it could be more, fucking take it, bro. You'll regret it for the rest of your life if you don't."

Chapter Fifty-One

Kasen

Brody's advice shook me to the core, as I was sure he'd intended. I'd spoken too soon, thinking that Emmie's family was backing off and giving us our space. No. Brody had been waiting in the dark, ready to pounce like an emotional ninja.

I'd showered, thinking of Emmie the whole time. Thinking about the way she'd felt in my arms the night we'd conceived our daughter. The way she'd laughed as we danced in the field. Everything about that weekend was burned into my heart. I remembered every detail of my time with Emmie, and everyone else I'd ever been with swirled together in a blur of nothing special.

I loved Ems. I knew I did. I was supposed to, right? I was supposed to love the mother of my child. That was me being a good man, a good dad. Two things that I'd promised her, months ago, that I would be. But that didn't mean I was *in* love with her.

I stood in her doorway, drinking in the sight of her. She was lying on her back, wearing a sports bra and some tiny shorts. She got overheated at night. She didn't like to wear a lot of clothes these days, and I was not complaining. So I thought she was smokin' hot. That also didn't mean I was *in* love with her.

Her laptop was shut beside her. She was done with her test. Her eyes were closed, but her hands were tapping her belly like she was playing with our daughter. "Ems?"

"Hm?"

I stepped into her room, glancing at the picture of me, her, and the bump I'd taken in the mirror. "Are you asleep?"

She smiled, opening her eyes. "Am I ever these days?"

"Our little girl giving you a hard time?"

She turned to look at me, lips pursed. "I don't think she's going to be one of those infants that naps all day."

I grabbed the headphones from the dresser then climbed into bed beside her, helping her roll over and get comfortable. Once my unborn daughter was propped against my side, I placed the headphones around Ems's belly and started rubbing big circles on her bare skin. "There you go, baby girl."

"She already has you wrapped around her finger."

"I'm not even ashamed." I dipped down and placed a kiss on her bump. "Can I ask you something?"

"Sure." Ems tucked her hands under her chin, resting her forehead against my arm and closing her eyes. "Nudge me if I doze off while I'm in the middle of a sentence."

"Why did you give me your virginity?"

"I thought you were going to ask me to name our daughter after another stripper." She picked her head up, meeting my gaze and taking a deep breath. "I don't know, you were the first guy I'd ever *wanted*, you know? You made me feel things I didn't realize even existed. And it felt *right*. It felt like it was exactly what was supposed to happen."

"Did you cry into your pillow when the sun came up?" I'd thought about her on the plane that next morning as I watched the sky turn orange with light. I'd wondered if she was awake, and if she was sad. I remembered the promise she made me while we'd been dancing, and I'd hoped that she'd kept it.

"No. Honestly, I woke up smiling." Her pink lips lifted at the corners, slightly. "I felt content and, like, happy."

I scooted down, resting my head on the pillow and putting my face near hers. "Maybe we were supposed to happen." I put my palm back on her belly. "Maybe it felt right because it was, because we were supposed to make her."

She nodded, her beautiful blue eyes filling with tears. "Yeah, maybe so."

"Ems?"

"Yeah?"

I glanced down, watching as she licked her bottom lip. Taking in the way the pulse in her slender neck started to race and her throat worked to swallow. "Nothing, I uh, get some rest." I kissed the top of her head, breathing in her sweet scent.

There were things I wanted to tell her, ask her, talk to her about. I wanted to share all the shit that Brody had stirred up in my brain because she was my best friend. We were honest with each other. We had to be for this to work. But I was scared. I didn't want to mess up what we had for what might be. There was too much at stake.

She snuggled down closer, her head resting on my chest.

This was all I needed.

Them safe and in my arms.

***

When I woke a few hours later, the house was silent. I rolled my head to the right, not all that surprised to find Emmie's side of the bed empty. It was getting harder and harder for her to sleep through the night. It wasn't only the baby keeping her up now, it was the fact that she had to pee all the time and her back hurt and her hips ached.

She was in her third trimester, and it was crazy to think we were coming up on the end. Our daughter would be here soon. I threw the covers off, getting out of bed to make sure Ems was okay because that was the right thing to do, not because I was *in* love with her.

I walked down the dark hallway, following the faint light coming from the kitchen. I shook my head, laughing quietly when I saw Ems, sitting on the counter, eating ice cream from the carton with a plastic spoon the size of her pretty little head. The fridge was open, a can of whipped cream sitting beside her. Her hair was a wild mess and her belly was still bare, the sports bra and tiny shorts she slept in all she had on.

She was stunning. I didn't think I'd ever be able to look at her and not notice her beauty. And my dad was right, I thought she was even hotter pregnant with our daughter. I tried to ignore it, but it was visceral. The way I felt about her body, it was possessive and raw. And fucking inconvenient. It turned me into a jealous dick. But it didn't mean I was *in* love with her.

"You gonna keep standing there like a weirdo, or you want some ice cream?" She turned to me, licking her lips clean.

I stuck my hands in my pockets, trying like hell to hide the semi the sight of her had given me. "I want some fucking ice cream." I stood in front of her, opening my mouth wide. "Give it to me."

She giggled, the sound like music in the quiet sleeping house. She gave me a bite, then grabbed the can of whipped cream and took a hit for herself. "Good?"

I nodded, reaching out to wipe some cream off her chin. "Very." I put my hands on her belly. "She wake you up?"

"Nah, this one was on me." She took another bite of ice cream. "It's hard to get comfortable."

"Come back to bed, I'll rub you until you're loose." I grinned, taking the can of whipped cream out of her hands.

She pursed her lips. "Maybe I should call Benson? He's so good at it, you know?"

I gasped playfully, tickling her ribs and making her squirm. I knew she was kidding, but his name on her lips wasn't what I wanted to hear. Ever. "No more rubdowns from Benson." I put my hands on her shoulders, kneading her tight muscles. "I'm the baby daddy. I do the rubbing."

"Your rubbing is what made you the baby daddy in the first place." She smiled, resting the ice cream carton on her belly. Our daughter kicked, making the carton wobble. Clearly, she didn't like being used as a table.

"What can I say? I give great rub." I winked, putting the lid on the ice cream and sticking it back in the freezer. "Come on, baby, let's go back to bed."

Time stood still, my words hanging in the air between us. I didn't mean them to sound the way they did, like she was mine, and her bed would always be mine too. I didn't mean to call her baby.

But it hadn't felt wrong, those words I'd so casually spoken. Then again, nothing ever felt wrong when I was with Ems. Not moving here to take care of her, not making her laugh, holding her hand, kissing her bump, or lying against her while we slept. Even in the beginning when I was unsure and she was so upset, even when we argued. Everything with that beautiful ballerina had always felt *right*.

I stepped closer, my hands cupping her face as I cursed Brody in my mind. "Ems?"

"Yeah?"

"I think I'm in love with you."

Her lips parted on a shaky exhale. "What?"

"I'm in love with you." I dipped down, softly kissing her lips for the first time in what felt like forever. That felt right too. Like coming home.

Her thighs wound around my waist as I kissed her again, deeper this time. She tasted like sugar, like perfection. Her tongue was cold from the ice cream as it tangled with mine and my hands moved to her hips, helping her hop down off the counter. Her fingers tugged at my hair, dragging my lips back to hers. I lifted her in my arms, carrying her down the hallway and back to the bed we'd been sharing. I laid her down, kicking the door shut behind me.

"Kase." She took in a shaky breath.

"I'm here, Ems, and I'm not going anywhere, ever." I knew she was scared, afraid that we were about to ruin everything we had. She'd told me once that she kept her expectations low so she wouldn't get let down. "Expect the world of me, Ems, because I'll never let you down."

"Don't make promises you can't keep, Kase. I won't survive you walking away from us." She swallowed thickly, her blue eyes watery with unshed tears as her fingertips trailed lazily up and down my bare back. Touching each other was second nature, even when she was nervous she held on to me. I was the person she drew strength from. I was the person she wanted when the world felt out of balance. Even if I was the one causing it.

"Emmie James, we both know I keep my word, always." I kissed her lips sweetly. "Please let me love you."

She took in another deep, shaky inhale, but nodded.

"Use words, baby."

"Love me."

I smiled as I rose up on my knees, pulling her boy shorts down her long, toned legs and then taking off my briefs. Her eyes were on me, watching my every move in the dimly lit room. She was propped up on a pile of pillows, her hair spread out like a fan of gold.

I'd never had sex with a pregnant chick before and I was a little apprehensive. I wasn't sure how to work around our daughter. *No. Whoa.* That didn't sound okay. I didn't know how to work around her belly. "Uh, Ems? How would you be the most, uh, comfortable?"

She pulled her bottom lip through her perfect white teeth, her hands resting on her stomach. "I don't know. I figured you would know how this was supposed to work."

"Me? Why would I know how to bang a pregnant chick?"

"Porn?"

"You think I watch pregnant porn? Are you serious right now?"

She covered her face, giggling, the sound making me smile. We'd made a big jump from *let me love you* to pregnancy porn fetishes. But she was laughing, and I was enamored. This was us honestly doing our best to figure out our life together.

I lay down beside her, helping her roll onto her side, making sure she had all the pillows she needed. I swept her long hair off her shoulder, placing soft kisses on her neck, her shoulder. I slid my palm down her side, over her hip. Curving around to her center, rubbing her clit and loving the soft gasp that escaped her lips. "You need to tell me if I'm hurting you or if you get uncomfortable. I don't want anything to happen to you or the baby."

"Kase. I have wanted you since the second you got on your knees and spoke to our daughter through my belly." Her fingers tangled in my hair, tugging gently. "Stop worrying about me. Stop overthinking this. Just, um, fuck me. Please."

I couldn't help the smirk on my face as I leaned down to scrape my teeth along the column of her slender neck. "In love." I slid my fingers farther south, slipping two inside her wet pussy. "In lust." She arched her back as I used my thumb to press on her clit. "Completely fucking into you, Ems." I pushed up her leg, making room for me. My dick had been begging to get back inside Emmie James since the moment I put him on a plane and flew him to another country. Slowly, I inched inside her core, letting my forehead rest against her back as I tried to gather an ounce of control.

"Fuck, Ems, you feel so good." I moved gently, her pussy tight around my cock, the pleasure already off the charts. I wasn't sure how long I'd last. She felt too perfect bare. I'd never fucked like this before. The emotion. Nothing between us. It was all so overwhelming.

I picked up my head to watch her face, her body, needing to make sure that she was okay, and I wasn't hurting her. Her lips were parted, soft moans escaping. Her hands were fisted in the sheets, her sexy spine was bowed. Her hips were dancing with mine, meeting me, making my every smooth thrust hit a little bit harder.

Emmie James was more than any man deserved. I'd been her first, and I was pretty damn positive I wanted to be her last. My gaze traveled up and down her beautiful body, enamored with the way she moved. I could watch her forever.

"Kase." Her hand came back, winding around my neck, pulling me closer.

The sound of my name whispered in the dark by the girl I'd fallen in love with was the best sound. Her soft voice alone had the power to unravel me. Goosebumps covered my legs, my balls tightened to the point of pain.

"Ems, baby, fuck." I wasn't making sense. I couldn't form a complete sentence. "Ohmygod."

She cried out my name, her pussy taking my dick in a viselike grip, tearing my orgasm from my body as she came.

Pregnant chick sex was fuckin' awesome.

Chapter Fifty-Two

Emmie

I woke up with my head on Kase's bare chest.

He'd told me he was in love with me, and then he'd kissed me. After that, he did lots of other stuff to me, and believe me, I wasn't complaining. But I'd be lying if I said I wasn't nervous about what this morning would bring.

Maybe he'd been in the heat of the moment. Maybe he'd wake up and think we made a terrible mistake. I took a deep breath, trying to gather all the strength I had inside me. If he changed his mind, I would be okay. I had to be. Our daughter mattered more. She came first. And as long as he never changed his mind about her, we would all be fine.

"I can hear you freaking out, Ems."

His voice was always rough first thing in the morning, and I usually loved to listen to him talk before he fully woke up. This morning, though, I was terrified to hear what he had to say.

"Hey, Em, I made pancakes, you guys want…" Cash was frozen in the doorway to the room Kase and I had been sharing. "Uh, I can see his dick."

I lifted my head, looking down, my cheeks heating instantly.

"Stop looking at it, dude." Kase moved the blankets, covering himself before rolling to me, burying his face in my neck. "And yes, we want pancakes. But Ems doesn't get syrup, she ate a carton of ice cream in the middle of the night and washed it down with a can of whipped cream."

"This isn't a bed-and-breakfast. Put some pants on and feed your girls." My gaze flew to Cash's. He winked before closing the door.

Your girls.

I got out of bed, pulling on a tank top and some yoga pants, which was basically my uniform at this point. I put my hair up, stepping into the adjoining bathroom to brush my teeth. I couldn't stay in bed with Kase. I couldn't breathe him in while he told me he'd made a mistake. I rinsed my mouth, then swiped some lip gloss on, buying time before I had to face him.

"Ems?"

"Yeah?" My heart was pounding.

"You coming?" I poked my head out of the bathroom to find Kase at the door, his hand held out, waiting for me. My eyes darted to his face. He was smiling. "Or were you planning on hiding in that bathroom for the rest of the day?"

"I was waiting for you to tell me that we'd made a mistake. That it was late and we weren't thinking clearly. That we can't complicate what we have. That it'll make things too hard." My body was shaking, and I could feel the tears coming.

He crossed the room, taking my face in his hands like he had last night. "It was late, and we weren't thinking clearly." I bit the inside of my cheek, trying like hell to fight back the waterworks. "If we had, we would've brought the whipped cream back to bed with us." He kissed my lips, his hands sliding around my hips to squeeze my ass before pulling away. "I'm in love with you, Ems. I meant it last night and I mean it this morning. I know it seems like it all came out of nowhere, but it didn't."

I let him pull me out of the bedroom and down the hall, too bewildered to respond. He was in love with me, and that was that.

Was I stuck in a twilight zone? He hadn't even asked me how I felt.

How *did* I feel?

I was so used to holding back my feelings for Kase that I was having a hard time trying to bring them to the surface. I'd been on edge, afraid that he would break my heart since day one. But he hadn't, not once. He'd been present and supportive. He'd given me everything I needed. All I had to do was ask. He was gorgeous and funny, and he called me out on my bullshit. He stood up to my family, over and over, protecting me and fighting in my corner. He'd kept every promise he'd ever made to me since the moment I met him.

Expect the world of me, Ems, because I'll never let you down.

Would he keep this one too?

"So you two *are* boning then." Jett pushed the chair next to him out and Kase helped lower me into it before going to make our plates. "No one sleeps butt-ass naked if they haven't used their dick."

Kase piled two plates high with pancakes, pouring syrup on one but not the other. "Is it really any of your business?"

"Yes. Us against the world. You knocked her up. You're part of our fucked-up shit now." Jett shoveled pancakes into his mouth, rudely talking around them. "But you've gotta be *honest* about said fucked-up shit."

"What's fucked up about it?" Kase sat next to me, lightly slapping my hand away when I reached for the second bottle of syrup that was on the table. "It's not like we haven't *boned* before." He rubbed my belly, grinning sarcastically. "And can we stop calling it that?"

"No. And right. But now the stakes are higher." Beau walked into the kitchen, going to the counter to make himself a plate. "You had that whole friends and co-parents thing going on."

"Where the hell did you come from?" Kase leaned back in his seat, looking toward the front of the house. "Cash, did you ring a fucking dinner bell or something?"

Jett held up his cell phone, waving it back and forth. "Mass group text."

I narrowed my eyes, reading the message as best I could. "Made pancakes, also, I think Kase and Emmie are doing it." I sighed, glaring at Cash. "Really?"

Whatever was happening between Kase and me was new. Like brand new. What we needed was to talk, to be alone and figure out where to go from here. But instead we were having breakfast with my cousins, discussing our sex life like it was as casual as the weather.

Cash shrugged, putting a tall whipped cream topper on his pancakes. "We wanted to make sure you were okay, that's all."

Kase rested his arm on the back of my chair, a wicked grin on his face. He waited until Cash took a big bite, then nodded at the can. "I'd be careful with that whipped cream, bro." He gestured to me. "My girl has a sweet tooth, you know what I'm saying?"

Cash choked, spitting food all over Beau's plate.

214

Chapter Fifty-Three

Kasen

Ems got up and walked out of the room without saying anything to anyone. I heard the back door open and close, and the rest of the table went still.

"Did you hurt her?" Cash was glaring at me. "I'll kill you if you hurt her."

"I'd never hurt her." I took our plates to the sink, rinsing them off, and then loaded them in the dishwasher. The kitchen was silent. No doubt, everyone was shooting daggers into my back. I turned around, leaning against the counter. "I told her I was in love with her."

My sister gasped dramatically, then rolled her eyes. "Of course you're in love with her."

I looked around the table. Beau, Jett, Devin, and Cash were all smiling. "Why are you looking at me like that?"

"Because you're such a dummy." My sister got up and wrapped her arms around my waist, squeezing me tight. "We've known for a while now that you're in love with Em. We were waiting for you to figure it out."

"You fell in love with your kid first, but Emmie was pretty quick after that." Beau balled up his napkin and tossed it into Jett's syrupy plate. "Hell, you told us all to fuck off at Thanksgiving when we were giving Emmie a hard time, and you hadn't even decided yet if you were going to stick around."

"That was the moment I knew you were here to stay." Cash was leaning back in his chair, his hands behind his head. "And then after you took that punch from Uncle Smith? The way you carried her in the house, the way you worried over her? I knew *then* that you were in love with her."

"You protect her. You stand up for her. You wear that apron and bake her cookies." My sister patted my chest, then started cleaning up the mess her husband had left making pancakes.

"Go talk to your girl, little fucker." Jett jerked his thumb in the direction of the backyard.

I found Emmie on the back patio, sitting on a porch swing, her legs kicked out in front of her. "Don't be that girl, Ems." I smiled as I sat beside her, demanding that she talk to me, like I always had.

She rested her head on my shoulder. "I think I'm in love with you too."

"Then why do you sound so sad?" I put my hand on her thigh, placing a kiss on the top of her head.

"You have my whole heart, Kase, and as much as it pains me to admit it, you always have." She put her hand on top of mine, threading our fingers together. "You were my first everything, and even though I tried not to, I fell for you a long time ago."

My feelings had tumbled like a downhill fall, gaining speed until they crashed into me, taking over my heart. But Ems? Apparently hers had been a steady descent down a rocky slope, with her hoping and wishing that she didn't break an arm on her way to the inevitable.

"Well, we're here now, having a baby and in love." I took our joined hands and brought them to my lips.

"Please don't hurt me." Her voice came out small and soft. "Please don't say these things to me unless you truly mean them."

I put my finger under her chin, making her see the truth in my eyes. "I don't lie to girls, Ems." I kissed the tip of her nose. "I love you. I'm here. I won't break your heart."

***

When I guided her back through the kitchen, we saw the house was still full of Emmie's family. They were posted all over the living room, something about a rainy day movie marathon. I didn't mind, not really. Cash and Katie moved the coffee table and made a big pallet on the floor. Ems and I were on the couch. I was lying behind her, my hand on our daughter.

Last night had changed us, but only that we were both being honest about our feelings for each other. We'd been terrified to ruin the normal we'd found, the safety we'd found in being friends and co-parents. But this? Being in love with the mother of my child? Brody was right, it was better than I could have ever imagined.

I smiled when I felt the baby kick. I'd miss this when she was out in the real world.

"Hey, have y'all picked a baby name yet?" Katie leaned her head back, looking at us.

Ems snorted. "No, but your brother has given me a long list of stripper names to choose from."

I tickled her ribs, which backfired because her tight ass wiggled against my dick. I groaned, putting my palms on her hips to keep her still before I lost control and simply carted her back to bed. "You could pop at any second, Ems. We really should pick a name."

"I'm not a bag of popcorn."

I put my lips against the shell of her ear, going out on a limb and playing with our *new* normal. "You could shoot her out of that perfect pussy of yours any second. We should pick a name."

She sighed. "Ugh, now I want more popcorn."

"Now I want to eat that pussy." I kissed the spot where her neck met her shoulder, watching in fascination as goose bumps broke out on her flesh.

Ems rolled onto her back, pinning me with her beautiful blue eyes. "I think I have her middle name picked, want to hear it?"

I pouted, playfully, because really the person birthing the kid should probably get final say. "Why do you get to pick her middle name?"

"Because you get to pick her last."

My heart fluttered in my chest, and I melted like fucking butter. "Are you serious?"

Ems nodded, smiling sweetly, her fingertip trailing lightly across my jaw. "I thought we could make James her middle name."

I didn't care who was watching, or who was listening. I kissed her deeply and wholly inappropriately, running my hands through her hair and swallowing her soft whimpers. I wanted to pick her up and finish this conversation in bed. I wanted to slide back inside her. I wanted to hear her come apart over and over again until neither of us could breathe.

"Get a room," Cash yelled, tossing a handful of popcorn our way.

I pulled away, fully prepared to take his suggestion and run with it. "Gladly, fuckers."

"No," Brody called out, stopping me from getting up. "I want to hear what name you guys chose."

"I've always liked Luca for a girl." Jett pressed pause on the movie.

I shook my head. "You don't get to pick our daughter's name."

"Luca James Cadence." Ems said it out loud, testing it all together.

I frowned. "Dammit. I love it." I glared at Jett, annoyed that the cocky fucker had chosen the perfect name for our girl. James was Emmie's last name, but it was also my sister's middle name. And Luca? It was different and sweet.

"I do too." Ems sighed. "I really love it. I don't think any other name will do now." She sounded as put out as I did.

Jett grinned, flipping me off before turning the movie back on. "You're welcome, little fucker."

I climbed to my feet, taking Emmie's hands and helping her up. "Come on, baby, let's go get a room." I ignored the commentary from her cousins, batting away the handfuls of popcorn that were thrown our way. I wanted her all to myself.

I was done sharing for the day.

Once we got into the room, I shut the door and threw the lock in place before pulling her shirt off, preferring her sports bra and panties uniform to all the clothes she was currently wearing. I crawled on the bed, patting the mattress suggestively, making her laugh.

"That night, *this* night." I rubbed her belly, grinning, when she lay down beside me. "I wanted to be more for you than myself." I paused, looking up at her, hoping she could see the sincerity in my eyes. "You've been making me a better man since day one, Emmie James."

"You were always a good man, Kase." She ran her fingers through my hair, tugging lightly.

"I moved from country to country, bed to bed, thinking only about myself." I'd lived. And I'd always been proud of my life. But being here, loving Ems, loving our daughter, it made everything else I'd done seem so small. So selfish.

"You knew what you wanted, and you went after it." She turned on her side, tucking her hands under her cheek against the pillow. "Always honest, never apologizing. I did the same, in a lot of ways. I wanted to dance, and I worked my ass off to make it happen. I missed family events, parties, hanging with friends. I missed everything."

"There's a difference between driven and selfish." She was trying to make me feel better, and I loved her all the more for it. "I hope our little girl grows up to be more like you than me."

Ems wrinkled her nose. "No. I hope she grows up to be the perfect mix of both of us."

"Your kind ambition."

"And your unapologetic strength." She smiled, and my heart swelled.

How had I not seen it sooner? Why did it take Brody to show me what I'd known from the very beginning? Emmie James was my perfect match. We were always going to happen, always meant to be. Inevitable.

"You want to hear something hilariously pathetic?"

"Of course."

I winced, slightly embarrassed to tell her. "I watched pregnancy porn this afternoon."

She snorted out a laugh, covering her mouth to contain her giggles. "When did you have time to watch porn?"

"I came in here while you were helping make popcorn." I'd snuck off to watch porn, and felt like a teenager with his first girlfriend.

"Why?"

"I wanted to make sure that it was good for you." I put my hand on her hip, squeezing. "I've never had a pregnant girlfriend before. I'm a little out of my element here." Or you know, a hell of a lot out of my element.

"Last night was perfect, Kase."

It had been for me, but I needed to make sure it was perfect for her too. So. I'd watched about five minutes of porn. Fast forward mode and silenced, hiding in the bathroom, hoping she didn't come looking for me. "You deserve more than perfect. You deserve mind-blowing and life-altering."

She smirked, rubbing her belly. "You've altered my life plenty, Kasen Cadence."

"You got jokes today?" I cupped her cheek, drawing her in so I could kiss her soft lips. "Here, sit up." I helped her slide toward the end of the mattress, adjusting a pile of pillows behind her back, helping her lie against them. I pulled off her leggings, then her lacy panties; her gaze was on me the whole time.

I moved down to the floor, spreading her thighs. I glanced at her, making sure she was comfortable. Her eyes had closed, her lips were parted, and her breaths heavy.

Anticipation.

I kissed my way to her center, flicking her clit with my tongue, her hips jerking off the bed. I licked her core, moaning at how fucking amazing she tasted against my tongue. I'd never get my fill of her. I slipped two fingers inside her heat, pumping them gently while I worked her clit with my mouth. She was panting, her fingers twisted in my hair. I had her right where I needed her. Wanting.

I stood, shed my shorts, and held her trim thighs in my hands. "Tell me if this doesn't feel good, okay?"

"You won't hurt me, Kase." She opened her beautiful eyes, meeting mine in the fading light coming through the window. "I trust you."

I swallowed past the ball of emotion in my throat, nodding.

I spread her legs wider, making room for me between them. I slid inside her warmth, groaning at how fucking fantastic she felt. Her pussy clamped down on my dick, holding me hostage. I moved slowly, dragging my cock in and out, drawing out her pleasure and mine. Her hands were twisted in the sheets, her bottom lip caught between her teeth.

I wanted her to feel good. I wanted her to feel my love for her, my commitment to our new family. I'd be here always.

"I love you, Ems, so fucking much."

"I love you too, Kase. Now don't stop."

I couldn't help but smile at her sweet whispered words. I wouldn't stop, not until I heard her scream my name.

I quickened my pace, pistoning into her harder. Her back arched off the bed, her hips moving to meet mine.

She was close.

I was closer, doing everything I could to hold my orgasm back.

She cried out, calling my name, her pussy milking my dick as she came.

My hold tightened on her thighs as I spilled my release into her body.

Chapter Fifty-Four

Emmie

I'd taken my last test for the semester, and it felt really good to be done. I'd worked hard, taking enough hours that I'd be able to take next semester off and still graduate in three years. I was getting a business degree, preparing to have my own ballet studio one day. I had this image in my mind of my daughter in a tiny tutu, twirling in the background waiting for me to get done teaching a class.

Kase and I had settled into our new normal, as he called it, which oddly enough included a lot of sex. And a lot of *I love yous*. And a lot of guitar playing for our unborn daughter. Eight months ago, my life had gone from picture perfect to stressful and unrecognizable. Now it looked a lot like that happily ever after I never thought I'd get.

"Hey, baby, how was your test?" Kase came into the kitchen, taking the Pop-Tart out of my hand and putting an apple in its place.

I frowned, grumbling under my breath. "When are you going back to work, little fucker?"

His eyebrows rose to his hairline. "Did you say something?"

"Oh, um, I was wondering when you're planning on going back to work." I pasted a smile on my face, which made him roll his eyes. He'd heard me. But it was his own fault. You shouldn't take sugar away from a pregnant chick.

"I don't know. Why?" He grabbed the jar of Nutella, setting it in front of me with a spoon as his form of a compromise.

"We've been living in this happy blissful in-between where we didn't really talk about what happens after the baby is born." I rested my hand on my belly. "But we're getting close to the end. I can't keep staying here with Katie and Cash, and I don't want to move back in with my parents, although they beg me to every day." They had become over-the-top supportive, trying to erase all the months they'd spent breaking my heart. "I think I should get a place of my own."

"Like build one here on the compound?"

"No. Maybe buy one in town? I don't think I want to live here with everyone else." I glanced down at my huge bump, pursing my lip. "I don't want her sneaking out in the middle of night to make out with Marley and Talon's son."

"Oh hell to the no." Kase paused, the spoon in his hand full of Nutella to put on my apple. "Our daughter will *not* be sneaking out to meet boys. Ever."

"She will if I live here." It was the nature of the beast. This place was magic. But it was also dangerous, and not what I wanted for Luca. She could be close with her cousins, and with all her aunts and uncles. She simply couldn't run wild like a little barefoot gypsy.

"Okay, so we'll get a house in town," Kase said the words casually, like they didn't carry the weight of the rest of our lives.

"*We?* Like, you want to get a house together?"

"Baby." He chuckled, leaning forward to kiss the tip of my nose. "We're basically living together already. I fell asleep with my dick still inside you last night. We're having a baby. We're *in* this, like in the thick of it." I smiled, not sure what else to say. "Come here." He wrapped his palm around my neck, drawing in for a kiss. "What am I going to have to do to make you see how desperately in love I am with you two?"

Chapter Fifty-Five

Kasen

We were sitting down to the first Friday family dinner Emmie's family had had in a long-ass time. Since all the spawn had walked away after Smith's outburst, it seemed no one was willing to try it again. But it had been reinstated, and I'd had to drag Ems off the couch and carry her here.

She was super fucking pregnant these days, and constantly uncomfortable. Everyone noticed. Brody had even come over last night and told me how to pop the baby out of her. He'd even demanded I take notes. We had a couple weeks left, but I put the instructions in the dresser in case I needed them.

"This is nice." Dash looked down the length of the table. They'd put the two tables end to end to make an incredibly long one. "I've missed this."

I knew Ems had too, even if she didn't want to admit it.

Brody knocked on the table, getting my attention. "You do what I told you?"

"What?" I shook my head when I realized what he was asking. "No. She's not due for two more weeks."

"Look at her bro, she's miserable." Brody pointed at Ems, who was slumped down in her chair, nibbling on a piece of bread. "Landry, tell Kase his kid is cooked."

Landry glanced down the table, checking to see if any of the parents heard him. The parents who didn't know that Ems and I were now way more than friends and co-parents. It's not that we were hiding things from them. We simply hadn't come up for air long enough to tell them. "I'm sure when Em has had enough, she'll let him know."

"That stupid method doesn't work." Beau rolled his eyes, joining the conversation.

"Hell yes it does." Marley pointed to her sleeping baby boy.

"See?" Brody laughed loudly. "You could never do it correctly."

Beau threw a green bean at his head.

"Don't listen to him, Beau, you pop me plenty good." Halen smiled at her husband, taking the second green bean he was about to launch and feeding it to their daughter. "Lennon was a stubborn baby, that's all."

"Ems, you want me to pop Luca out?" I rubbed my palm on her belly.

"Let's give her another week, then sure, you can hit me like a ketchup bottle."

Brody threw his head back, laughing so loud that it was hard not to join in.

"A ketchup bottle?"

"That was the visual I gave Beau." Brody rested his hand on Beau's back, shaking him playfully. "But he wasn't the best student, apparently."

"You're such a dick." Beau shoved Brody away, making him laugh even louder.

"Are you guys talking about my daughter and sex again?" Dash shook his head, looking a bit nauseous. "Please stop."

"Brody." Jacks sighed, pointing down the table at his son-in-law. "We *know* you got the babies in there, and we *all know* you got them out. But can you please, for the love of fuck, stop bringing it up at the damn dinner table?"

"Dude, I'm trying to spread knowledge here." Brody pointed at Ems, her eyes going wide. I stiffened beside her. It was like watching a train wreck about to happen, and feeling powerless to stop it. "Emmie is miserable, she needs that baby out. And Kase—"

"And Kase what?" Smith's gaze darted between Ems and me.

Brody clamped his lips shut, then hung his head, whispering under his breath, "My bad, bro."

"Um, yeah, so, you see—"

"Kase and I are dating." Ems cut off my rambling.

I stood and moved behind her chair, refusing to let her go through anything without me right by her side. Because, where the hell else would I be?

"We're more than dating, sir. I'm in love with your daughter, and mine. I'm completely in love with my girls." I glanced down at Ems to see her smiling back at me, with those seemingly ever-present tears in her beautiful blue eyes.

She was always meant to be more. I think I knew that from the first moment I'd met her. I never thought I wanted this life, the life I'd accidentally created with Emmie James. But I did. I wanted what we had, and I wanted it forever.

"I'm here. I've always been here, and I'm not going anywhere. Ever. I promise." I dropped down on one knee, which was entirely unplanned. "Marry me, Ems." Unplanned, but so damn *right,* like everything between us.

"What?" Those tears were spilling over now.

"Marry me." I took her hands in mine, enjoying the hell out of the shocked gasps that came from the peanut gallery. "Let me spend the rest of my life being there for you."

"Okay."

I couldn't help but laugh. "Okay?"

She smiled through her tears, taking my face in her hands. "Yes. I meant, yes. I'll marry you."

"Huh, would you look at that?" Jett held out his hand palm up to Marley. "Em saved that virginity of hers for her husband after all. I want my fifty bucks back."

Epilogue

Six Months later
Emmie

I woke up alone, reaching my hand out to Kase's side of the bed to find it warm. We'd been watching a movie, and honestly, I couldn't remember making it past the opening credits. Luca was teething and she'd refused to nap today while Kase had been out at the compound.

He helped my family from time to time, creating videos for RiffRaff. He was even more talented behind the camera than he was in front of it. But the best side of Kase wasn't the model or the artist. It was him as a dad.

The most gorgeous man you've ever seen holding a baby against his bare muscled chest? I can't put the magnetic attraction into words. I could understand now how women had babies nine months apart because the moment I'd been cleared by my OB, I'd straight jumped Kase.

He was sweet too, doting and helpful. He changed diapers and begged to take late-night feedings. You name it and he did it with a goofy grin on his face. Which was the reason I knew where my guy and my girl were right now.

Luca didn't sleep through the night. It seemed she never had from the moment she was conceived. Avory's boyfriend had said that Luca was a new soul and sleep came hard for those experiencing the world for the first time. Crue, of course, said that was a load of bull and our family didn't believe in all that hippie shit. But I thought it was incredibly insightful, and I clung to it on nights when I was beyond exhausted.

Avory had finally brought her new guy around, and the reaction was so volatile it was on the edge of explosive. For the most part, Crue stayed away when Avory and her guy were there, but every once in a while the three of them were on the compound at the same time and the whole place felt like a powder keg.

I tossed the covers aside, then padded down the hallway and the stairs. They creaked with every step, alerting Kase I was making my way through the house. I rounded the corner, smiling when I heard an old Bob Dylan tune playing softly through our sound system.

His voice calmed her as it always had. After she was born, Kase had switched to "Make You Feel My Love" as the song he sang to her. I loved that Bob Dylan's voice soothed our daughter. I loved our old house. I loved the ancient building we'd bought on the town square for our future businesses. I loved that we chose things that had withstood the test of time.

I watched Kase dancing with our sleeping daughter for a few moments and then I went to join them. His eyes were closed, but he felt me, opening his free arm so he could hold us both. I rested my head on his shoulder, swaying to the beat.

When the song was over, it started playing again. He'd put it on repeat, and I wondered how many times he'd already listened to it. We were so lucky, Luca and I, to have his love.

My life hadn't gone according to plan. But I'd met a guy, fallen in love, and had a baby. I guess in the end, I'd found my way to exactly where I'd always wanted to be.

***

Kasen

I thought my life would be full of constant excitement and new experiences, never two days the same. I'd thought I would travel the world and have adventures until my body gave up or gave out. I thought that was what I wanted, what would make me happy.

But I was wrong.

Nothing could possibly make me happier than the two girls dancing with me.

Our house in town was old. Built in the early 1900s, it had a legit white picket fence. There were columns and shutters, and wood floors that creaked whether you were walking on them or not. We had a baby swing in the oak tree out front and an SUV in the driveway. Our daughter would not be sneaking out to run wild on the Devil's Share compound. Although we'd make sure her cousins would be an ever-present fixture in her life.

Ems and I had bought a building on the town square that was going to be our studio: half for her and half for me. She'd teach ballet classes and I'd keep creating content. We weren't in any hurry though. We were both enjoying our time with our daughter.

Luca was six months old, and all indications were she'd start crawling any day. I loved her so damn much, and I was *in* love with her mother in a way that consumed me.

My two girls each had half of my heart.

I kissed the top of Emmie's head while my hand rested on our baby's back. We'd all been in our bed, and had fallen asleep while watching a movie. But Luca had woken up. She still got a little restless in the middle of the night. Since she'd already spent enough time keeping Ems up when she was pregnant, I made sure I was the one to dance my daughter back to sleep now that she was here.

No, my life had not turned out the way I'd thought it would. It'd turned out better than I could have ever imagined.

I didn't need to travel to see the world.

Not when I was already holding it in my arms.

PLAY LIST

Harvest Moon by SYML
Let's Be Still by the Head and the Heart
Home by Edward Sharpe & The Magnetic Zeros
All My Days by Alexi Murdoch
Better Than Love by Griffin House
I Found by Amber Run
Forever Young by Bob Dylan
Make You Feel My Love by Bob Dylan

ABOUT THE AUTHOR

L.P. lives in Austin, Texas with her husband, daughter, two rescue dogs, and one adopted cat. The first group of chickens met with a sad and unexpected death. They have been replaced. The dwarf goats are a story for another day. And now there are ducks.

Writer, business owner, and office manager, L.P. says she loves to read as much as she loves to write. Reading a good book is her reward after writing one. In her spare time—ha!—she fosters puppies for a rescue organization based in Austin.

Connect with L.P.:
lpmaxa.wordpress.com
facebook.com/pages/LP-Maxa/1442560722667127
twitter.com/lpmaxa
instagram.com/lpmaxa

www.BOROUGHSPUBLISHINGGROUP.com

If you enjoyed this book, please write a review. Our authors appreciate the feedback, and it helps future readers find books they love. We welcome your comments and invite you to send them to info@boroughspublishinggroup.com. Follow us on Facebook, Twitter and Instagram, and be sure to sign up for our newsletter for surprises and new releases from your favorite authors.

Are you an aspiring writer? Check out www.boroughspublishinggroup.com/submit and see if we can help you make your dreams come true.

www.ingramcontent.com/pod-product-compliance
Lightning Source LLC
Chambersburg PA
CBHW031324170626
46807CB00002B/556